THE MERCURY MAN

Happy Christmas
Love
Re Coadys

ABOUT THE AUTHOR

John Glavin is a garda stationed in Killorglin, County Kerry. A winner of the Hennessy/Sunday Tribune Literary Award in 1993, his first novel, *Bog Warriors*, was published by TownHouse in 2000. He lives in the seaside village of Cromane, County Kerry with his wife, Deirdre and their three children, David, Christopher and Anna.

The Mercury Man

John Galvin

TOWN
HOUSE
DUBLIN

First published in 2002 by

TownHouse and CountryHouse Ltd
Trinity House
Charleston Road
Ranelagh
Dublin 6
Ireland

1 2 3 4 5 6 7 8 9 10

A CIP catalogue record for this book is available from the British Library.

ISBN: 1-86059-172-8

Cover design by Splash, London
Typeset by Claire Rourke, TownHouse, Dublin
Printed in Great Britain by Bookmarque Ltd, Croydon, Surrey

To my parents, Jack and Eileen

CHAPTER ONE

Gerry Feeney had never meant to kill his wife. At least, that's what his senior counsel told the jury in his closing statement on the last day of the trial at the Central Criminal Court. Her death, he explained, had been the final chapter in the tragic story of a man driven to the brink of insanity, and eventually beyond.

Who in their right mind would be capable of picking up a long brass poker and beating a wheelchair-bound woman to death while she slept?

Certainly not Gerry Feeney.

Gerry Feeney was of unsound mind when he had committed this heinous act.

For the previous two days, the jury heard how he

had changed from a loving spouse into the monster that society had now created. How he had cared for his wife after her accident for more than twenty-five years. How he had constantly worried about her health and the growing medical bills that snapped greedily at their modest pensions. His slow descent into the comfort of alcohol and the subsequent deterioration of his mind.

And who had helped him in his hour of need? No one. Not the health board. Not the social services. He was just another forgotten sixty-five-year-old citizen, getting the same pittance as the rest.

This once kind and loving man had not killed his wife! An uncaring society had killed Anne Feeney.

The jury deliberated for just under three hours. As they returned, one of the female jurors had patted the corner of her eye with the tip of a white handkerchief.

It was a good sign.

The verdict: 'Not guilty by reason of insanity.'

Gerry had rubbed his hands together and given a barely noticeable smile. It was the first gesture he had made throughout the entire trial.

The judge looked down pensively at the documents on his bench, the assessments of both psychiatrists, one saying that Gerry Feeney was of unsound mind when the crime was committed, the other saying that he was not.

He massaged his temples for a moment and scratched with one finger at the wig that irritated his scalp before looking down at the defence council.

'I believe,' he stated, 'that I would be failing in my duty if I were to release the defendant back into the society which you have so vigorously condemned. The verdict is that of not guilty by reason of insanity. Whether it was temporary or not will be a matter for further assessment. Your client will be detained indefinitely at the Central Mental Hospital in Dun drum for that purpose.'

Indefinitely had totalled out at just less than nine months. Gerry had been a most popular patient with the staff. His life-long array of filthy jokes had gone down well with some of the male nurses he had befriended. He spoke openly about his experiences to the resident analyst. Got it all off his chest. No one could understand how such an amicable and cheerful individual could be capable of bludgeoning a helpless old woman to death. And so, after eight months and twenty-six days, Gerry was sent home.

The attitude of the people to him in the council estate where he lived had changed. Mothers jerked at their children's wrists as they passed by his small gateway, their heads turned away from the house of the man who had killed his wife. The man in the corner shop now engrossed himself in conversation with another customer whenever Gerry went there to buy the paper. Gerry soon learned to leave the correct sum of money on the counter and walk out.

Their attitude to him did not improve with time. If anything, it got worse.

How he dreaded Hallowe'en! On the last two such occasions, a gang of teenagers on the estate had thrown eggs at his house and had broken two of the front windows. When he had gone out to chastise them, he had stumbled over the wheelchair they had found in the nearby dump and stained with blood from the local butchers. Their cruel inventiveness was a constant source of amazement to him.

Nobody ever spoke to him. Nobody ever called. And so, it was with a gasp of surprise that he sat up on that sunny June morning when the doorbell rang. He paused for a moment in the kitchen, his hands shaking as he pulled the braces over his shoulders. It was too early for the local pranksters. They only came, as all cowards do, during the hours of darkness.

He smoothed the front of his shirt and patted his hair. He could see the caller through the frosted glass of the front door. Certainly not one of the 'knock and run' incidents that had become so popular with the local children. He took a deep breath and opened the door.

A middle-aged man in a brown hound's-tooth jacket turned around to him with a look of surprise and smiled. He ran a nervous hand through his thick, greying hair, and then extended it.

'Good morning to you, sir,' he said cheerfully. 'It's Mr Feeney, isn't it?'

Gerry took the hand cautiously and they shook. He relaxed as the firm grip warmed him. It was the first handshake he had received in three years, the last being from the male nurse at the door of the Central Mental Hospital, wishing him good luck.

'Are you selling something?' he asked. 'Because if you are, then I have to tell you...'

The man shook his head and lifted his dark briefcase, his other hand held up to dismiss the very mention of it.

'It's about your pension, Mr Feeney,' he explained.

'I take it that you got the letter from our department some weeks ago about the increase? I'm just calling to check on why you didn't fill out the form and return it to us.'

'What increase?' asked Gerry as he pulled the door open wide and stood back with his arm held out in a gesture of invitation.

The pension official muttered under his breath in frustration as he struggled with the catch on his brief-case.

'Well, I'm not surprised that you didn't reply if we didn't send it out to you. Those people in administration would really want to get their act together. It would make my job a whole lot easier,' he said, loosening his tie.

Gerry watched him as he bent down on one knee and placed the briefcase on the hall floor.

'Here. Come in here,' he offered quickly, the thought of extra money spurring him on.

He crossed the narrow hallway and reached above the heavily glossed green door, rubbing his hand along the architrave for a moment before taking down the key.

'I don't usually use this room,' he explained as the man watched him unlock it.

He pushed it open, and again held his hand out for the man to go inside.

Although the sun shone brightly outside, the room was darkened by the ashen net curtains. A bluebottle buzzed in a desperate struggle for survival in a cobweb above them on the ceiling. The room smelt of stagnant dampness.

'You can sit down there,' said Gerry, pointing to

the faded-brown, two-seater sofa, 'Mr... eh?'

'Landers. James, if you like,' the man replied casually as he inspected the stained cushions beneath him.

Once he was seated, Gerry pushed the small coffee table in front of him. Landers placed his briefcase on it and clicked it open.

'Well now, Mr Feeney,' he smiled, 'let me give you some good news.'

Gerry raised his eyebrows in pleasant surprise and eased himself down on the matching single-seater opposite his guest.

'I could do with some of that,' he said gruffly.

'Mr Feeney.' The man's tone was apologetic. 'It appears from your file that we have overlooked a number of increases in your pension for some time, and as a result we now owe you a considerable amount of back payment.'

'How the hell did that happen?' asked Gerry.

'Well, now, Mr Feeney,' Landers began to explain, smiling to ease the tension, 'our department has been in turmoil since we moved three years ago. I can assure you that you're not the only victim of this fiasco. But at least we're putting things right as of today.'

Gerry looked at the man for a moment and then nodded with a grin. There was something very pleasant about this Mr Landers.

Here was someone who didn't care about Gerry's past. A man who spoke to him without fear in his voice. A man whose sole purpose it was to solve the problem and make life a little more comfortable.

Who did his manner remind him of? Gerry watched

his every move as he tried to remember. Of course! The nice, softly spoken solicitor who had visited him on the night of his arrest. They were even dressed alike. Hound's-tooth jacket with shirt, tie and dark slacks. Even the smell of their aftershave was similar.

Gerry's blank expression suddenly turned to a frown.

Indeed, the solicitor had been very pleasant at first. But later, when Gerry had begun to cry as he told his story, the solicitor had just kept on writing with apparent indifference. Maybe he hadn't been such a nice person after all. Maybe this pension official was the same?

'I'd kill for a cup of tea,' said Landers with a smile, as he busily arranged his papers on the low table. 'That is, if it's not too much trouble... and only if you join me,' he added.

Gerry stared at him for a moment, and then stood up.

'I'd better make a cup for the both of us then,' he said without emotion. 'Milk and sugar?'

'Yes. Two sugars and a little milk, thank you.'

Gerry hummed to himself as he made his way to the kitchen. He clicked the press open and removed two mugs, blowing at them to dispel the light coating of dust. He wondered how much he was owed by the government. Eight hundred euro? Maybe more.

He switched on the kettle and threw the tea bags into the mugs.

'What am I owed?' he called out, folding his arms and resting back against the sink as he waited for the kettle to boil.

'I'm just calculating that at the moment,' came the

reply that echoed down through the small hallway. 'I believe that it should be in the region of around eleven hundred euro.'

Gerry stifled a snigger of excitement, his shoulders shaking.

The tea made, he returned to the room, holding the steaming mugs at arm's length.

'Here you are,' he announced, bending down to place one of them on the coffee table. The other man moved his documents quickly to one side. 'Eleven hundred euro, you say?'

'Yes, indeed.' Landers nodded as he lifted the mug and watched Gerry sit down opposite him once more. 'It appears that payment was stopped to you for a number of months about three years ago.'

Gerry leaned back in the chair and smiled to himself as he looked into the mug. He sipped gently at the tea and then rested his head back against the top of the chair.

'Yes,' he said, still smiling. 'There's a bit of a story attached to that.'

Landers lifted the mug to his lips, watching Gerry over the rim. He lowered it suddenly and rubbed at his mouth.

'Is it too hot?' enquired Gerry leaning forward and placing his own mug on the table.

The man shook his head in apology and smiled as he held the scalding tea out to him.

'Just a little.'

Gerry took the cup from him and threw his eyes up as he left the room. He had just been ready to give this government messenger-boy the shock of his life, and now it had been ruined because he couldn't drink hot tea.

'Would you like to hear my story or not?' His voice growled in frustration as he opened the fridge and took out the pint carton of milk.

'Yes. Yes, I would, Mr Feeney.'

Gerry poured half of the tea from the mug into the sink and filled it back to the rim with cold milk. He could afford to be generous now. After all, he was eleven hundred euro better off.

'I guarantee that it's cool enough for you,' he promised as he returned to the room and held it out.

Landers took it from him and eased back on the sofa to listen.

Gerry sat down and took his own mug from the table. He paused for a moment before he spoke, trying to get the words into the right order. He would only get one crack at it. He wanted maximum shock value.

'I killed my wife,' he announced and gave a half-laugh. 'Three years ago. That's why I didn't fill out any of those forms you sent me then. I was... how should I put it?... in the nut-house.'

Landers's eyes widened in shock as he put the mug back on the table in slow motion.

'You... you did... what?' he stuttered.

Gerry nodded vigorously with a wide grin as his hand pointed down at the carpet.

'Right in this very room in fact.'

Landers swallowed hard. His breathing got faster.

'Do you recognise the name now?' asked Gerry, visibly pleased with the reaction to his story.

The man looked down at his documents, his hands

shaking as he fingered through one of them to the name of the pensioner.

'Gerry Feeney,' he mouthed to himself.

Gerry took a long gulp from his mug as he watched him. This was much more fun than he had anticipated, watching the paled expression of this desk-driver from the pension department. Admittedly, Mr Landers was a pleasant man, just like the solicitor who had sat back and watched him crying in the interview room. Anyway, after today, he would probably never see him again.

'Yes,' he smiled. 'That's me. The madman who killed his annoying and disabled bitch of a wife with a big poker.'

He continued to smile as he glanced around the room. He gulped at the tea again and stood up, pointing to a faded-black stain on the wall behind the sofa.

'Look,' he said enthusiastically. 'There's still some of her dried blood as a reminder.'

Landers glanced over his shoulder in horror and then rose quickly to his feet as if he had been zapped with an electric cattle prod.

Gerry laughed. The first loud laugh he had given since the one he had faked for the gardaí the night they had arrested him for the murder of his wife.

Landers turned and looked at him with fear in his eyes.

'Now,' smiled Gerry, 'I think that we've had a long enough chat. Are you going to write out my cheque for the eleven hundred euro? Or do I have to... wait... until...'

He stopped suddenly and grimaced in pain, his

yellowing teeth bared as he lifted his hand to his throat.

Landers relaxed his expression of horror. He reached over and took the mug from a frightened and pained Gerry, then calmly sat back down on the sofa to wait.

Gerry staggered backwards and steadied himself, frantically pointing to his neck, his other hand held out in a wide-eyed plea for assistance, his nostrils opening and closing as he snorted for air, a trickle of blood running from the side of his mouth.

'I know that you killed your wife, Gerry. I know *all* about it,' said Landers calmly as he shuffled the documents and replaced them in the briefcase. He snapped it shut with purpose and stood up, waiting and watching until Gerry slumped down on his knees before him on the mouldering carpet.

He placed the briefcase on its end on the coffee table and removed a pair of green rubber surgical gloves from the pocket of his jacket, along with a clean square of white flannel.

Busily, he set about cleaning the room and table of his prints, before taking the two mugs to the kitchen and washing them under the gushing tap. When he returned, Gerry was on his back, a pink mixture of blood and saliva boiling from the side of his mouth down his left cheek and dripping slowly onto the carpet. His eyes opened and closed in fading wonder as the man above leaned over him and gave a faint smile.

'Poison in your tea, Gerry,' he clarified. 'Time to pay for your crime.'

Landers arched his back as he surveyed the room.

He had been careful about what he had touched, and had done so without arousing the suspicion of his victim. He waited until Gerry's eyes closed for the last time before snapping the glove from his right hand and checking for a pulse on his victim's neck. The vein gave two weakened thumps, then stopped.

Landers stood upright. Another job well done. He smiled and then exhaled slowly in victory. With his left hand, he reached into the inside pocket of his jacket and took out the printed business card, which he placed on Gerry's lifeless chest: 'Messenger of the gods.'

He lifted his briefcase and walked out of the room, shutting the door behind him.

Once outside the front door, he pulled it closed and rubbed the bell-button with the white flannel cloth. He paused for a moment on the steps, craning his wrinkled but muscled neck to look out at the passing traffic. He slowly unrolled the surgical glove from his left hand and walked out casually past the small, rusting gate and turned right. The children screeched excitedly as they played on the large green in the middle of the estate.

Two hundred yards away, a ten-strong group of people stood waiting at the local bus stop. He swung the briefcase in time to his brisk pace as he walked towards them, then stopped and nodded a smile of greeting at a stern, heavy-set woman who scowled back at him. He whistled merrily to himself as he waited.

The bus pulled to a stop with a loud groan and a hiss.

He stood back and touched his forelock as he allowed the large woman to board in front of him.

'Daycent man,' she muttered to the driver as he followed her inside.

Landers smiled to himself as he dropped his fare into the cash box and then took the first seat by the window. He looked out as the bus roared up in protest through the gears and passed the gate of Gerry Feeney's house. He settled back in the seat and closed his eyes in thought. All had gone well. This one had been easy. The next one, however, would be something of a challenge.

CHAPTER TWO

The sole purpose of the Metropolitan Crime Squad is to deal swiftly with matters affecting the security of the state and its citizens. It consists of one superintendent, an inspector, three sergeants and twelve detective gardaí. An elite group of men who answer only to the commissioner, and that is a rare enough occurrence.

Needless to say, complaints about their methods are endless. The MCS don't really care that much, once the job is brought to a successful conclusion. Ordinary gardaí look on them as secretive and opinionated, preferring to steer well clear of them whenever they have business in one of the city stations.

Their base is at the rear of Garda Headquarters. A large office with twelve tables, like that of a newspaper room, but without the partitions, the purpose of this being that all present can contribute to matters relevant. There are no secrets among the men in the squad. There is only one nest to be feathered.

The sergeants have their own office in the hallway, as have the inspector and the superintendent. The latter is naturally the plushest. It has sliding blinds on the windows and a leather reclining chair behind the desk. In addition to this comfort, there is a kettle and a tray, which is restocked daily with cellophane-wrapped biscuits from Bewley's.

Two young detectives stood outside the office door, the smaller one looking up with a whisper of confidence.

'I'll do the explaining,' said Andy Fox, a Clareman who had been in the squad for seven years and had gained the reputation of being reckless but extremely effective.

His colleague, Bob McGrath, Dub born and raised, looked down at him and closed his eyes in trepidation.

'Oh, Jaysus, no,' he whispered, reaching for the handle.

The superintendent was nibbling on one of the biscuits. He looked up as they entered his office. His eyes were weary. This was the third time that they were about to have this type of conversation.

'This was a most unusual incident, gentlemen,' he said, gesturing to the two chairs that he had placed in front of his desk, trying his best to remain calm.

He dropped his gaze to the file, muttering the words he chose from it.

'Accidental shot fired... civilians... fear... indiscriminate...' His eyebrows lifted. 'Two arrests... no one dead... Well, that's fairly marvellous, now, isn't it?'

Andy Fox smiled as he eased himself down on the chair and lifted one of his frayed Nike runners on to the desk. This impromptu summoning to the superintendent's office had forced him to tuck his T-shirt inside his denims, and tear the bristle from his face with a year-old razor that he had found on the floor of his locker.

'Another successful defence of the title, Super,' he said, and then turned to grin at McGrath who scowled back at him and widened his eyes in warning.

The super did not look up from the report sheet. He nibbled at the biscuit and spoke softly through the crumbs.

'Fox, what age are you?' he asked casually.

Fox looked puzzled.

'Thirty-three, Super,' he replied with a shrug.

'And you're with us... how long?'

'Seven years.'

'Mmmm. Seven years. Tell me, Detective, in all that time, did I ever invite you to put your big, smelly hoof up on my desk? *Get it off, boy!*'

McGrath slapped his fist into Fox's thigh.

'You had to be there, Super.' McGrath stood up to his six-foot three to explain and pointed down to the file on the table. 'It certainly wasn't as dangerous to the public as that report suggests,' he said, then sat back down.

Fox eased his leg from the desk, at the same time rubbing at his thigh and glaring at McGrath. 'He's right, Super. It reads a lot worse than it was.'

The superintendent looked up at McGrath.

'How many *accidental* shots did you fire, Detective?' he asked, already knowing the answer.

'None, sir,' replied McGrath, rubbing a nervous hand across his close-cut hair.

The superintendent nodded slowly at him, then turned with narrowed eyes to Fox.

'And you, Machine-gun Kelly,' he frowned. 'What rush of blood went to your head that explains the shot you fired into the air in the busiest street in this city?'

Fox sat up eagerly and then leaned forward with his hands held out in a gesture of explanation.

'Fear is the key to any conflict, Super,' he smiled. 'If a gouger fires a shot at me, then I fire back and keep firing until the white flag comes up. God bless the Uzi and the Israeli who invented it.'

The super looked down at the file and closed his eyes. 'Mother of Jesus,' he whispered in desperation.

Fox smiled at both of them.

'Super, is this the part like on the TV where you shout, "How the *hell* am I going to explain this one to the mayor downtown?"'

McGrath pursed his lips to stifle a smile. The superintendent rubbed his hand across his face in a vain attempt to do likewise.

Fox looked from one to the other.

'I think that the whole thing went *really* well,' he said surprised at their attitude of concern. 'Two gows on remand, money retrieved and the guards laughing all the way to the court. What more could you ask for?'

The super drummed his finger across his lips for a moment as he stared across the desk at Fox.

'Well now, Detective, I'm sure the commissioner will be absolutely thrilled with all of us,' he said, his tone heavy with sarcasm. 'A successful job, no doubt.'

He lowered his voice to a growl and threw the half-eaten biscuit on the table.

'That is, if only we could leave out the bits about losing control of a sub-machine gun... and telling an old-age pensioner – who, by the way, gentlemen, now resides in the hospital suffering from post-traumatic shock syndrome – to...'

He pointed at the sheet on the desk and ran his finger along it.

'"Get down ya old bollocks or you'll be shot." His family were simply over the moon with delight when they heard it. We can expect to see the whole thing in the Sunday papers next week. And no doubt a question in the Dáil as well, if they run out of shit to talk about up there.'

He picked up the file and then threw it dramatically across the desk. It slid along the polished surface and floated to the floor.

'They all gave interviews to the papers at the scene.' He frowned. 'One big guard, one small guard, armed to the teeth and shouting foul abuse at old people – the very people who we should be out there protecting. Can you imagine the headline? "Abbot and Costello take Grafton Street". Sweet mother of Jesus!'

Again, Fox leaned forward in explanation.

'You had to be there, Super,' he said. 'Everybody else hit the ground outside the bank except that old "have a go" hero. He stood straight in the line of fire looking back at us, waving his walking stick and shouting, "What's going on here, ye young blackguards?" Bob had to physically drag him by the neck out of there.'

McGrath glared at him in shock as he picked up the file, then looked down at the super.

'I think you'll find that I escorted him from the scene, sir,' he corrected, placing the file down on the desk.

The super erupted and slammed his fist down on the file.

'The complaints crowd are up my arse again with the pair of you,' he shouted. 'Only that ye happen to show a little competence from time to time, ye'd now be sorting old uniform trousers next door. Can either of you go into a situation without shooting and swearing at everyone?'

He did not wait for an answer. His voice rose in a commanding roar.

'For Christ's sake, Fox, will you exercise a little restraint?'

The two detectives looked at each other in the ringing silence. They turned back to the super, who narrowed his eyes and pointed his finger from one to the other.

'One other thing,' he said, waving the finger across and back in front of the two of them. 'Nobody told me that we had entered a "who can dress up like a gouger" contest. Look at the state of the two of you.' His tone smacked of disgust.

Fox and McGrath looked each other up and down. Their attire was, indeed, questionable.

The super ran an irate hand across his brow.

'Forget it,' he muttered, then leaned forward, resting his elbow on the table, his finger pointed upwards. His eyes were closed as he spoke, his voice lowered to an ominous whisper.

'If I see either of you two detectives in this office again for anything other than a bravery medal ceremony, then I'll dismiss you both on the spot. Not to mention that this matter is far from over. Do we understand what is happening here?'

Fox and McGrath looked sheepishly at the floor.

'Do we understand what is happening here?' he roared.

'Yes, sir, we do,' said McGrath as he punched Fox on the shoulder to respond in kind.

'Yes, we understand,' muttered Fox.

'Right. Leave my office, *now.*'

Both men rose and placed the chairs back in front of the desk. The superintendent picked up his half-eaten biscuit and ground it between his teeth.

'What file are you dealing with at the moment?' he asked as they left.

They turned at the door.

'The Bunker case,' Fox replied.

The super nodded his understanding.

'Good,' he sighed quietly. 'A nice, peaceful investigation that doesn't involve any sweeping gunfire or scaring the bejaysus out of the public.'

Fox nodded in agreement. Still, he couldn't resist the urge.

'Well, sir. You can never tell how these things will end though,' he shrugged.

The super stared angrily at him.

'Can you remember what I've just told you?'

'Yes.'

The super spun around in the leather chair and looked out the window.

'Good. Get out.'

Fox pulled the door shut. They looked at each other in the hallway.

'We really dumped on the course this time,' whispered McGrath. 'I wonder what kind of punishment he has in store?'

Fox tossed his head back as he walked away.

'Ah, no big deal,' he said dismissing the worry. 'It was a simple mistake. Could happen to anyone.'

McGrath followed him quickly and pulled him to a stop outside the inspector's office.

'A simple mistake,' he whispered incredulously. 'Have you finally lost it? A shot fired into the air. You could have killed someone... someone innocent.'

Fox shook his arm free.

'It went up in the sky,' he protested. He snorted a laugh. 'Good job there was no hang-gliders around.'

'Aw, sure that's great news,' said McGrath, the gravity of the situation evident in his voice. 'So that means that you *actually meant* to fire that shot.'

Fox shoved his hands in his pockets and glanced around the corridor for a moment.

'All right, all right,' he finally admitted with a whisper. 'I pulled the trigger by mistake when I jumped from behind the car. Fuckin' thing,' he added with disgust.

He sighed. 'Frightened the bowels outta me, I can tell you,' he muttered.

McGrath smiled down at Fox and sniggered. He slapped him on the back and led him away.

'The super will put us both in jail the next time.'

'Uh-huh,' nodded Fox. 'But he'll have to get replacements first.'

***

Detective Inspector Frank Donegan stepped gingerly through the puddles of blackened water in the dark hallway, muttering and then cursing loudly as a drop fell from the ceiling and landed with pinpoint accuracy inside the collar of his white shirt.

'I see the firemen went mad again.' He frowned at the young detective beside him. 'Can they not put out a blaze without flooding the city?'

Detective Sergeant Alan Reidy slapped in frustration at the speck of ash that settled on his jacket sleeve. He stepped to one side to allow a man in a white forensic suit to pass.

'They're fairly enthusiastic about their job all right,' he agreed, looking down at the floor and following Donegan along the soot-stained cavern.

At the end of the hall, a second, older man in a white scene-of-crime suit struggled to balance a glaring spotlight on the blackened debris. He looked up from his task at the approaching detectives.

'Frank the man,' he called by way of greeting. 'Welcome to the party.'

Donegan laughed and looked back at Reidy.

'Alan, you know Dan Malley. Better known as Dr Doom. And take no notice of his jokes. Twenty-five years at this crack has turned him into a total head-case.'

'Now, now,' scolded Malley smiling. 'Every job must have its experts, even if we are a small bit de-ranged.'

Reidy said nothing, choosing instead to nod in agreement and give a thin smile.

Donegan placed his hands in his pockets and looked around him and up at the ceiling.

'So, somebody torched the place. I'm sure it's all very upsetting – but why call us? Surely this is a job for the local lads.'

Malley lifted a gloved hand and beckoned them along the hall.

'Follow me, good men of the MCS,' he whispered as he turned away.

Donegan looked at Reidy and threw his eyes up.

Malley stopped at the entrance to the sitting room and held out his arm.

'Tell me now, Frank. In all your years of service, have you ever seen anything like this?' He grinned, and then stood back to await their reaction.

Donegan moved to the charcoaled doorway and peered in. Reidy moved behind him and glanced over his shoulder. He brushed gently past, into the room, his hands in his pockets as he looked around at the walls and up at the ceiling.

'Looks like something out of Dante's *Inferno*,' he muttered as he ran his fingers over and back beneath his clean-shaven chin.

'Aw, Jesus Christ,' gasped Malley, rubbing his gloved hand across his forehead, disappointed at the low-key reaction the scene had received. 'Not *another* college graduate in the job, surely.'

Reidy fixed his stare on him. 'No,' he said calmly. 'Just someone who can read.'

Donegan remained silent as he stepped into the room.

'Who is it?'

Reidy took a silver pen from his breast pocket and used it as a pointer.

'Jimbo, the Wolfman. Do you not recognise the teeth?'

Donegan bent down, resting his hands on his knees, to examine the charred corpse that was bound with wire to the steel skeleton of a chair.

'A fitting end to a really beautiful person,' he muttered. 'Burnt alive.'

'How do you know that he was alive?' enquired Reidy as he moved in for a closer examination.

Donegan stood upright. He and Malley smiled at one another. He looked down at Reidy who was examining the jagged teeth of the corpse.

'Not much point tying him up if he was dead. Would you agree, Sergeant?' he said.

Reidy gave an embarrassed cough and stood upright. To be corrected was a rare occurrence and he didn't like it, especially not in front of the smart-arse from the Bureau.

'Yes, yes, of course,' he agreed, clicking the pen twice and replacing it in his pocket.

'So.' Donegan turned his attention back to Malley.

'You still haven't answered my first question. Somebody barbecuing a local heroin-dealer isn't really a job for the MCS. Fair enough, he was a scumbag of the highest order, but I don't think that he was a threat to national security.'

Malley narrowed his eyes and gave a series of purposeful, furtive glances around the room, wiggling his gloved fingers as he did so.

'Come on, for Christ's sake,' growled Donegan, growing tired of the mad scientist charade. 'We have better things to be doing than acting the mick with you.'

Malley took him by the shoulders and moved him gently to one side.

'Look what else we found,' he whispered, kneeling down beside the chair and picking up a small, ash-covered steel cash box. He took a pair of tweezers from his pocket and carefully lifted the lid, revealing a gleaming interior that contrasted with the darkness and filth of the room.

'What do you think of this?' he asked quietly as he pinched the edge of a white envelope and lifted it out.

The three men gazed at the black lettering:

FOR THE IMMEDIATE ATTENTION
OF THE GARDAÍ

'Looks like this madman is looking for a chase,' smiled Malley. He nodded back at the cash box in his hand. 'Are ye up for it, I wonder?'

In the envelope were a folded letter and a business card.

'Messenger... of... the gods.' Donegan read the business card slowly, craning to see into the envelope that Malley held carefully open.

Reidy pursed his lips and nodded gently. 'That would be Mercury,' he announced.

Both older men looked at him.

'Roman mythology.' He narrowed his eyes at them as he explained, content that he had once again assumed the role of youngest, smartest detective in the group. 'Mercury was the messenger of the gods. Or, if your choice is leaning more to the Greeks, then the messenger was Hermes.'

Malley hissed in disgust as he carefully replaced the envelope in the cash box.

'And who was the third commissioner of the job you're in now, smart-arse?' he said. 'I bet you don't know, do you?'

Reidy gave a casual shrug. 'Really intelligent people don't give a shit about such trivia,' he said, knowing that his tone would incense the Bureau man.

'I knew it,' Malley grunted. 'You know more about the friggin' Romans than your job.'

Donegan gave a soft cough of warning. 'I wouldn't put too much money on that now, Dan,' he said, the comment drawing a faint smile from Reidy. 'When can we get our hands on the contents of that letter?'

'Some time this evening. There was something else found, beside a socket over there. It's going back to the Bureau as we speak. Some type of crude device. Anyway, as regards the letter, I'll speed it up as much as I can. I take it that it's a job for you lads after all?'

Donegan moved out of the room, followed by Reidy. He looked back.

'Well now, that all depends on what's in the letter, doctor.'

He and Reidy stood for a moment outside on the pathway before Donegan raised the line of crime tape for Reidy to pass beneath.

He spoke in a hushed tone as they walked past the group of onlookers and snapping cameras. Three uniformed gardaí carrying clipboards were already moving from house to house on inquiries.

'If someone's going to kill a drug-dealing spunker like the Wolfman, why leave a note for us along with a business card?'

'Anybody could have been responsible for that,' offered Reidy. 'I mean, how many enemies does a drug-dealer have?'

Donegan didn't reply, but thought for a moment.

'What are Fox and McGrath working on at the moment?' he asked, as he unlocked the car door. 'They must have known this Jimbo guy from their time in the Drug Squad.'

Reidy lifted an eyebrow in disgust. 'I'd say those two headers are working on a very quiet case at the moment after the Grafton Street incident.'

Donegan snorted a laugh as he pictured in his mind the meeting of Fox and McGrath with the super. He looked across the roof of the unmarked car at a frowning Reidy.

'What a wonderful couple they make,' he grinned.

CHAPTER THREE

Landers moved with an air of purpose across the lobby of the city-centre hotel. He placed his briefcase on the marble counter at the reception and drummed his fingers on it as he waited. The receptionist was speaking in broken German to an elderly couple as she pointed to a map on a small pamphlet. The husband and wife looked at one another, shaking their heads in confusion. The young receptionist glanced around in desperation searching for assistance.

'Hallo. Verzeihung,' said Landers with a polite smile and edged his way along the counter towards them. 'Kann ich Ihnen bitte helfen?' The receptionist watched as he gently took the pamphlet from her hand and turned to the couple. He spoke to them in fluent German, enquiring, explaining and even pausing to crack a joke about the Irish weather. The Germans smiled and then nodded in understanding and thanked him. He bade them a good evening with a quick touch of his forehead before turning to the relieved receptionist.

'Thank you, Mr Landers,' she sighed, her eyes sparkling in admiration at his linguistic prowess.

Landers was a very likable guest. Not at all like the demanding others who complained about this and that. The air-conditioning controls, the weather, the lift.

But not Mr Landers. He was a middle-aged, courteous gentleman who had been staying for the past six weeks, and not once had he given any of the staff a reason to grumble amongst themselves. He reminded the young receptionist of her favourite uncle.

'I really don't know how you deal with all these foreigners,' he smiled at her. 'Any messages for me?'

She turned her back to him and searched through a bundle of envelopes for a moment before holding one up. She checked the name and then placed it on the counter in front of him together with the key of his room.

'That's the one,' he said, picking it up and putting it in the inside pocket of his jacket.

'Will you be eating in this evening, sir?' she enquired.

'Yes. Yes, I will. And I would like a table for two at nine,' he replied. 'An associate will be joining me.'

She opened up the leather register and began to write.

'I'll ensure that you get the best table then,' she promised. 'I owe it to you.'

Landers rubbed his hands together and smiled.

'That's very good of you,' he said, taking his brief-case and key from the counter.

He walked across the lobby and took the lift to the second floor.

Back in his room, he threw the briefcase on the bed and sat for a moment on the sofa beside the window looking out at the city street. He glanced at his watch, then eased his head back and closed his eyes. There would be just enough time for a short nap, a shower and a change of clothes. He ran through the events of the morning in his head.

Gerry Feeney had been old, weak and vulnerable. An easy target. He had felt no sense of victory, at least not the same sense of victory he had felt after he had dispatched Jimbo Ryan, the drug-dealer. Of the three so far, Jimbo had given the greatest job satisfaction.

The bigger they are, they harder they fall. Always a challenge.

Cancelling the snooze, he reached into the inside pocket of his tweed jacket and took out the white envelope. He tore it open and removed the contents. He balled the envelope in his fist and dropped it into the wastebasket beside the sofa. He then leaned forward on his elbows and unfolded the paper.

Let it be worthwhile, he thought to himself as he glanced down through the photocopied file page. A smile of pleasure crept across his mouth as he read the heading under *Crime*. This was a job that would take careful planning. A job outside the safety of the bustling city, a city where anonymity had been so easy.

In less than a week's time the primary task of the mission would be accomplished and he would receive payment in full for his efforts.

He folded the paper slowly and knelt down beside the bed. He snapped the briefcase open and removed the top sheet of paper, glancing down through it for a moment before placing both papers inside and locking it.

From beneath the bed, he pulled an identical briefcase and meticulously checked the contents.

All was in readiness.

He showered, changed into a dark grey suit, and in a matter of thirty minutes was passing back through the lobby of the hotel, the second briefcase swinging from one hand, his other hand giving a quick wave to the receptionist. She smiled and turned to tell her story to her colleague beside her, pointing furiously at Landers as he passed through the revolving door.

He strolled casually along the street, stopping for a moment to check his appearance in the large window of an electrical shop, and again to buy the evening paper from a vendor on the corner.

He folded the newspaper twice and placed it under his arm as he walked on, looking like any other businessman coming from work. An accountant perhaps.

He crossed the street and entered into the coolness of the high-rise car park. The attendant in the small cabin glanced up at him from the football magazine and tossed his head in indifferent greeting.

It took Landers less than a minute to locate the car. His two weeks of surveillance told him that the black BMW would be parked in the reserved zone. He allowed himself a moment of silent congratulation.

He looked around before putting the briefcase on the roof and opening it. He put on his surgical gloves and clasped his hands together to tighten them.

A child cried in protest at his mother in the distance.

'Now... Now... I want them now!' The screeched demands echoed through the mass concrete.

He drummed his fingers impatiently on the roof. He didn't like to be kept waiting.

Christ, give the child what he wants and move on.

Finally, the engine started and purred into the distance. He took his home-made picklock from the briefcase, started his stopwatch and set to work. His expression of concentration changed to a smile as the central locking whirred open. He worked with an air of urgency in the driver's seat, the briefcase resting on his lap, the trickles of sweat running behind his ears, his nostrils assaulted by the smell of new leather. He removed the battery from its wrapping and fitted it in its place in the device he had prepared. He opened the glove compartment, carefully placed the device inside and closed the flap.

The job complete, he stepped out and eased the heavy car door shut, then stooped down once more to work until the locks whirred. He stood up and checked his watch.

Not a record, but fast nonetheless.

Taking a white handkerchief from his pocket, he rubbed his face and neck. He left by the pedestrian exit into the side alleyway and moved around to the front of the building, crossing the wide street and carefully choosing a vantage point that faced the entrance to the high-rise.

Now, all he had to do was wait.

***

Fox sat at his desk looking down at the mass of paper in front of him. He leaned back on the chair and threw his hands up with a purposefully loud yawn.

'Jesus, I could do with a bite to eat,' he grumbled. 'Will we head off?'

McGrath eyed him for a moment from the adjoining desk and then resumed writing.

Fox, not getting the reaction he had hoped for, picked up one of the sheets from the file and pretended to read it.

'What the hell are we doing stuck in here anyway?' he sighed, throwing the paper back down on the desk. He laid his palms down on the strewn sheets and shuffled them noisily.

'Well now, Andy,' replied McGrath, without raising his head, his tone sarcastic. 'Allegedly, we're detectives. And now we're preparing a file on a case we've solved. The wonderful paperwork side of the job.'

'Yeah. That's hilarious altogether.' Fox was indignant. He leaned forward on the desk and picked up one of the sheets. He glanced down at it and then blew his lips in disgust.

'This is *some* boring shite,' he muttered. 'I mean, he's pleading guilty to the possession of the guns, isn't he? We spend eight months catching him, three more months taking statements. Another month making a book out of them. And for what? Five minutes in court.'

McGrath closed his eyes and cupped his hands over his ears. He waited until the ranting had faded to a silent protest of head-shaking and then leaned back slowly on the chair, his elbows resting on the arms as he rolled the pen between his fingers. He glared at Fox for a moment before speaking.

'I started work at six o'clock this morning,' he began in a low voice. 'It is now...' he looked at the clock above the office door, '... a quarter to five and, to be honest with you, so far, it's been something of a shitty day.'

Fox gave a casual shrug and then grimaced.

'You speak the truth, Detective.'

'So,' continued McGrath, his voice rising, 'I would like very much to get out of here some time in the next couple of hours.'

He picked up the statement from the desk and read through it. He frowned as he searched through the pile for another, holding them both out as his eyes moved across from one to the other.

Fox sat back and rolled his thumbs as he watched the confusion grow.

'Problems, Detective?'

McGrath leaned across the desk.

'Explain these contradictions to me,' he said, both statements outstretched.

Fox took them and whistled softly for a minute as he read them through.

'No contradiction,' he said finally, and placed the statements back on the desk.

McGrath listened as he outlined the slight differences but stronger similarities in the evidence. He silently cursed himself for his hasty reading and then braced himself for the inevitable put-down.

'Anything else I can help you with... eh... Guard, is it?' smiled Fox.

'I can't understand how you find anything in that

desk.' McGrath knew the retaliation was weak. 'It looks like a burst mattress.'

'I was never any good at this paper crack,' explained Fox.

'You mean that you never *wanted* to be any good at it,' he corrected. 'That's why I'm the one who always ends up doing it. Isn't it?'

Fox pointed across at him.

'You're the one with the degree,' he offered. ''Twould be a fright to let all that smartness go to waste.'

'It's a degree in criminology, not doing files.'

'Coffee,' suggested Fox, changing the subject. 'I'll go and get us two coffees.'

The chair clattered behind him as he stood up. McGrath winced at the noise.

Fox moved to the door and then stopped for a moment, looking up at the clock. He snapped his fingers suddenly and turned around.

'You've a date, haven't you?' he grinned. 'That new bird.'

McGrath pretended not to hear, engrossing himself in the file. He closed his eyes as he sensed Fox return.

'It's with that beautiful, intelligent, wealthy girl, isn't it?'

McGrath remained silent.

'Oh boy, I can't wait to meet her. All those fabulous qualities – only to be struck down with blindness in her prime.'

He turned away towards the door. McGrath sighed as he eased back on the chair, tossing the pen on the table, resigning himself to the fact that he would have to introduce his partner to her sooner or later. God, how he dreaded it!

Fox whistled loudly as he made his way along the corridor. The superintendent appeared in the doorway of his office, jacket on, keys in hand.

'Finished for the day, sir?'

The superintendent glanced at him from the task of locking his office door and gave a weary shake of his head.

Fox walked on a few yards and then clapped his hands.

'I'd *really* love to be an officer,' he gushed.

The superintendent turned and called after Fox.

'Things will never get that bad around here, boy. I hope that file you're dealing with is going to see the light some time.'

Banter completed, he turned and walked away without waiting for a response.

Inside in the small canteen, Fox plugged in the kettle and checked the press and fridge. He shook the scant contents of the coffee jar and then reached for the phone beside him. He dialled and then hummed as he waited for a reply.

'Bob, my friend,' he smiled. 'Old Mother Hubbard here. How do you like your coffee again? Ah yes, I see, strong with milk and two sugars. What about fairly weak with no milk and no sugar?'

He sniggered as McGrath cursed down the line at him. In the background he could hear Inspector Donegan enquiring as to his whereabouts.

'Get him and get in here.'

He hung up and slammed the coffee jar back on the

draining board, hurriedly making his way along the corridor. Donegan beckoned to him in the distance before he and Reidy disappeared into the inspector's office.

'What's this about?' he asked as McGrath appeared from the detectives' room.

McGrath shrugged. 'Dunno. He looks a bit worried though.'

Fox pushed him towards the office door.

'Admit nothing,' he whispered as they went inside.

Reidy sat on the window ledge of the office with his arms folded. He closed and opened his eyes slowly at them by way of greeting.

Donegan removed his coat and threw it across the back of the chair behind his desk. He took the cigarette from his mouth and pounded it in a large glass ashtray.

'Malley just phoned me on the mobile,' he said, as he took his seat.

Fox and McGrath looked at one another and then moved to opposite sides of the room and pulled chairs to the middle of the office.

'What's the story, Kig?' Fox was in first.

'Jimbo the Wolfman was tied to a chair in his house and burnt to death late last night.'

Fox looked at McGrath and winked.

'Told you there was a God.'

'Yeah, maybe,' muttered Donegan. 'Thing is, there was a business card and a message for us left at the scene of the fire.'

Fox leaned forward and opened his mouth to speak.

Donegan raised a silencing hand.

'Thank you for thinking of the question, Detective.

The answer is that it was in a fire-proof cash box.'

Fox nodded and eased back on the chair.

'What was the message?' asked McGrath.

As if on cue, the fax machine clicked and buzzed to life.

'This should be the full version now,' he said. 'Malley only gave the first couple of lines.'

Fox and McGrath stood up and moved towards the fax machine. Reidy remained seated on the window ledge. Donegan threw his eyes up and pointed outwards.

'Sit down.' He scolded their eagerness. 'I'll read it out.' They reluctantly returned to their places and waited.

The fax machine hummed for a further moment and fell silent, Donegan whipping the page away before it fell on the tray. He sat back in the chair and took a deep breath before he began.

'Dear Gardaí,'

'Sounds like a nice enough fella,' Fox grinned.

The inspector glared at him. Fox's head lowered. This was not the time for cracking jokes.

'The whip, it cracks loud, then the chase, it begins,
For the ones who have yielded their souls,
Its doors open wide, fate lingers inside,
As the coach of redress onward rolls.

Sincerely
Best wishes

The Mercury Man.'

Donegan frowned at the page for a moment and then flattened it on the desk. He looked up at the others.

'Malley is doing the usual checks. Source of paper, ink used, fingerprints.'

Something snapped in the silence of the room and Fox and McGrath turned to look at Reidy who was preening his fingernails with a small gold cutter. 'I told him that Mercury was the messenger of the gods,' he smiled. 'But he's such an ignorant arsehole.'

Fox leaned forward and took the sheet of paper from the desk. He sat back and raised his eyebrows as he read it in silence. When he was finished he held it out to McGrath.

'Well, he's a piss-poor poet, Kig. We've established that anyway.'

He became more serious when he looked up and saw the expression on Donegan's face.

'OK.' He changed his tone. 'Let's look at what we have. Someone goes into Jimbo's house and torches him. Now, Jimbo wasn't exactly the flavour of the month with his rivals. Or his customers for that matter. Not forgetting the hundreds and thousands of parents who have a thing against drug-dealers.'

'Why leave a poem, Detective?' asked Reidy behind him. 'Why do that?'

Fox turned. Reidy always asked the awkward questions. He shrugged as he settled back in the seat.

'Who knows, Sergeant?' he replied casually. 'The reality is that when you get involved in the drug scene you run the risk of being tied to a chair and toasted. Face it, they're dropping like flies around us every day. Why should Jimbo be any different?'

McGrath looked up. 'Is this not an ordinary murder investigation, Kig?'

Donegan shook his head and then changed it to a nod.

'Well, it is and it isn't, Bob. The local lads have started the door-to-door and the preliminaries. But I want us to get in on the edge, just in case it turns out to be some headball going around topping our favourite people. I want you and Andy to do a bit of background on Jimbo. Talk to...' He paused and threw his eyes up. 'Whoever it is you fellas talk to.'

Fox and McGrath looked at one another. Already they had both picked the same snitch without thinking that hard about it.

McGrath looked back at Donegan.

'What makes you think that it might not be a one-off drug-related killing?' he asked.

Donegan moved around the desk and took the fax paper from McGrath. He lifted it up and turned the sheet around, his finger pointing at the top.

'*For the ones*, gentlemen,' he said. 'The words, *for the ones*.'

CHAPTER FOUR

Landers craned his neck as he looked across the street, his heart rate increasing as he watched the young man in his early twenties make his way to the entrance of the high-rise. He took three steps back and rested against the corner wall of the bread shop, one hand taking the mobile phone from his trouser pocket, the other putting the briefcase on the path. Briefcase settled, he placed his free hand inside his suit pocket and closed it around the remote-control device.

He looked down at his watch, calculating the time it would take for his victim to arrive at the black BMW.

Young Henry Williams kicked the empty cola can with his milk-white runners, much to the annoyance of the car-park attendant who scowled out from the small booth.

Williams looked in as he passed and laughed.

'Cheer up, for fuck's sake, will you,' he said.

He walked on for a minute, taking the car keys out of his designer tracksuit pocket and pressing the remote. The car flashed orange lights in the semi-darkness and greeted him with a short beep. He removed his tracksuit top, threw it onto the back seat and sat in.

The mobile phone rang.

He looked around for a moment and then glanced down at the floor of the car. He stepped out and knelt down to look beneath the leather seat. The green dial illuminated for a second then stopped. And then it rang again.

'So that's where you were hiding,' he muttered.

He reached in for his phone and examined it. As he sat back in he pressed the receive button and lifted it to his ear.

'Hello,' he said. 'I'm not here at the moment, so go and jump.' Then he laughed.

'Young man. I want you to listen very carefully to what I have to say.'

'Who the fuck is this?' William's tone was vexed.

'Open the glove compartment and tell me what you see.'

Without thinking, Williams reached across quickly and pulled at the catch, sitting back suddenly as it flapped open.

'Well?'

'It's a flashing red light,' he said, his voice lowered in fear.

'No, Mr Williams, it's a bomb. And if you get out of the car, it will go off.'

'Who the fuck is this?' Williams repeated, looking wildly around him in panic. 'What do you want? Is this some kind of joke?'

Landers fell silent. It was important that the victim felt alone.

Would the bomb go off now? Was there any more to be said? Landers smiled to himself as he pictured the young man, sitting in his expensive, explosive tomb, counting the seconds, his eyes closed as he waited for the bang that he would never hear.

'Repentance, Mr Williams,' he hissed.

'What?'

'You heard me, you spoilt brat rapist.' His tone softened. More like the semi-scolding of a child. 'Tell me, do you remember Sheila?'

Williams lifted a trembling hand to his forehead and rubbed the sweat back into his hair. He put little thought into the answer.

'I... I don't know anyone called Sheila.' He stuttered like a drunk.

He closed his eyes as the anonymous caller's voice lowered to a sinister whisper.

'Please don't upset me, or I will be forced to terminate this conversation... and you.'

Williams clenched the phone in his hand.

'Are you talking about the trial?' His voice stammered as he looked at the flashing red light in the glove compartment.

'Ah, yes, yes, very good. Continue.' The tone lightened again.

Williams took a deep breath and tried to clear his mind. He would have to choose his words more carefully. Play along. Say what had to be said. He looked again at the tiny, flashing red bulb in the glove compartment and his courage sagged.

'It was a party at a friend's house,' he blurted out, his voice cracking as he felt the tears rise behind his eyes. Not tears of sorrow for his victim, but tears of fear and self-pity for his own impending demise. 'You know it was me. What the fuck do you want?'

'Yes. We know all this. But the real question is, do you repent? You and I both know that you slithered through some legal loophole or other. But what I want to know is, are you really sorry for drugging and raping a fifteen-year-old girl?'

Williams swallowed hard. There were so many answers he would like to give. So many inane explanations for his actions: I was drunk, I was high, she was a little tart and she was asking for it. Common sense dictated that there could be only one.

'Yes, yes, I am,' he said, mustering as much sincerity as he could in his voice.

And then silence.

Outside, Landers waited for a mother pushing her child in a buggy to pass.

'Well,' his voice lowered in contempt, 'I'm afraid that I don't believe you.'

Williams gritted his teeth in angry defiance. He knew all along that the faceless accuser's verdict would go against him. Why put a bomb in a car if you're not going to use it? No suave, fast-talking senior counsel to snip the blue wire this time.

There was only one thing to do. He had nothing to lose by trying.

He eased his hand down slowly to the side of the driver's door, his clammy fingers caressing the handle for a moment, his eyes closing as he pulled gently at it, his jaw aching in a clench of fear and determination. The door clicked open, and in a second he was rolling out and throwing himself on the ground beside the car.

'Mr Williams?'

A pause.

'I hope that you haven't left the car,' the voice scolded gently.

Williams crawled out from the parking space and lay on the ground. He knew that if the bomb went off now that he would have a better chance of survival. It always happened in the films.

'Mr Williams?' The voice was a distant buzz at the end of his arm.

It was surely decision time now. Time to choose between life and death. Time to race the devil. He was already half way there.

He jumped to his feet, his mobile phone gripped like a relay baton.

And then he ran faster than he ever had before. Twenty yards. Thirty. Fifty.

He stopped suddenly and looked back, his runners squeaking on the smooth concrete. He panted for a moment before lifting the phone to his sweating face.

'Fuck you, whoever you are, and that little bitch too,' he roared in triumph. 'Go ahead and blow it up now, you, you, fucking – sicko.'

'Tut tut tut tut tut.'

'I'm out and I'm going straight to the cops,' shouted Williams, as he raced past the parking attendant who leaned out quizzically through the hatch, on and up towards the awaiting safety of the evening sun.

Across the street, Landers narrowed his eyes and waited for his quarry to appear. Williams stood at the entrance to the high-rise, his head moving left and right quickly as he searched the now almost empty street for help. A taxi lounged by the footpath some two hundred yards away and he moved towards it in long purposeful strides.

As he neared it, his courage grew even stronger.

'I don't know who you are,' he all but shouted. 'But the cops won't be long finding out.'

Landers smiled.

'If you want to know who I am... just look across the street.'

He waited for a moment, waited and watched as his fourth victim stopped ten yards from the taxi.

'No, not him. Down here.'

Williams turned his head slowly, his eyes checking the few remaining pedestrians. They narrowed as they settled on the well-dressed man at the corner who was leaning against the bread-shop wall.

'You really should be more careful where you leave your phone, Henry.'

Landers gave him a little wave. With his other hand, he squeezed the remote in his pocket.

The last sound that Henry Williams heard was a short buzz of interference in his mobile phone, just before the explosive device inside detonated, shredding his hand and removing the left side of his head.

***

The unmarked car cruised at a leisurely twenty-five miles an hour along the street. Fox shuffled in the passenger seat for a moment before grappling with the adjuster and turning it twice. He settled back on the headrest and looked out the window.

'Isn't the city grand at this time of the evening?' he mused. 'Everyone gone home. No traffic to get in the way.'

McGrath glanced sideways at him.

'I never took you for the peace-loving type,' he said dryly. 'Or maybe you're changing for the better.'

Fox smiled in contentment.

'You don't understand,' he said. 'What I mean is, why isn't there ever a car chase or a bit of bang-bang at this time of the evening when a fella could really cut loose? Why does it always happen when there's a line of young wans with their first provisional licence in front of us on their way to work?'

McGrath sighed as he reached forward and turned on the car radio.

'Yeah, that's a bit of a shame all right.'

The DJ waffled on in a false American accent about some competition where the lucky winner would win a year's supply of Coca Cola, and finished with a 'Yeeehaaa' before the music started again.

'Gobshite,' Fox muttered as he turned his head to look at the radio. 'How does he know how much of that stuff a fella would drink in a year? Or maybe they post you out a bottle a day.'

McGrath laughed. 'Where are we going to find Beano at this time of the evening?' he asked when he had finished. 'Give him a ring.'

Fox groaned in protest as he unclipped the phone from his belt and fingered through the numbers.

'Where'll we meet him?' he asked as he lifted it to his ear.

'Find him first,' replied McGrath.

The phone rang twice.

'Yeah,' came the reply.

'Beano, my old friend,' Fox said with a smile. 'I'm just calling to wish you a happy birthday.'

He turned to McGrath with a frown of mock disappointment.

'Inconvenient, did you say? Now where did an illiterate bollocks like you get a big word like that? And can you tell us the name of the man who gave it to you so that we can learn big words from him too?'

He smiled at the response. Fast, nervous breathing.

'Well, now, Beano,' he said glancing at his watch. 'It is a quarter to eight. And if I don't hear from you by eight, then the next time I see you, I'll be using big words myself like... illegal substances... warrant... habeas corpus... and so on and so forth. Tarry a moment while I put you on to my colleague, if it's not too much of an imposition.'

He handed the phone to a smiling McGrath.

'Beano, seriously, this is a matter of urgency.' He turned and looked at Fox. 'Nah, don't mind him. He doesn't mean a word of it.' There was a short pause. 'Where? Good man.'

He held the phone out to Fox and gave a knowing wink.

Fox understood, clearing his throat before he spoke.

'That's u-r-g-e-n-c-y,' he spelled out, then pressed at the phone to end the call.

McGrath waited for a clear street ahead and then checked his rear mirror before doing a U-turn. Once it was complete, he lowered the speed back to thirty.

'The Rising Salmon in half an hour,' he announced.

Fox puffed with disgust as he clipped the phone back on his belt.

'Why did you let him pick that place? I hear it's an awful kip,' he said. 'The Rising Salmon, my arse. The Retching Wino's more like it.' He lay back on the seat and closed his eyes.

McGrath tried without success to keep a straight face as he spoke.

'It's one of his haunts. Ah, c'mon now. It's not that bad. I hear that they do a fabulous toasted special.'

He laughed suddenly as he pictured what the bar might be like. He stopped at the traffic lights as the siren of a patrol car neared, the wailing growing louder until the flashing blue lights passed in front of them. Fox was already sitting upright, switching on his walkie-talkie and changing channels until the voices cut in. He waited until the conversation stopped.

'This is Charlie nine-one. What's the big panic? Over.'

'Some guy's mobile-phone just blew up,' came the hurried reply.

McGrath laughed unintentionally, then stopped suddenly when he realised the seriousness of what had happened.

'Jesus,' he said. 'Who says they're not hazardous to your health?'

Fox switched off the walkie-talkie and threw it back on the dashboard.

'Blew up, if you don't mind,' he said pensively. 'I wonder if he's badly hurt?'

He looked down at his own phone clipped to his belt.

McGrath caught him.

'Yep,' he said casually as he accelerated away slowly. 'I reckon that one of those things could cause quite a bit of damage to the lower region when they go.'

Fox tossed his head back nonchalantly. Much as he wanted to remove it and put it in the boot of the car, he would not give in to McGrath.

'They're as safe as your driving,' he quipped.

They arrived outside The Rising Salmon ten minutes earlier than planned. Fox muttered a low curse under his breath as they went through the door. McGrath, walking behind him, glanced back to where he had parked the car a short distance away.

They both knew that it was not the most law-abiding sidestreet in the city.

'Now isn't this just wonderful,' said Fox sarcastically as they stepped into the darkened, smoke-filled bar. 'I always wondered what cancer looked like.'

McGrath nudged him towards the small counter, behind which stood a bald giant in his fifties wearing a black T-shirt with the words 'Transvestites really get on my tits' in bold white lettering. He eyed them both as they entered and then, as if giving his approval, made towards them and rested his hands on the brown timber counter dotted with cigarette burns.

'What can I get ye, lads?' he enquired in a pleasant tone that surprised them both.

'Eh, two pints,' replied Fox looking back at McGrath who nodded in silence.

They pulled a couple of shaky metal stools from the counter and sat down to survey the premises.

The barman moved to the Guinness tap at the far end and picked up a glass.

'You should bring your wan here on a date some time,' smiled Fox. 'I'd say she'd be thrilled.'

McGrath looked at him in panic and stood up from the stool. 'Oh, Christ!' he said as he looked at his watch, then scanned the room for a public phone. He certainly wasn't going to use the mobile with Fox listening in. He walked quickly along the bar to where the second pint was being pulled.

'Where's the phone?' he asked, trying to disguise the urgency in his voice.

The barman nodded to the toilet door. 'In there on your right. Do you need change?'

McGrath shook his head without turning back and went inside.

At the other end of the bar, Fox drummed his fingers on the counter as he looked around.

Just inside the door in the corner, a woman sat whispering threats to her semi-drunk husband. 'If I catch ya again, Paddy, I'll fuckin' kill ya. Do ya hear me?'

Paddy's head bobbed in understanding.

In the other corner a lone drunk sat teetering on a bad chair for a moment before falling to the ground, his head giving a dull thud as it struck the corner of the stone fireplace. Blood started to drip from above his eye onto the manky brown carpet. Fox was in no doubt that it was not the first time that this carpet had tasted blood.

He started to rise from his stool, then changed his mind. Nobody else moved to help the old drunk. And he didn't want to look out of place.

The barman returned and placed the pints on the counter. Fox nodded back over his shoulder.

'Looks like yer man is in a bit of bother,' he said casually as he placed the tenner on the counter. The barman took it and looked down, then shook his head in dismay.

'Aw, Jaysus, Billy,' he muttered to himself, and moved quickly inside the bar to the hatch, grabbing a damp beer towel from the sink as he passed. Fox looked on in wonder as the hulking barman picked the drunk up from the floor with one hand and held the towel to his bleeding head with the other. He lifted the remaining half-pint from the table and cupped it in the drunk's hand.

'Drink this and go home for yourself, will you,' he advised gently.

Fox was glad he was on his own. If McGrath was with him at the time, then they would surely at this stage be rocking with laughter. Rocking with laughter that is, just before all hell would break loose and he'd be forced to save their lives by shooting the gigantic barman in the knee.

He turned his attention back to his drink and took a long gulp from his pint.

Mother's milk, he thought. Why was it that all the kip pubs sold the best pints?

He watched as McGrath returned from the phone, looking curiously at the barman who edged past him with the bloodied towel.

'Well, are we in the doghouse with the wan?' enquired Fox.

McGrath shook his head and smiled as he took his pint and sipped.

'She's a very understanding person,' he said and wiped the white froth from his lips. He leaned forward and lowered his voice, his eyes narrowing.

Fox opened his arms in a grand gesture. 'When am I going to be introduced to this fabulous female anyway?' he grinned.

McGrath looked him straight in the eyes. How could he explain to his colleague that the girl that he was currently dating, was a refined and stunning brunette with a wealthy father, living in Dublin 4? Fox's taste in women confined itself to loose women in tight leggings who chewed gum and swore at will.

'This looks like a nice enough place,' he said wryly.

'Absolutely.' Fox glanced around. 'All they're missing is a bald retard with a banjo.'

McGrath snorted in laughter. 'God, yeah. That was a great film.' And he commenced to pluck an air-banjo.

'What's the story with yer man?' he nodded his head in the direction of the barman.

'Well,' said Fox, 'I have two possible theories that will answer that.'

McGrath relaxed into the stool, relieved now that the train of conversation had turned from the phone call.

'What are these theories?' he asked with enthusiasm.

'One, he's being very nice to us because he knows that we're the law, or the "filth" to give us our proper name in this particular establishment.'

McGrath thought about it for a moment, and nodded. 'And the other?' he asked.

Fox lowered to a barely audible whisper.

'He's the biggest, nicest and strongest homosexual barman in the city, and you're his new boyfriend.'

Fox and McGrath laughed out loud.

The drunk with the bleeding forehead, the cross wife and her humbled spouse looked up at them for a second and then turned back to their drinks.

'Jesus, the smell is cat in here,' said Fox getting serious. His nostrils widened and narrowed in disgust. 'I'd say the toilets are a wonder to behold.'

'Are we pub spies now or what?' said McGrath.

The door opened behind them and a thin man in his mid-twenties stood inside, glancing furtively around, his hands in the pockets of his stained suede jacket, his faded denims torn at the knees, not because of a fashion trend, but more as a result of wear and falling. Fox and McGrath looked at him and he winked, reaching around and tightening the rubber band that held his black, greasy ponytail.

The drunk stared at him as he rubbed the drying blood from his face with a wrinkled hand. He slurred a foul-mouthed greeting.

'Beano... ya... shtupa... baastar... ya... Ga us a pie.'

Fox nudged McGrath and they both turned back to the counter.

'Oops. That's his cover blown I'd say,' said Fox.

McGrath snorted for a moment, then picked up his drink.

Beano had a confidential and hurried conversation with Billy that ended with the advice that he should 'shut up and fuck off' all at the same time. He then moved to the counter where he placed his elbows down beside Fox and McGrath.

The barman approached and raised his eyebrows in question.

'Pint,' said Beano. He looked around and waited until it was safe to speak.

'The Wolfman got it last night,' he said.

'Well now, aren't you a mine of information,' said Fox. 'Where did you hear that? On the evening news?'

Beano winced and nodded in the direction of a vacant table.

They sat at the table beside the toilet, a safe distance away from any listening ears. Fox was in no mood for waiting. The poor lighting and the smell of stale urine that emanated through the hole in the bottom of the toilet door was making his stomach churn.

'Who did him, Beano?' he urged. 'Tell us, and we're gone.'

Beano licked his lips. He looked more nervous than usual. His eyes moved from Fox to McGrath and then focused on the carpet.

'That's just it,' he said, looking up. 'No one has a clue. No word at all. Not even a rumour.'

He rose to his feet and waited until the barman placed the pint down on the counter.

Beano rattled the change in his pocket, then took it out and flicked the coins from one hand to the other.

Fox and McGrath looked at one another in silence as he moved away to get his drink.

It was not good when Beano had nothing to contribute. He had been their tout for nearly ten years, and he had never let them down before. But information did not come cheap, and Beano was no different.

'Maybe he's frightened,' whispered McGrath.

Fox shook his head.

'Bollocks. He knows a lot more than he's letting on. I'm going to put the frighteners on him.'

He leaned forward with his elbows on his knees and watched as Beano returned and took a long gulp from the pint before he sat down.

'You were a runner for the Wolfman at one stage, weren't you?' he asked indifferently.

Beano lowered his pint slowly on to the table. His eyes darted nervously from one detective to the other.

'Hold on a minute. You don't think that *I* had anything to do with it?'

There was no response.

'Now, lads. I know that he was a real bad ass. He even stiffed me a couple of times.'

'That's very upsetting,' said Fox lifting his pint. 'But we're not really interested in your drug stories, Beano. Think hard now, like a good man.'

Beano ran a trembling hand across his lips and then tightened his ponytail again. He stared at the floor as he ran through every possibility. He looked up suddenly at the two of them.

'What about all that bad shit that he sold a couple of years ago? The stuff that he cut ten times. Fuck knows with what.'

'What about it?' asked McGrath quickly.

'Well, it killed a few of them, didn't it? The whole city knew that he did it, but yous lot could do nothing about it.'

'And?'

'And maybe some of the survivors set out to get him. There must have been at least twenty of them.'

Fox lowered his head.

'For fuck's sake, Beano,' he muttered. 'What are you saying? That there's a gang of vigilante junkies going around whacking dealers?'

'No, just *that* dealer.' Beano attempted to continue but McGrath fanned him to silence.

'Beano, that has to be the wildest statement that ever came out of your mouth. And I'm sure that when that murky haze of cannabis clears, you'll agree with me. We are not going back to our boss and telling him that we're currently looking for a very large gang of angered addicts.'

'I'd help ye if I could,' said Beano, half-pleading. 'But the word outside is zero.'

'Then get it somewhere,' said Fox. 'And while you're at it, find out who the Mercury Man is.'

'The who?'

'The Mercury Man,' repeated Fox as he placed two folded twenties under his beermat and slid it across the table to a smiling Beano. 'You have our number.'

He and McGrath stood up to leave.

Beano smiled as he eyed the beermat.

'Ye'll be the first to know,' he said, slipping it along with the twenties into his jacket pocket.

McGrath patted him on the shoulder.

'Be talking to you,' he whispered.

Fox took a series of deep breaths outside the door until his head spun. He shook the dizziness away and walked in front of McGrath in silence. They were both thinking the same thing. Never before had they left Beano without some slight lead to work on. Things were back to square one for the time being.

'What do you reckon?' asked McGrath as they crossed the street to the car.

'Well, it doesn't look good when Beano has no word on it,' Fox replied, looking at McGrath across the roof of the car.

'You don't think that he had anything to do with it, do you?' offered McGrath as he looked down to unlock the door.

Fox gave a short laugh before sitting in. The laugh changed to a series of controlled snorts before he answered.

'Bob, you know as well as I do that Beano couldn't organise the drowning of a cat. If he tried to burn the Wolfman, he'd probably have set fire to himself instead.'

McGrath laughed.

'He's a total fuck-up at everything,' Fox continued. 'Except two things, that is. Listening and remembering. And that's what makes him worth his weight in gold.'

McGrath nodded in agreement as he started the car. He looked over his shoulder as he pulled out from the kerb.

'He'll come up with something for us,' he said casually. 'Wait and see.'

CHAPTER FIVE

Landers stood in front of the steamed bathroom mirror turning his face left and right for inspection. He took a bottle of expensive cologne from the shelf and gently patted some of it on his face. Happy with his appearance and his evening's work, he returned to the bedroom, put on his suit jacket and then treated himself to a straight scotch with ice from the mini-bar. He sat back on the large armchair and sipped at it as he thought about Henry Williams.

A perfect execution. His explosives mentor would have been proud.

He looked around the plush surroundings of his room and nodded his approval.

His previous work had never been as good to him as this. This was the life he craved. Easy work, easy money. All the training, the violence and the torture was paying off at last. His skills in weapon handling, explosives, surveillance, counter-surveillance and intelligence-gathering were equal to none. Why waste such ability?

He rested the drink on the arm of the chair, took his briefcase from beneath the bed and opened it. He removed a file on victim number five and sat back down. His lips pursed in thought as he ran a quick inventory through his mind of what would be needed for the task, his eyes fixed on the sheet as he picked up the glass of scotch. He was jolted from his thoughts by the sharp buzz of the telephone on the bedside locker. He rose slowly from the armchair, straightened his jacket and picked up the receiver.

'Mr Landers. Your guest is waiting in the lobby.'

'Thank you.'

He replaced the receiver and left the empty glass on the locker. Having returned the file to the suitcase, he locked it and pushed it back to its place of safety beneath the bed. He walked to the long mirror beside the door and gave his appearance a final check, straightening his tie and again pressing at the front of his dark suit.

He swung the key of the room on his finger as he made his way along the corridor and down the wide, marble stairway, his eyes scanning the lobby. He stood at the foot of the stairs for a moment, his eyes searching each face.

A newspaper was folded in the corner and the

reader looked directly at him, smiling as he stood up and approached.

'James. A pleasure to meet you again,' said the elderly man extending his hand, his other holding a soft, brown leather briefcase.

Landers returned the smile as he took the man's hand and shook it, then gestured towards the door of the hotel bar.

'Shall we have an aperitif?' he offered.

'Indeed, why not.'

Landers ordered two whiskies and soda then took a table in the corner near the window, out of earshot. Landers's guest listened with obvious fascination as he related the methods that he had used to dispatch the first four victims. This was indeed money well spent.

Landers was pleased with his reaction. So pleased, in fact, that he mentally abandoned the simple plan for his fifth victim and gave a much more elaborate one instead. His guest rubbed his hands together in wonder. No sooner had Landers explained the plan than he was inwardly cursing his own boastfulness. What he said was indeed possible, but would take a lot more work and involved much more risk.

Still, his client was happy. Perhaps he could squeeze a few extra thousand out of him in his present state.

A waiter approached. 'Your table is ready, Mr Landers.'

Landers's guest gave him a congratulatory pat on the shoulder as they followed the waiter to the dining room, like a boss happy with his employee's work.

The conversation between them as they ate was

much more coded than it had been in the bar. When Landers broached the question of extra funding for the fifth victim, his guest smiled at him and said, 'Certainly, that can be arranged. You will have it by tomorrow evening.'

When they had finished dessert, both of them refused the offer of coffee, each opting instead for a large brandy. Landers's guest reached down beside him, picked up his briefcase and placed it on his lap. He looked across the table.

'I understand,' he began, 'that this is not part of your contract.'

Landers raised his eyebrows with interest.

'And I know that you have a great deal of work to do at the moment. But this is something that really made my blood boil when I read it.'

Landers sat back in the chair and held his hands out in a gesture of curiosity.

His guest was pleased. He took out a file sealed in a plastic cover. He looked down at it for a moment as if deep in thought and then held it out to Landers.

'I'm sure that it will have the same effect on you,' he said.

Landers wanted to open the file there and then, so strong was his interest. He restrained himself, deciding that it would make some light bedtime reading.

'If you agree to deal with this matter – and, of course, the decision is yours – there will be an additional payment of... shall we say, thirty thousand?'

Landers simply nodded and placed the file on the table beside him. He lifted his brandy glass and smiled.

'We'll see,' he said. He was making no promises. He

had already loaded more work on himself in an attempt to impress. He would not make the same mistake again.

They remained in the dining room until it was almost empty. Landers changed to mineral water after the second brandy. Finally his guest rubbed his hands gently together.

'I hope to hear from you soon,' he said as he rose from the chair and picked up his briefcase. Landers took the file and rolled it in his hands. They walked to the lobby together where they shook hands. Landers held the grip as he looked around.

'One final question,' he said, releasing his guest's hand. 'When does all of this go to the media?'

His guest gave a brief smile.

'Soon. Very soon. Good night, Mr Landers.'

'And a very good night to you, Mr Doyle.'

Landers remained where he was until his guest had left the hotel, and then turned to the stairs. The combination of a four-course meal, the whiskey and the two large brandies had made him tired. His eyes were heavy with sleep. He was certainly not as fit as he had been up to his middle forties. He decided to start with the first few pages of the file and then get a good night's rest.

He returned to his room and threw his suit jacket on the armchair. He removed his shoes and lay down on the bed, the file resting on his chest for a moment before he tore the plastic cover from it and began to read.

It was almost 2am when he finished it. His heart pounded with anger in his chest. He would almost consider doing this one for free. Almost. Already the plan was unfolding in his head. It would not be difficult.

He would deal with this matter swiftly.

***

Fox sat with his feet up on the desk, stirring the teabag through the milk and sugar. When he was satisfied with the strength, he squeezed the bag against the mug and catapulted it with the spoon into the wastebasket some ten feet away.

One of the detectives who had seen this feat clapped slowly, and Fox acknowledged the admiration with a gentle bowing of his head.

McGrath sat opposite him head in hands, his shoulders rising in a huge yawn.

'When are we on rest-days?' he groaned as he exhaled.

Fox sipped at his tea and shrugged. 'Some time in 2008 by all accounts.'

McGrath sat back and folded his arms as he looked around the office.

'Why is everyone in the squad in at 6am?' he enquired casually.

Fox put his mug down on the desk and swung his feet off, his weary eyes glancing around at the other detectives who stood chatting in small groups. He smiled to himself when he saw Reidy at the top table, his head down, moving each sheet to one side slowly as he read them, glancing up now and then at the men who moved around the office. Fox searched his own desk for a sheet of paper, selected one, balled it and threw it basketball-style into the air. It bounced on the top table, struck Reidy on the sleeve and spun for a moment.

'You little swot, Sergeant,' he scolded.

Reidy did not look up. He brushed the ball of paper from the desk and resumed turning the pages slowly.

'What's this all about, Sergeant?' Fox called out. 'Why are we all here?'

Reidy looked up and stared for a moment, then licked his thumb and looked back down.

'You're unusually eager for this time of the morning, Detective,' he said with sarcasm.

Fox looked at McGrath and threw his eyes up.

'I'm not eager,' he snapped, his patience wearing thin. 'I'm tired and pissed off.'

'Then you should try doing some of that paperwork to cheer yourself up,' muttered Reidy.

Laughter filled the room. It was not often that Reidy showed a sense of humour. All eyes settled on Fox.

McGrath looked across with a wide grin at his irate partner, raising and lowering his eyebrows. 'You're not going to let them away with that, are you?' he said.

Fox looked around, searching for a victim amongst the smiling detectives.

'I don't know what you're laughing at, Dunne,' he said, pointing to the red-faced, middle-aged man. 'You're only a kick in the hole away from a finished fool yourself.'

'Why you smart little...'

The heavy-set detective rose to his feet, a half smile on his face.

The laughter died quickly as the superintendent and Donegan entered the room. Everyone moved back to their desks and sat down, looking earnest.

Donegan sat down beside Reidy who in turn placed sheets in order on the desk in front of the concerned-looking inspector. The superintendent remained standing behind them and cleared his throat.

'Gentlemen, it would appear that we have ourselves a vigilante. Sadly, he's not one of those run-of-the-mill gobshites with a shotgun, as Inspector Donegan will soon make clear. All other matters are to be put in the desk drawers until he's found.'

Some of the detectives who were close to finishing files groaned their disapproval. Fox looked across at McGrath and smiled as he rubbed his hands together.

The superintendent coughed and closed his eyes for a moment as if he were about to commit a mortal sin against the state.

'Overtime will be compulsory and unlimited.'

All present looked around at each other. The cow had just given birth to a bull calf.

'As of eleven o'clock last night, this has become a matter for the MCS. However, we will be working on this one with the co-operation of the local squads. And I stress that word co-operation. We're all policemen, and don't forget it. I want twice-daily reports on progress, Inspector.'

He looked around. 'Any questions on what I've said?'

McGrath winced and closed his eyes when he saw Fox raise his hand.

The superintendent looked down with a blank expression and nodded.

'Sir, does all this mean that Detective McGrath and myself are back on active service?'

There were a number of sniggers in the room. Donegan rubbed his hand across his face. The superintendent looked down at the floor and turned to the door.

'Yes, Detective Fox,' he muttered as he left. 'Sadly, that's exactly what it means. Carry on, Inspector.'

Donegan stood up and took the first sheet from Reidy.

'Jimbo the Wolfman,' he announced, holding it aloft. 'Drug-dealer, scumbag and not really a very nice lad. The night before last at approximately eleven o'clock, some person or persons gave him a taste of what his afterlife is going to be like. We all know what happened.'

All present nodded.

'A note and a poem were left at the scene for us. It's difficult to say why.'

He pointed to a closed file of paper.

'There's a photocopy of each for everyone in the audience. Some headball calling himself the Mercury Man is responsible.'

He paused for a moment as he placed the sheet back on the table and took the second one from Reidy.

'It wasn't really a job for us, until this happened. Henry Williams – anyone know him?'

Two detectives raised their hands. One of them spoke.

'Is he Williams who drugged and raped some girl on the northside a couple of years ago and got off on some mistake by the DPP?'

Donegan nodded.

'That's him. Well, half his head was removed last night by a mobile phone. They're still picking bits of it out of his brain.'

'That was yer man,' Fox whispered with urgency to McGrath.

Donegan took a breath before continuing.

'According to forensics, the phone contained an explosive device that was detonated from a remote.'

A senior detective raised his hand in objection.

'Surely a small amount of explosive couldn't do that much damage, Kig.'

'Course it could,' Fox sat up and spoke with an air of expertise. 'We've all seen what a teaspoon of Semtex can do. You pack that into a mobile phone and with all the components inside as shrapnel, you've got yourself a pretty good grenade when it goes off. Especially if you're holding it to your head.'

Donegan lowered his eyebrows as he looked down at Fox.

'Thank you, Alfred Nobel,' he muttered. 'Now then, lads, let's not get bogged down too much in how this device was made. That's a job for Malley and company. The reality is that there's a young fella lying in St James's morgue with a lot of his head missing. Our job is to find *who* did it. A simple device with a flashing red light was found in the glove compartment of his car in the high-rise. When the army EOD opened it, they found a battery wired to a bulb, and the same calling card as the one left at the Wolfman's house – "Messenger of the gods". A full print job is being done on the car as we speak, but I don't hold out much hope.

If this bastard is clever enough to set up a hit like that, I doubt if he'd make a silly mistake like leaving a fingerprint behind for us.'

McGrath sat up in his chair.

'How far into it are the local lads?' he asked.

'Well, they've only just started, so we can't expect much yet. Which brings me to the work detail. As the super told you, we'll be hand-in-hand with the other squads on this. I don't want to see any of the one-upmanship or the bickering bullshit I saw the last time we had to work together. Most of you are too old to get promoted at this stage anyway.'

Laughter echoed around the office.

'And as for Fox and McGrath – the one thing they have in common with the commissioner is that all three of them are gone as far in the job as they're going to get.'

The laughter grew louder. Fox and McGrath joined in.

'Teams of three,' announced Donegan quieting the room as he opened the folder and then called out the names, sending three men to join the Wolfman squad, the next three to the Williams squad. The six of them stood in front of the desk.

'I want every questionnaire, every statement, every shred of evidence copied and brought back here, where you'll give it all a thorough examination. Take one of those. It's what we have so far,' he said as Reidy held out the thin files, giving one to each of them.

The detectives were reading it as they sat back down.

It was scant to say the least.

'Fox, McGrath,' said Donegan looking down at them, 'I want a list of everyone who was acquitted, got off or got off lightly for serious crime in the last three years. Murder, rape, all violent crimes against the person. And not forgetting drugs. Sergeant Reidy here will be your third man, but I doubt if you'll see him. He's going to be dealing with the Bureau reports as they come through, so you'll have to manage on your own for the time being.'

Fox lowered his head.

'Christ,' he mumbled, before looking up.

'What then, Kig?' he asked trying to hide his irritation.

'Come back to me when you have the list and I'll tell you,' said Donegan.

Fox looked across at McGrath.

'That should be sometime around Christmas,' he whispered in disgust.

McGrath shook his head casually.

'No problem,' he whispered back. 'Half an hour on the computer.'

'Good man, Bob,' smiled Fox, happier now that his partner had taken the weight of paperwork from his shoulders for the umpteenth time.

Donegan stood up at the table and straightened his loosened tie. The remaining detectives turned from him, muttering amongst themselves as they compared the inane tasks they had been set.

'I want you to squeeze everyone on the street for information on this. Are we all clear on what has to be done here?' he asked. He looked around the office for a moment, some detectives already starting their enquiries by phone, others hastily scribbling notes at their desks, and then finally accepted the fact that there was no reply to his question as a 'yes'.

Knowing that Fox and McGrath had the best touts in the city, he looked down at them, waiting to catch their attention, then beckoned them with a backward nod. They were both laughing at some smart comment as they stood up and walked to the top table.

'You should have that job finished in about an hour,' he said. 'I want the two of you out of here by eight o'clock and blood-hounding.'

'Excellent,' Fox said with a grin. 'Thank you so much, Inspector.'

'When you give me that list, I'm going to pick the most likely out of it. That'll be later in the day, though. So you have a free hand until I call you back.'

Fox and McGrath nodded in acknowledgment and left the office. In the corridor, Fox punched his partner on the shoulder as they made their way to the computer terminal.

'Told you we were great.' He almost laughed.

McGrath looked curiously at him as they walked. 'What do you mean?'

'Well, it's obvious isn't it?' said Fox, disappointed that McGrath was not thinking along the same lines. 'He put all the others in groups of three, but he fobbed it off that Reidy would be coming with us, even though he had another job lined up for him. Just as well, anyway. He's a real depresser.' He smiled to himself. 'He thinks we work better on our own.' His tone smacked of vanity.

McGrath sighed inwardly and shook his head as they walked down the stairs.

'Nah,' he said. 'He just doesn't want to destroy a promising career.'

Donegan stood beside the desk, waiting as Reidy gathered the remaining paperwork, and quickly clarified a number of enquiries from the passing detectives. The young sergeant already had a head start on the rest of them, having stayed up for most of the night to read through the reports until he knew every one of them by heart. Donegan was confident that nothing would be left to chance by Reidy, a thirty year old with his inspector's exam done, and a certainty to be on the next list for promotion. Although he spoke very little during investigations, whenever he did, he said something intelligent. Replacing his ability in the squad would not be easy. Although his neat and shaven appearance and constant dress of trendy sports coat with matching shirt and tie did not fit in with the casual and downright grungy outfits of the others, he was an integral part of every investigation. The older men admired his individuality and the fact that he kept himself very much to himself. Even Fox and McGrath could not deny that he had a razor-sharp investigative brain.

'He's smart all right,' Fox had once admitted. 'But he's about as much *craic* as an undertaker with cancer.'

Donegan waited until all questions had been answered and then signalled his intentions with a nod towards the office door. Armed with what paperwork they had, he and Reidy made their way down the corridor to the superintendent's office.

'Come in, lads. Come in,' he greeted them. 'Take a seat.'

He stood behind his desk, removing his jacket and placing it on the back of his chair.

'Now then,' he said as he rolled up his shirtsleeves and made his way to the kettle that was already beginning to steam. 'Tell me what the plan of action is.'

Donegan waited while Reidy placed the paper on the superintendent's desk and sat back in his chair.

'Well, as you said yourself, Superintendent, this is no ordinary vigilante,' he began. 'At present, we're running a check on all persons with a possible motive for the Wolfman incident.'

He looked at Donegan and continued.

'Needless to say, it's going to be one hell of a long list.'

The super stood beside the kettle listening and watching it as it clicked to a finish.

'How big a list?' he asked quietly.

'Well, sir,' Reidy answered, 'that's not really the problem. The problem is evidence.'

The super turned around to them with a curious expression, holding the kettle.

'I think what Sergeant Reidy is trying to say,' said Donegan, 'is that the scene is in complete shit, for want of a better description. The fire brigade, bless them, went a bit haywire with the hoses. The cash box and documents are clean of any print. Forensics are presently examining the remains of a small device that was found at the scene, so the only thing we have to go on at the moment is the corpse. That, of course, and anything that might turn up in the house-to-house.'

'Somebody saw something,' insisted the superintendent as he poured the boiling water into the three coffee mugs and turned around to them. 'A person doesn't just walk into an estate, set fire to a drug-dealer and walk back out again unnoticed.'

He held out the two piping mugs to Reidy and Donegan.

Reidy leaned forward and smoothed his tie as he took one.

'Well, sir, that appears to be part of our problem. Which brings me back to the big list. The Wolfman was hated in the estate,' he explained, as he spooned two sugars into his mug from the small bowl on the desk. 'I'd go so far as to say there was a celebration when the residents found out that he'd been torched. The first run of questionnaires has given us about another fifty suspects. There is a great sense of relief on the estate.'

The superintendent sat down and rubbed pensively at his forehead.

'Jesus, what's this country coming to?' he said quietly, then looked up. 'So what you're telling me is that we're going to get no help whatsoever from Joe Public on this.'

Donegan shook his head once.

'No, not really, Super. I mean, if your next-door neighbour was dealing heroin and other drugs to kids on your estate, wouldn't you be happy if he was topped?'

The superintendent looked across the desk at him and raised an eyebrow.

'I'm going to pretend that I didn't hear that, Inspector,' he warned.

Donegan shrugged.

'Well, maybe I'm making my point too strongly.'

'Yes, Inspector. I'd have to agree with you there.'

Reidy looked at them both for a moment and decided to change the mood.

'Things look a bit better at the Henry Williams scene,' he said, reaching for the file on the desk. 'Forensics are presently trying to identify the explosive used, and the parking attendant has given a few possibilities to the local lads.'

The superintendent looked down at the paper in Reidy's lap and then back to the eager detective.

'The explosive used,' he said. 'Could it be our subversive friends?'

Reidy shrugged and held out the preliminary report from the lab.

'We can't rule that out,' he replied. 'Some type of powerful home-made plastique. First examination suggests that they haven't seen anything like it before.

The super took the sheet and glanced at it. It was all gibberish to him.

'I'll read this later.' He sighed as he handed it back. He looked at Donegan. 'The squad has been given their assignments, Frank?' he asked, the earlier morality debate now forgotten.

Donegan nodded and went through each man's task for the morning in detail, assuring him that hourly reports on progress would be sent back to the office. In addition to this, he told of the check being made by Fox and McGrath on the possible victims and the steps that he would then put in place.

The super waited until he finished and then held out a plate of wrapped biscuits, which were politely refused.

'We're doing all we can do at the moment, then.' He appeared pleased. 'As you know, I must give a report to the AC this morning at ten. Whatever about the Wolfman, this Williams business is going to be all over the news and he wants some answers for the press office.'

He rubbed at his forehead again and then unwrapped one of the biscuits.

'Good God,' he said as if to himself. 'Blowing people up on the street.'

He stirred from his misery and his tone strengthened.

'We're keeping this Mercury Man name out of the story for the moment. The last thing we want is some bullshit phantom hero on the front page. Understood?'

Neither detective responded. It had gone without saying that the information to the press would be the usual crumbs to keep them from the door.

'I'd like to talk to you in connection with another matter, Inspector,' he said and looked at Reidy.

The sergeant gathered his documents under his arm and left without speaking.

The superintendent waited until the door closed and then sat back on his chair. He locked his fingers together, then his thumbs rose up with his eyebrows.

'This Fox and McGrath incident, Frank. This could turn out to be very serious for them,' he warned.

Donegan couldn't help but smile as he pictured the two detectives.

The super was unmoved.

'C'mon, Frank, you've seen the report,' he said, and waited for Donegan to confirm this fact.

'I mean, what the hell did they think they were doing? I had the two of them in here yesterday, and the most frightening aspect of it all is that Fox thought they had done a great job altogether.'

Donegan laughed loudly as he stood up. This conversation was going nowhere, and he certainly didn't have the solution. The super threw his hands out in lone desperation.

'Am I the only one who sees anything wrong with this?' he asked no one in particular.

Donegan turned around when he was halfway to the door.

'Kieran, how many accidental shots were fired in the seventies and there was never a word about it?' He laughed as he remembered a particular incident.

The superintendent frowned.

'Now, Frank, don't be digging up the past to make excuses for those two.' He almost smiled. 'They were different times. If a gouger fires a shot at you in this day and age the instruction is that you duck and call his psychiatrist immediately.'

His face relaxed and he gave a faint smile as the thought came to him.

'Wait until all this is over,' he promised. 'I'm going to bury the two of them in paper.'

Donegan paused with his hand on the door handle and looked back at him.

'I really think that would be a complete waste of your time and theirs, sir,' he said as he left the room.

CHAPTER SIX

Landers sat on the edge of the bed for a moment and then stood up. He rolled his shoulders as he padded gingerly across the carpet towards the bathroom, cursing himself silently for his indulgence in alcohol the previous night. He turned on the shower and tested the water with his hand before stepping under it. He gasped and then panted air as the freezing torrent ran over him. It was the only way to clear the muggy feeling in his head.

After the initial shock had passed, he relaxed and moved his face over and back through the flow. Soon his mind was clear and his thoughts turned to the file that lay on the bedside locker. All the information he needed was in it.

This matter could be dealt with very quickly. Today, perhaps, if all went well. Why complicate things?

After showering, he stood for a moment in the doorway of the bathroom, looking across the room at the file. Where was Doyle getting all his superb information? And, more importantly, why was he paying such an exorbitant amount of money to rid the country of a few lowlifers? He shrugged the questions from his mind and gave them the same answers that he had given the first time he had asked himself. Why should he care? He dressed quickly, took the file from the bedside locker and placed it in his briefcase.

At reception, he picked up one of the fresh daily newspapers and made his way to the dining room where he sat down the same table where he and Doyle had sat the night before. The room was empty except for the two waitresses who stood at the far end with their hands clasped in front of their gleaming white aprons.

He held the paper aloft, his eyes scanning the turning pages. There was the story, ten lines at the bottom of page five with the heading 'Unanswered questions in city death', followed underneath by the tragic story of young Henry Williams. He crunched the paper closed and then slapped it down on the empty chair beside him in disgust.

When would his craft be recognised? How long more would it be before the country's criminals quaked in terror at the very mention of the Mercury Man? Doyle had promised that it would be soon. He would just have to wait.

He faked a smile as the waitress brought his customary light breakfast of cereal and black coffee.

'Will there be anything else, sir?' she asked pleasantly.

'No, thank you,' he replied, as he lifted the heavy silver coffeepot. 'This will be fine.'

After breakfast, he went outside and hailed a taxi. The driver nodded at the instruction in silence and flicked the meter as he pulled away from the kerb.

'It'll take about twenty minutes,' he called over his shoulder. 'The traffic is dire this morning.'

Landers looked at him through the rear-view mirror.

'It's not a problem,' he said. 'There's no rush.'

The taxi driver shook his head in dismay.

'I don't know how they're going to solve this gridlock,' he said. 'It gets worse and worse every morning and evening. Are you from Dublin yerself?' He swerved the car violently and braked, at the same time winding down the window and gesturing with his finger at a small car that was attempting to pull into the lane in front of them.

'Get a fuckin' helicopter, why don't ya,' he shouted at the wide-eyed female.

Landers looked out the back window at the strained face of the young woman and then back at the thick neck of his driver.

'Refrain from using that kind of language,' he said without emotion. 'Turn on the radio, please,' he demanded, his voice deepening.

The driver obeyed with a grunt and then slumped back in the seat as he waited for the traffic ahead to move again. There was no further conversation between them until they reached their destination.

'You should try this job for a week,' the driver said, trying to justify his earlier outburst as he took the fare over his shoulder.

Landers opened the back door.

'You should get a job that you like,' he advised, as he stepped out. 'Keep the change.'

The driver muttered something under his breath and pulled away.

Landers turned and walked through the tall glass door of the private gymnasium and sports complex. He had become a member on his arrival in Dublin. Although the fee of two thousand euro had disturbed him, keeping physically fit was one of his job requirements, but the real reason was the private locker that came with membership.

The smell of chlorine filled his nostrils as he passed the smiling attendant dressed in shorts and T-shirt at the desk. He made his way along the carpeted hallway.

He removed the key from his suit pocket and looked down as he walked along the rows to locker number 240. He glanced around before opening it and checked the contents. Satisfied that nothing had been touched, he changed into his grey sweatsuit and made his way to the gym where he did a light workout on the weight-machine and bag. Thirty minutes later, he was back at his locker having showered and changed into a fresh, blue tracksuit. He tore the map with the copy of the photograph from the file and tucked them into his pocket along with the item he had selected. He closed the locker and grasped the key in his hand, as he made his way back towards the reception area.

'Going for a long walk again today?' asked the smiling girl behind the desk.

'Yes,' he said, tossing the key up in his hand. 'I need to clear these cobwebs away before the weekend.'

Once outside, he went a short distance from the door of the gym and then stopped. He took the map from his pocket and looked around to get his bearings. He calculated that it would take him at least an hour at a fast walking pace to reach his objective. Then, it would just be a matter of waiting for the opportunity to present itself.

***

McGrath rolled his thumbs as he waited for the printer to begin. Beside him, with feet up on the desk, Fox was engrossed in an article in the *Garda Review*.

'Do you see this?' he asked, nudging McGrath's elbow.

'What?'

Fox held the magazine out.

'The promotion line-up for sergeant,' he said. 'Would you look at who's after getting stripes?'

McGrath narrowed his eyes at the long list on the folded page and then gave up. He turned back to his task and tapped on the keyboard.

'Who?' he asked in frustration.

'Do you remember Muffy in Unit C, the judo black-belt?'

'Muffy?'

'Yeah. Muffy. She was off duty one night and got stuck in to a gouger who was beating up his girlfriend. She showed him her ID and he punched her in the face and called her a pig. Do you remember? She kicked the living shit out of him and dragged him to Store Street. There was a big inquiry because she nearly bit his arm off. C'mon, think now, man.'

McGrath moved closer to the screen, his head moving left and right as he read the details.

'No,' he replied absently.

Fox swung his legs off the desk.

'Muffy,' he said with urgency. 'Mad Unstoppable Female From Youghal. Her voice would bring a tear to a glass eye.'

'What about her?' asked McGrath, not really caring.

Fox eased himself back on the chair and spoke in a tone of disbelief.

'She's only after going and getting herself promoted. C'mon Bob, tell me that you remember her. Unit C, big girl, everyone afraid of her.'

He elbowed McGrath again. 'C'mon. Think now, Bob.'

McGrath leaned back from the screen and held his palms out.

'Do you want to do this?' he asked, without turning to him 'Or do you want to read in silence?'

As there was no reply, he resigned himself to the fact that he would have to answer the question. 'Yes, Andy. I know who you're talking about,' he sighed.

'Describe her, then,' said Fox, testing him.

'Blonde hair.'

'Yeah.'

'Big.'

'Correct so far.'

'Sounded like Gregory Peck.'

'Ah, you have her,' laughed Fox as he leaned to his side and creased the page as he pointed to the name. 'Look at that, will you?'

'So what?'

'So what!' said Fox incredulously. 'So what! Here we are, the two of us, breaking our balls after every lowlife in the town, and this – this cannibal gets promoted.'

McGrath narrowed his eyes and turned back to the screen.

'Get over it,' he said dryly.

Fox shook his head in disgust and threw the magazine down.

'How much longer are we going to be here at this crack?' he asked, pointing to the screen.

'This is the last one.'

'How many are there?'

McGrath leaned to his side and picked up the sheets from the mouth of the printer and thumbed through them. 'Twenty-five in all,' he replied, and slapped them across Fox's chest before turning back to the screen.

Fox pursed his lips as he went through the list, then snorted a laugh.

'What do countries have police for at all?' he asked. He held one of the sheets up. 'I mean, look at this one.'

'I've read them already, thank you.' McGrath cut him short.

Fox was unshaken. There was unusual anger in his voice.

'This – this – *fucker* walks into a playground and takes a seven-year-old girl.'

McGrath nodded as he listened.

'He sexually assaults her, strangles her, then dumps her in a drain beside a building site.' Fox threw the pile of paper on the desk. 'And where is he now?' he asked, knowing that McGrath knew the answer. 'He's out and about with all the rest of us,' he said. 'And all because some sleepy bollocks with a wig doesn't know what it's like to live out in the real world.'

McGrath sat back on the chair and waited for the printout.

'It's the sad reality of modern Ireland, my friend,' he said casually. 'The day of worrying about the victim is gone. We worry more about the criminal now. No such thing as justice anymore.'

His voice faded to a distant muttering as his lips began to read the last screen.

Fox stood up slowly and took a step back. McGrath, hearing the noise, turned and watched the expression of shock on his colleague's face.

'What? What is it?' he asked in surprise, then flinched as Fox quickly pulled his Smith and Wesson automatic from the belt beneath his T-shirt.

'You're the Mercury Man,' he exclaimed, holding the gun out between his hands at arm's length. 'Help, lads. Help,' he called out in fake distress.

McGrath slapped it away and turned back to the printer. 'You eejit,' he muttered.

Fox laughed and sat back down in the chair, swivelling from left to right as he examined the weapon. 'Are we going to get breakfast or not?' he grumbled. ''Tis almost eleven.'

No sooner had he asked the question than his mobile phone rang.

'Yeah.'

He sat upright.

'Beano...'

McGrath turned while at the same time stacking the papers on the desk without looking.

Fox's expression changed to one of anger, the bones whitening high on his cheeks. The spittle sprayed from his mouth as he spoke through grinding teeth.

'You're where? Beano, Beano, you better hope they execute you before I get up there.'

He slammed the phone down on the computer desk and sat back, his chest rising and falling quickly with temper.

McGrath waited for a moment. 'Well?'

'Well? Well, what?' snarled Fox. 'The stupid bastard is after being arrested.'

'Arrested? What did he do?'

Fox eyed him.

McGrath understood immediately.

'How much did he have?' he asked.

Fox stood up and placed the gun back in his belt, then picked up his mobile phone.

'A nine-bar and fifty ecstasy.'

McGrath gave a soft whistle as he turned and gathered up the printouts. 'It's going to take a fair bit of sweet-talking to get him out of this one,' he said. 'Was it the locals or the Drug Squad that lifted him?'

Fox stood with his hands in his pockets, his head down.

'Squad,' he said dejectedly. 'Brian Finn.'

McGrath slapped him on the back. 'Well, there's still hope so,' he said cheerfully. 'Finn is a clever enough fella. C'mon, let's see if we can sort it out. I'll just drop these back to the Kig's office.'

Fox sat on the steps outside as he waited. He was angry for two reasons. Firstly because their best tout was now locked up, and secondly because all of the lecturing to Beano about the hazards of dealing had fallen on deaf ears. All the promises were empty. 'I'll smoke a bit myself, but I'll never deal again, lads. And yez have my word on it.'

Fox stamped the ground with his runner.

'Bollocks.'

The door swung open and McGrath ran down the steps.

'Let's go,' he shouted, walking quickly to the car. 'The sooner we get the eejit out, the sooner he can get back to work.'

Fox followed slowly behind, and then stopped at the passenger side.

McGrath looked across the roof at him. He knew that Fox had put an unusual effort into keeping Beano out of the dealing scene. And this was totally out of character for his colleague, who believed that all drug-dealers should be given the rope.

'Did you ever hear the one about the old man and the pit-bull terrier, Andy?' he asked as he unlocked the door.

Fox tried to laugh as he sat in.

'No, Bob,' he said as he watched McGrath start the car. 'What's that one?'

'Well, now,' started McGrath, 'once upon a time, there was an old man who lived alone, and had no friends.'

'Like the super, you mean,' Fox interrupted.

McGrath laughed.

'Anyway, one day he was out for a walk on his lonesome, when he heard a crying noise coming from a hole beside the road. And when he looked in, lo and behold, there was a cloth bag, and the bag was moving. So the old man reached into the hole and took out the bag, opened it, and there looking up at him was a weakened and frightened pit-bull terrier pup.'

'Aw Jesus,' muttered Fox as he settled himself in the seat. 'Is this a *long* story?'

'Anyhow,' McGrath continued, unruffled by the interruption, 'he took the little pup home in his arms and nursed it back to health. But he knew that the breed was dangerous, so he fed it only on milk and bread. And the pup grew up to be a fine, strapping dog. This was a most unusual pit-bull, a pit-bull who played with children in the park during the day and lay at his master's feet at night.'

Fox turned to him with a frown. 'For the love of Christ, where's the point in this?' he snapped.

'All through the years, dog and master were inseparable. Then one day, the old man went outside with the dog's feed of milk and bread, tripped and fell and cut his hand on a sharp stone. The pit-bull ran to his aid, but when he saw the blood, he jumped on his master, and began to savage him.'

Fox nodded and threw his eyes up. 'Lovely story, Bob. Now can we...'

'*And*,' shouted McGrath, 'as the old man lay dying on the ground, he looked up in wonder at his once loving pet and asked, "But why?" And the dog replied,

"I'm a pit-bull terrier, old man. What the fuck did you expect?"'

Fox shook his head in confusion and looked out the window.

'Thanks a million for that,' he said with sarcasm. 'A story about a vicious talking dog. I'm all cheery now.' However, as he sat in silence, the significance of the story was not lost on him.

The car stopped at the traffic lights and Fox looked at McGrath. 'So that makes me a lonesome old man, does it?' he asked sharply.

'No,' corrected McGrath, driving away again. 'It just makes you someone who thought he could change something that couldn't be changed.'

Fox thought about it for a moment. Much as he hated admitting it to himself, McGrath was right.

Beano had been born and reared in the drug scene. His father had been the first victim, followed quickly by his two older brothers, one serving a ten-year sentence, the other one buried less than three months before, the stereo on the coffin filling the almost empty church with the thundering of Chris Rea's, 'Let's Dance', a song chosen not for its heart-lifting lyrics, but because it was the verbal gauntlet used by his brother to initiate the many fights he had gotten into. It was, of course, preceded by the words, 'C'mon so, ya fucker.'

Still, there had been something decent about young Beano. Behind all the hard talk and endless knowledge of illegal substances, Fox believed that there was a decent young fella struggling to get out and live a normal life.

He folded his arms and gazed out at the passing street. 'Just wait until I get my hands on the bollocks. Then he'll see what a talking pit-bull looks like.'

CHAPTER SEVEN

Landers stopped at the corner of the tree-lined street and removed the small map from his pocket. He glanced across at the four-storey, red-brick house and noted the number on the white ceramic plate on the gate pillar. His head bobbed as it turned and counted down along the row of houses to number 52, a hundred yards away.

He replaced the map in his pocket and moved towards the house. The street was unusually quiet for that time of the morning and it made him feel uneasy and vulnerable. Perhaps it was not such a good idea to rush this job.

This was not the estate of Jimbo the Wolfman or Gerry Feeney, where no one noticed who came or went and, even if they did, would not get involved in the subsequent investigation. This was a wealthy, middle-class cul-de-sac where every window had eyes and where the residents would have no hesitation in talking to the police.

'A middle-aged man in a blue tracksuit, dark, greying hair and a slight paunch, officer. I saw him walking up and down the street and he was paying particular attention to the poor man's house. Who would do such a terrible thing to such a lovely person?'

The shadow of the tall oak trees gave him some cover as he walked on, passing the house and glancing across to check for any signs of movement. An elderly woman appeared in a gateway a few yards ahead, pulling a tartan shopping trolley out behind her. He turned his face away from her and crossed quickly to the other side. He went to the end of the cul-de-sac and stopped, then leaned down and undid the lace of his runner. The woman had gone the other way, and the street was quiet again except for the noise of the traffic that passed at the junction of the entrance.

He tied his lace and then moved backwards to the park bench situated beneath the cluster of tall oak trees in a small grassy area. He sat down and looked out from the cooling shadows as he considered his options. How easy it would be to simply knock on the door and get the job done quickly. He immediately cursed his impetuosity.

All the other jobs he had completed with such success had been carefully planned. But not this one; this was the behaviour of some enthusiastic amateur.

He glanced along the side of the street, the houses

with their small, well-maintained lawns and perfectly trimmed hedges. Did any of these people really know the man who was living alone in number 52? The congenial Ivor Danby who lived alone amongst them with total anonymity. A friendless and private man who wanted to keep it that way. The same Mr Danby who, through his organised paedophile ring, had been responsible for the abduction and subsequent deaths of at least fifteen children. The very same Mr Danby who himself had abducted a seven-year-old girl from a playground in southern England to rape and strangle.

The words on the file Doyle had given him ran through his thoughts. He cleared his head now as he stood up. Anger was not an emotion that he should entertain.

This was not the time. It was too risky by day. He would return that night and complete the task that was set. And he promised himself that he would do so with relish.

He walked slowly back towards the main road. As he neared the steps of number 52, he tried to shut his thoughts out to the pictures that flashed before him. The child trapped in the dark room, shaking with fear, shoulders rising and falling in whimpers as the tears ran down her cheeks.

He cursed himself out loud and turned quickly and up the steps. He paused at the large, red door and looked back onto the street before pressing the doorbell with his elbow. Why should this man enjoy another twelve hours of life?, he asked himself as he listened to the approaching footsteps inside. He intentionally turned his back to the door as the latch clicked, his eyes scanning the street.

The door creaked open slowly, and a man in his late fifties squinted out at him through gold-rimmed reading glasses, the wisps of jet-black, dyed hair resting on top of the rims. Landers did not turn at first, waiting until the door was opened further. The man stood there in a dark shirt and slacks, one hand still on the latch of the door, the other hand holding a book that was page-marked with his index finger.

'Yes?' he enquired in a mild English accent.

'Mr Danby, if I'm not mistaken.' Landers turned and smiled, convinced that the street was now clear and that any view of the doorway was obscured by the mature trees.

Danby looked him quizzically up and down for a moment before giving a slow and cautious reply.

'Yes, I am Mr...'

Landers took one quick step forward, his fingers jabbing out with the speed of a cobra bite at the man's throat. Danby fell backwards into the hallway, the book catapulting from his hand and striking the wall. Landers turned back calmly to check the street before he stepped inside. Danby lay in the foetal position on the cold black-and-red terracotta tiles, his face a light shade of purple, his tongue out as he gasped for air.

Landers looked down at him in disgust, as he closed the front door with the heel of his runner, and then froze to the spot as the heavy sitting-room door at the end of the hall moved with a groan. He mentally prepared himself for hand-to-hand combat, taking deep, controlled breaths, opening and closing his fists at his side.

His chest fell with a snorted laugh of relief as he

watched a grossly overweight King Charles spaniel waddle through the gap in the door and out into the hall. Its head wavered from side to side as it patted gently towards its master, sniffed once at him, looked up with large brown eyes at Landers, and then sat down to wait.

Danby continued to wheeze on the hall floor, his questions a confused series of gurgles.

'Hoookk, whaaaa?'

Landers stepped past him and checked the downstairs rooms, the King Charles panting behind as it followed like some large, curious slug.

At the kitchen door, Landers bent down with the intention of pushing it inside and closing the door. By the time he heard the high-pitched growl, it was too late. The dog snapped and closed its jaws in the centre of his palm. He grimaced in pain as he reached quickly for the collar and twisted it in his free hand until the dog hissed for air and the jaws opened. The dog swung from the collar, snarling and snapping before Landers slammed it against the doorjamb and threw it with force onto the kitchen floor. He cursed under his breath and pulled the door closed. The dog did not bark. The house was silent again.

He looked down angrily at the two crimson puncture wounds in his palm, the blood dripping from them onto the hall tiles as he turned his hand over to examine the other side. Thankfully the teeth had not broken the skin there.

He would have to move quickly now. Danby, almost recovered from the throat blow, was sitting up, but still struggling to clear his airway.

As Landers approached from behind, he took the three-foot length of thin wax rope from the pocket of his tracksuit. In one swift movement he secured it on his hands and looped it around Danby's neck. He placed his runner between Danby's shoulder blades and gave a quick but effective tug. His victim slumped to his side, the neck and spinal cord severed at the base of the skull. He released the rope from one hand and pulled it free. He looked around as he rolled it in his hand before replacing it in his tracksuit pocket. He winced in pain as he took out the pair of green surgical gloves and pulled one on to his injured hand. He went to the sitting room and removed a paisley covering from one of the sofa cushions, and set about the job of wiping any evidence.

The handle of the kitchen door, the blood that had dripped from his wound on the tiled hallway, the faint print that his runner had left on the tiles just inside the front door. Satisfied that he had done the job properly, he folded the cushion-cover, tucked it inside his tracksuit top and returned to the hall. He reached into his pocket and took out his business card, wiped it across the front of his tracksuit and placed it on Danby's forehead.

Now came the hard part. Getting away.

He opened the front door a fraction and peered out through the small gap. There was no movement. The street was quiet. He stepped quickly onto the outside step and pulled the door behind him, slipping the glove from one hand as the latch caught. The warm blood trapped inside the other glove eased the pain somewhat. He put the gloved hand in the pocket of his tracksuit top and walked slowly down the steps to the footpath. And then he looked left and right, crossed the street and walked briskly up to the junction.

***

Brian Finn of the Drug Squad leaned against the wall at the end of the corridor, a cigarette hanging limply from his mouth, his head down, reading the interview notes. He looked up as he heard the approaching footsteps and then smiled, holding out the sheets of paper and waving them.

'He's for the high jump this time, lads,' he grinned.

McGrath faked a laugh as he took the notes from him and glanced down at them, pretending to read.

'I bet he told you where you can find Shergar,' he mused.

'Or maybe who's going to win this year's All-Ireland,' Fox added.

Finn looked at them. The smile was gone. The only thing that he and these two detectives had in common was their ability to annoy their respective superintendents with their breach of dress code.

'There's no bargaining this time,' he said gruffly. 'I spent three weeks trying to get this little ferret.' He spoke as if it had been his life's work. 'Funny how it's always you fellas that he calls when he's in the tank.'

Fox held his cool.

'Look, Brian,' he said politely. 'We're stuck in the middle of something at the moment.' He pointed to the interview-room door. 'And Beano there is the best lead that we have.'

McGrath looked up from the notes and held them out with a shrug.

'Looks like an open and shut case to me,' he said. 'You have our congratulations, Brian.'

Finn looked at the two of them. His heart sank. He knew that the trap was already being laid. It had happened so many times in the past. Even when they had worked together in the Drug Squad, Fox and McGrath had always come up with a better plan. A plan that would inevitably lead to a better capture, but one that would thwart many of his own arrests and convictions.

Besides, a nine-bar and fifty Es was not much of a catch if Beano was helping in a major investigation. That is, if Fox and McGrath were telling the truth.

'What's the case?' he asked.

McGrath looked back along the empty corridor. 'Double murder,' he whispered. 'The Wolfman and young Williams.'

Finn gave a gentle whistle as he rolled the paper between his hands. He lowered his head and paused for a moment in thought.

The two detectives glanced at each other before looking back at him.

'What's in it for me?' he asked, eying both of them.

'You'll be mentioned in the file, of course,' said McGrath.

'Bullshit. I want his supplier. And I want the name before he walks,' said Finn.

McGrath and Fox nodded.

'Seems fair,' said Fox. 'Give us ten minutes with him.'

Finn smiled. 'I think it's going to take a bit longer than that,' he said, as Fox opened the door.

McGrath turned back to him in the open doorway. 'What odds are you giving on that?' he grinned as he followed Fox inside.

Beano sat with his head resting on the table, his suede jacket now discarded and hanging on a chair beside him, his dirty, striped grandfather-shirt, giving him the proper appearance of a prisoner.

He lifted his head and gave a half-laugh of relief as Fox and McGrath entered.

'Shite, lads,' he smiled. 'I thought it was yer man again. I was pretending to be asleep.'

The smile disappeared when he saw the expression on Fox.

'I know yez are tick with me,' he explained as he watched the two of them slowly pull chairs from beneath the table and sit down close to him. He looked nervously from one to the other.

They stared back at him in the silence.

''Twas only a bit o' smoke and a few Es,' he whispered, his shaking hands reaching back and tightening his ponytail. ''Twas for meself.'

Fox leaned forward slowly towards him, his jaw clenched. His lips barely moved when he spoke.

'It was half a pound of cannabis resin, and fifty poison tablets, you – little – prick. So, what are you telling us?' His voice rose. 'Personal use? There's a party in Beano's kip and everyone's invited. Is that your story?'

Beano leaned back from the table, his hands urging silence as he glanced at the door.

'I can explain everything,' he whispered. He looked nervously at both of them. 'This can be sorted out, can't it?'

It was time for McGrath to speak. 'Well, now, my purveyor of all things illegal,' he smiled. 'As you can well imagine, my colleague here is more than a little upset that you have returned to your wicked ways after all this time.' He paused for a moment with a puzzled frown. 'Or perhaps, you never gave up your dealing, and just trailed us along for the ride.'

Beano looked at Fox and shook his head quickly.

'No, no, lads...' he started.

The knowing glare from Fox silenced him.

'Beano,' said McGrath calmly. 'There's a very irate drugs officer just outside that door. And he's waiting for one thing. The one and *only* thing that can save your hide.'

Beano leaned forward, his breathing faster, his head nodding vigorously. There was light at the end of the tunnel after all.

'What is it? Tell me what he wants,' he asked anxiously.

McGrath sat back on the chair and looked across at Fox.

'Your supplier,' said Fox, the anger still apparent. 'Like all good policemen, he's prepared to throw back the flea's bollocks in order to get the horse's pair.'

'Sure, I've no problem telling yous, lads,' Beano fidgeted nervously, not in the least bit upset about the flea's bollocks remark. 'It was the Wolfman.'

The words hung for a moment before Fox stood up slowly and allowed the chair to clatter on the floor beneath him. He looked down at Beano.

'Very smart,' he said with disdain. 'Well, this is one you're not going to cop out of with a story like that.'

He signalled his intentions to McGrath. 'C'mon Bob,' he said in a low voice and took a step towards the door. 'Rot in hell, Beano,' he snarled.

'Wait, wait!' Beano was on his feet and pleading. 'It's the truth. It's the Wolfman's gear. I got it two nights ago. I was to hold it until he phoned me with a contact the next morning.'

McGrath, who had remained seated, looked up at him.

'And?' he enquired.

Beano looked down at him, his eyes darting back and forth to Fox as he rushed his explanation.

'He never contacted. So I phoned him and there was no answer. I went to his house at around dinner-time and I got no answer. I thought that he'd gone out of town.'

Fox picked up the chair and sat back down. He rested his elbows on the table and examined the expression on Beano's face for a moment before pointing to the empty chair beside him.

'Why did you not tell us this last night, you – you lying little drug-dealer?'

Beano was immune to the insults at this stage. He sat back down and spoke like a true professional mover of drugs. His voice was steady as he spoke.

'Wolfman would never handle the stuff himself,' he explained. 'The gear would be out on the street before any order was made. The customer would phone Wolfman and he would phone some other runner or me and make arrangements for the gear to be delivered. That way, he'd never handle it himself and the trail would never go back.'

'So you were holding for him two days ago?' said McGrath.

Beano nodded.

'When I heard that he'd been whacked, I decided to keep the bar and Es for myself and deal them when the heat was off.' He laughed suddenly. 'C'mon, lads. They weren't going to do the Wolfman much good, were they?'

'When did you last see him?' asked Fox, ignoring the question.

'Monday, around ten that night,' said Beano.

'And then he disappeared?'

'Well, I couldn't make any contact. And he wasn't at home.'

Fox edged towards him along the table. Their faces almost touched. He could smell Beano's foul breath.

'If you're lying to me – so help me, *Jesus*, if you're lying,' he warned, 'I'll make it the focus of my remaining years as a policeman to make your life a living hell.'

Beano eased back from him and gave a worried laugh.

'I swear, lads,' he said. 'It's the truth. Why would I lie now?'

'We won't answer that,' said McGrath dryly as he took out his notebook and then jotted a reminder on it. He replaced it in his pocket and then clapped his hands.

'Well, now,' he said, looking across at Fox, who was still eyeing Beano. 'I'd say that just about covers things for the moment. Would you say so, Detective?'

'Who's the Mercury Man, Beano?' asked Fox.

Beano lowered his head. 'You asked me that already and I told you I don't know,' he said. 'Get me out of here and I'll suss the word on him. I'll work on it, I promise.'

Both detectives rose in silence and walked to the door. Beano remained seated, his hands held out in a plea for freedom.

'C'mon, lads,' he called, 'gimme a chance. I can find him for yez.'

The door closed behind them and they stood in the empty corridor. Finn had tired of waiting even though ten minutes had not yet passed.

McGrath leaned back against the wall and folded his arms, looking up at the ceiling.

Fox paced slowly away from him, his hands in his pockets, his head lowered in thought.

McGrath turned his head slowly against the wall.

'What do you reckon?' he asked.

Fox paced back and forth.

'Beano tells us that the last time he saw the Wolfman was on Monday night, the night before he was toasted.'

'Yeah,' agreed McGrath.

'That means that his killer was in the house early that morning and held him prisoner for the day. That's why he didn't answer his phone or the door for Beano.'

McGrath looked down at the cream tiles of the corridor for a moment before lifting his head as the revelation dawned.

'Maybe his killer wasn't there at all when Beano called,' he said slowly.

'What?' snapped Fox, looking up at him.

McGrath moved away from the wall to the centre of the corridor.

'The Wolfman answers his door on Tuesday morning. His killer takes him prisoner and ties him to an armchair. Gags him. And a few minutes later he walks out the front door.'

Fox raised a questioning finger.

'Who lit the barbecue then? That didn't start until midnight.'

No sooner had he asked the question than he realised the answer.

'The device that Malley found at the scene,' he said. 'It was a fire-starter.'

'And the killer would have been gone,' added McGrath.

Fox was already walking away, a pointed finger held back. 'Contact Donegan,' he said. 'Let him know what we have.'

McGrath remained where he was. 'Where are you going?' he shouted.

'I'm going to get a rat loose,' he shouted back, as he rounded the corner at the end of the hall.

Brian Finn stood at the station orderly's desk, flicking through the morning newspaper. He looked up at Fox as he entered and then glanced down at his watch. Fox beckoned him out to the secrecy of the corridor with a backward nod.

'This better be good,' said Finn as he slapped the folded newspaper on his thigh.

Fox held his hands out in explanation.

'I've got the supplier,' he said.

Finn was visibly impressed.

'Before I tell you, Brian,' continued Fox, 'you have to give me your word that you'll release him straightaway without charge.'

Finn looked at him. He knew from Fox's demeanour that he had some startling piece of information. Fox stood breathless before him, his face a grimace of anticipation. Still, Finn had seen this act before.

'Tell me who he is first,' he said.

Fox knew his act would not work.

'All right. OK,' he said in a voice of defeat. 'His supplier was the Wolfman.'

Finn laughed loudly and slapped Fox on the shoulder with the newspaper.

'Sure, that prick is dead,' he continued to laugh. 'You're a gas man, Andy, there's no doubt about it.'

He turned away for the day room. Fox grabbed him by the arm.

'C'mon, Brian,' he appealed. 'Cut him loose and if he doesn't come up with something in the next three days, then you can give him the full whack. And if he does, then I'll see to it that you get full credit.'

Finn pretended to think about it for a moment. This feeling of power over a member of the MCS pleased him. However, he knew that Fox and McGrath would be on the winning side eventually, as they always were. And he wanted to be there right beside them when that happened.

'Fair enough,' he said. 'I'll give him the time because you asked. But if he doesn't come up trumps, then it's back to square one.'

Fox smiled and winked at him.

'Good on you, Brian,' he said. 'You'll be there when they're giving out the medals, I promise.'

Finn gave him a sharp glance and turned away. 'Yeah. I bet I will.'

CHAPTER EIGHT

The three chairs remained empty behind the long, rectangular table. The dark-blue cloth with the stark white emblem of An Garda Síochána, gave it the appearance of the top table at a Garda dinner dance, apart, that is, from the collection of microphones that cluttered together along the front.

The group of journalists chatted and joked amongst themselves as they waited, asking each other questions and guessing the answers. Two cameras stood on sturdy, black tripods at the back of the room, their operators checking the lenses and then politely nudging at any human obstruction that hindered the view. One of the assistant operators backed slowly along the narrow aisle between the rows of chairs, a cable unfolding from his hands until he reached the table and began to connect yet another microphone.

His eyes widened with surprise as the side door opened and three men appeared. He genuflected on one knee in front of the table as he hurriedly twisted the microphone into the awaiting holder, then backed away in a bowed position from the table. He knew that the camera at the back of the room would already be rolling.

The three men stepped up sombrely onto the low stage and sat behind the table, the journalists jostling quickly to the front as they vied for the best seats. The clatter of chairs on tiles ended as suddenly as it had begun.

The room fell silent.

The superintendent gave a short cough as he shuffled his notes in front of him. He was immaculately groomed. His gleaming white shirt and navy-blue tie matched perfectly with the colours of the table in front of him.

'Ladies and gentlemen of the press,' he started. 'I am Superintendent Kieran Harrington. To my left is Detective Inspector Frank Donegan. And on my right is Detective Sergeant Alan Reidy. I will make a brief statement, and I will then hand you over to Inspector Donegan and Sergeant Reidy to answer any questions that you may have.'

It was the way of things. The briefing at the assistant commissioner's office had gone as expected. The superintendent had done his best to explain the progress to date. After listening for twenty minutes, the assistant commissioner had tapped his fingers together with a studious frown and advised that perhaps the superintendent was the more suitable and better informed to face the press. The superintendent, in turn, had made the same proposition to Donegan, who, after much cajoling, had convinced Reidy that this was the career booster he had been waiting for.

'I wonder if we had arrested the killer, would we be going through this door?' Reidy had asked him outside a minute earlier.

'No, boy,' Donegan had replied wearily. 'We'd have been told to take a ciggy break in the jacks.'

The superintendent fingered one of the sheets of paper and began. The journalists waited with pens at the ready. All that is, bar one.

'The Metropolitan Crime Squad, in co-operation with local Garda units, are currently investigating the suspicious death of James Ryan, who, as you all know, was found burnt to death in his terraced house in the early hours of yesterday morning. The circumstances in which the body was found would suggest that the fire was not accidental, and therefore a full-scale murder investigation has now begun.

'Yesterday evening, at approximately 7.45, an incident occurred just off St Stephen's Green, where a young man, Henry Williams, lost his life. This matter is also the subject of an investigation by the MCS, to determine whether the death was suspicious or not.

'Finally, on behalf of An Garda Síochána, I offer my sincere sympathies to both families concerned, and I would like to take this opportunity to appeal to any members of the public with any information to come forward, no matter how small or insignificant they may feel that information is. Thank you.'

His job was done. He had spoken for sixty-three seconds and had said nothing that every dog in the street didn't know. He sat back in the chair, looking out at the crowded room, his palms held out to the men on either side, in an open invitation for their savaging to begin. It did not take long. The hands shot to the air as in an enthusiastic class.

'Why are the MCS involved in this investigation?' a shout from the back.

Donegan leaned forward to the microphone and then back quickly as it whistled in protest. 'We were brought in at the request of the local investigation teams,' he replied softly.

'Why? Surely the death of James Ryan – or the Wolfman, to give him his proper name – is not a matter of national security?'

'The investigating teams felt that our expertise would hasten the solving of this murder. Many members of the MCS are experienced ex-Murder Squad or Drug Squad detectives.'

Another hand wavered in the front line and Donegan nodded.

'Are you saying, Inspector, that the ordinary local squads are not capable of solving these murders on their own?'

Donegan bit down hard on the bullet.

'No. That's not what I said,' he snapped, and turned his head to the other side of the room where more nerve-jangling questions awaited at the end of raised hands.

'Is this a drug-related killing, Inspector?'

'We haven't ruled out that possibility.' He pointed at the journalist in the next seat.

'The superintendent said that the body was found in suspicious circumstances. Can you elaborate on that?'

'I'm afraid I cannot comment on that at this time.'

He moved along the line, his confidence growing, yet at the same time knowing that the tougher questions had yet to be asked.

'In light of James Ryan's connection with the drugs trade, and his involvement in the death of a number of persons in recent times, is there a possibility that this was a revenge killing?'

'The investigation has just begun. At this stage, we are ruling out nothing.'

He knew that the house of cards was about to crumble. He inwardly cursed the superintendent who sat smugly beside him, lips pursed, arms folded as if holding himself aloof from the rabble. He glanced past him at Reidy, who looked cool and unruffled.

And then it came, through the garbled chattering, 'Inspector.' The call was low at first. Then it grew in urgency. *'Inspector.'*

And grew louder until the room fell silent once again. '*Inspector*.'

Donegan searched the room until his eyes settled on the balding journalist to his right on the front row who glared up at him and then changed his expression of annoyance to a weak smile. He sat with his legs crossed, the notebook resting on his thigh, a notebook that Donegan saw was devoid of any writing.

'Inspector,' he began, 'perhaps you might explain for us, the presence of the army explosives disposal team at the scene of Henry Williams's death last evening?'

Reidy leaned forward on the table, his eyes narrowed at the journalist. 'Mr – eh...?'

'Farrell,' the journalist smiled. 'Tom Farrell, Sergeant.'

'If I might take that one, Mr Farrell,' he smiled back, 'it is policy that the army team be called in the event of such incidents. It's a precautionary measure.'

'For explosions, you mean, Sergeant?'

'That matter has yet to be determined.'

'Tell me, Sergeant, was anything found by the army team?'

'Yes, but I'm unable to comment on that at this time.'

Reidy turned his head away.

Farrell was unperturbed by the rebuff.

'Is there a connection between these deaths, Sergeant?' he asked.

The hands lowered slowly. This was a most unusual question. All eyes fixed on Reidy.

'Nothing has come to light to suggest that at the moment,' he lied with all the composure of a tutored perjurer.

Farrell sat back and smiled up at the three of them as the questions started again. He raised an eyebrow at Reidy and gently shook his head in quiet reprimand. Reidy stared hard at him for a moment before a shouted question jolted him from his thoughts.

The questions continued for a further ten minutes, varying from the intelligent to the semi-intelligent, and off the scale to the downright stupid. Reidy fielded them all with calm alacrity.

'Thank you all very much, that's the end of the press conference,' announced the superintendent as he stood up and was joined by Donegan and Reidy.

Farrell stood up and placed the clean notebook in his pocket. He followed the three of them towards the side door. Donegan turned as he felt the presence behind him.

'I'm sorry, Mr Farrell. The press conference is over.' He held his hand out.

Farrell looked around the room and then back, directly into Donegan's eyes.

'I know what's going on here,' he whispered with a smile. 'And to be quite honest with you, I've never seen such an incompetent cover-up in my life.'

Donegan looked him up and down. He had, in the past, been the unwary victim of a journalist's bluff. 'You're entitled to your opinion. Now, let's see if you have the bottle to print it,' he said calmly, and turned to follow the others.

'This Mercury Man person has you worried, hasn't he?' said Farrell behind him.

Donegan whirled around and stared for a moment at Farrell, before taking him roughly by the arm and pulling him into the corridor and out of sight.

***

Landers grimaced as a young man brushed past him on the crowded footpath, their shoulders colliding. A cold sweat broke across his back as the searing pain shot from his palm to his elbow. He cursed silently and walked on, the combination of the hot sun and the claustrophobic street adding to his nausea. He knew that the safety of the gym was less than ten minutes away where he could remove the glove and soothe his throbbing hand under cool, rushing water.

Still the pain increased.

He wanted to remove the gloved hand from his pocket and hold it above his head to ease the agony that drummed in perfect time to his rapid heartbeat.

What the hell had the paedophile's best friend been eating before he sank his fangs into his palm?

The sweat that he rubbed from his brow was instantly replaced by a fresh coating. Soon the glass doors of the gym came into view at the end of the street. He stood outside for a moment to steady himself before going inside. The young receptionist looked up from her sports magazine as the door swung open.

'Mr Landers,' she welcomed him, 'can I speak to you for a moment?'

He turned and looked at her as she reached into the drawer of her desk and removed a small laminated ID card.

'These have just come in,' she explained with a smile, still looking down at her desk and selecting a sheet of paper. 'We've had to change them.'

She lifted the paper onto the counter and placed a pen beside it.

Her expression changed to one of shock as she raised her eyes to him.

'Jesus,' she blurted out as if by accident, then stood up looking at the paled and sweating face outside the counter. 'What happened to you? You look very sick.'

He tried to smile as he shook his head to dismiss her concern.

'It's nothing,' he said. 'I think I might have overdone the exercise today. Too much, too quickly. I'm not as young as I used to be, you know.'

Still, she was not convinced. She reached to her side and picked up the receiver.

'I think I should call a doctor for you all the same,' she said. 'I've seen a few people suffer from heart problems here before. I've had to give cardiac massage to two people, you know.'

Landers rested against the counter and smiled at her through the pain.

'I'm really not *that* old,' he said. 'Anyway, I'll see my own GP when I get a chance.'

'It's no problem,' she said as she began to press out the numbers on the handset.

The pain in his hand and her disregard of his wishes were beginning to irritate him.

'I'd prefer to see my own doctor,' he insisted. 'May I have my membership card now, please?' he said, reaching inside the counter.

'You can understand my concern,' she apologised as she handed it to him. 'In my profession, we always have to look out for signs of weakness.'

'Me too,' he smiled as he took the card and turned to go.

'Mr Landers?' she called him.

He stopped and looked back to see her with the pen outstretched. 'Will you sign the sheet to verify that you got it, please?'

He returned cautiously and held out his left hand.

He looked down at the other signatures.

Thankfully, most of them were illegible scribbles. He rolled the pen between his fingers and looked up at her.

'You can give me cardiac massage any time you want to,' he joked. This crude comment went against all his professional instincts, but he had to buy time.

She gave an embarrassed glance, then blushed crimson as she looked down at her desk, giving him the chance to scribble awkwardly beside his typed name. He placed the pen down on the paper and shook his head.

'I'm sorry, that was very rude of me.' He smiled apologetically.

'It's OK,' she whispered shyly, her eyes gazing down steadily at the counter.

'Good day to you.'

'See you,' she said mildly.

Landers checked the locker room before making his way to the showers and toilet. He waited for a moment before selecting a cubicle, went inside and secured the latch. It would be the best way to dispose of the surgical glove. He removed his hand from his tracksuit top and looked down. The sight of it shocked him. The blood had darkened the green surgical glove to his fingertips. He held it over the toilet bowl as he peeled it off, the coagulated blood dropping in a glob from his palm into the water. He flushed the toilet and ran his hand under the swirling water, then stood up quickly and slammed himself back against the cubicle wall as the acid-like pain burned. Whatever chemical was being used in the waste system had little regard for his wound.

His breathing grew sharp and his head spun. He sat down on the edge of the bowl, his wrist clasped in an attempt to stem the pain. Although the bleeding had stopped, the bite marks were now an ugly crimson black. He would have to seek medical attention. Tetanus shot at the very least.

He sat upright as the outside door thudded open against the wall.

'Mr Landers,' called a male voice, 'are you in here?'

Landers composed himself quickly.

'Yes, yes I am,' he croaked, then cleared his throat. 'Is there a problem?'

The steps neared and he could see the spotless white runners at the foot of the cubicle door.

'Shannon was worried about you. She said you were ill,' said the voice. 'Are you all right?'

Landers squeezed his wrist harder. Anger boiled inside him. Still, this was not a time for a confrontation with the overly concerned youngster.

'I'm perfectly fine now,' he replied as politely as the situation would allow. 'It must have been something I ate, if you know what I mean.' He managed a faint laugh.

There was a cough of understanding from outside, followed by a stifled giggle.

'I know what you mean, Mr Landers,' the voice rose slightly. 'It's always best to work these things out on your own.'

Landers couldn't help but smile as he heard the door outside close. The young man's humour had brought some temporary relief. He pulled at the giant roll of paper beside him, tore several sheets from it and clasped them in his sore hand.

He stood up on his weakened legs and quickly planned his solution. The bleeding was no longer a problem. At least that was something.

He would rinse out the irritant from the wound, get some antibiotics and disinfectant from a chemist shop, and take a tetanus shot later. Doyle could surely arrange that.

He removed the tissue from his hand and looked down at in disgust. Killing Danby had been done on impulse and now he was paying the price. He knew that he should have waited, should have planned it like the others. For the first time in a long time, he was worried. His hand throbbed again to remind him of his stupidity. It would have to be cured, and quickly.

He would certainly need both hands for the next job.

***

Donegan stood with his back to the room, looking out the window as he spoke into his mobile phone.

'I had it switched off, Bob,' he explained. 'We were at the press conference. Not too good.' His tone was filled with accusation as he turned around and looked at Tom Farrell.

'Yes, yes, I know what you've told me. I'll tell Malley to speed things up. In the meantime, you contact the local lads and tell them what you know. Yes, it is unusual. And it puts us back a day as well. Tell them to start again. No, I doubt if they'll be pleas-ed.'

Tom Farrell rested back in the chair, smiled and

folded his arms as he listened to the cryptic conversation.

He was almost fifty, still freelance and still wearing the brown tweed jacket with leather patches that he had bought after his first story had been published. He was regarded in his profession as extremely dangerous, preferring to stick to the ridiculous stories, adding his own twist to them as he went along, rather than do the donkeywork of real investigative journalism. The newspapers he had submitted his work to had, on many occasions, been the subject of severe and costly lawsuits as a result of his works of faction.

He leaned forward in the chair as Donegan turned his back to him to whisper something into the phone. The superintendent sat on the opposite side of the office rolling his thumbs. Reidy stood like a nightclub doorman with his back to the office door, his hands clasped in front of him, examining Farrell with his eyes.

Farrell waited until Donegan had finished the telephone conversation.

'Do I need a solicitor present?' he asked smugly, already knowing the answer.

'Well, now, that depends,' replied Donegan, trying to unnerve him.

'Certainly not,' the superintendent reassured him and then glared at Donegan. 'If you have information that can be helpful in this investigation, I am confident that you will give it to us.'

'I want to help in any way I can,' said Farrell.

'Where did you hear the name Mercury Man?' asked Donegan.

Reidy moved silently from behind him to the desk in front and flipped open the file cover of the A4 copy.

The superintendent leaned forward and rested his elbows on his knees.

'First things first, gentlemen,' smiled Farrell.

'What does that mean?' snapped Donegan.

'It means that I want the exclusive on the story, Inspector,' he replied and then shrugged casually. 'Not that I don't have it already,' he added with a grin at the three of them. 'You tell me what you know and I'll tell you. That's the way it works, isn't it?'

'Now wait just one...' Donegan started.

'Mr Farrell,' the superintendent interrupted.

'Please, call me Tom,' said Farrell.

'Em, Tom. As you well know from your experience in journalism, there are certain things that can be said, and there are other things that must be kept under wraps until the case is solved.'

Farrell looked at him and gave a contemptuous laugh. 'You mean like the fact that a vigilante is going around the city killing people who have evaded justice. Is that what you mean, Superintendent?'

Reidy closed the file cover and walked around the desk. He stood behind the seated inspector and folded his arms.

'You realise of course, *Tom*,' he said, 'that withholding evidence in a murder investigation is a serious criminal offence – an offence that is punishable by imprisonment.'

He stared hard at him for a few seconds as he waited for a response.

'Thank you for the legal advice, eh, Sergeant,' said Farrell. 'However, the fact remains that I am the only one who can get this show on the road. But I must tell you now, I don't work for nothing.'

'That's not what I heard,' Donegan muttered under his breath. His comment drew another angry glance from the superintendent.

'It is my intention,' continued Farrell unperturbed, 'to have my story appear on the front page of a leading newspaper next Sunday. I've even thought of a catchy heading. "Mercury Man – Divine Justice from the Gods".'

Donegan rose quickly from behind his desk. His fists were clenched as he rounded to the front.

'Now listen here, you – you little – bollocks,' he warned, 'if you hinder this investigation in any way, I'll see you swing from the highest pole.'

Farrell smiled up innocently.

'But I'm a journalist, Inspector. It's my job to tell the public the truth.'

Donegan was struggling for words.

'You're a journalist,' he sneered. 'I'll tell you what you are, you're a...'

'That's enough, Inspector.' The superintendent was on his feet. He looked down at Farrell.

'Tom, what information do you have on this Mercury Man?' he asked.

Farrell unfolded his arms and signalled them back to their seats. He was now in complete control of the proceedings, and he knew it. 'Gentlemen, please,' he urged.

Donegan returned reluctantly to his seat behind the desk. Reidy sat down beside the superintendent on the couch. All three of them looked at the irritating journalist.

'This morning,' began Farrell. 'I was going through my post and I found this.'

He reached into his inside pocket and removed a white envelope with the tips of his fingers.

'I have two copies,' he informed them as he placed it on the desk. 'Once I realised what it was, I was very careful how I handled it.'

'What's in it?' asked Donegan, disguising the fact that he was impressed at Farrell's care not to destroy any possible evidence.

'It's a short note, Inspector. A short note and a list of four names.'

He reached into his other inside pocket and removed a sheet of paper.

'This is a copy for you,' he smiled holding it out.

Donegan took it from him and unfolded it. He read aloud.

'Mr Farrell

The following have boarded the coach of redress and have reached their final destination.
Lilly Carey
James Ryan
Gerry Feeney
Henry Williams

The coach has returned and is now empty. For a while at least.

Sincerely
Best wishes

The Mercury Man'

He handed the sheet to Reidy and then fixed his stare on Farrell.

'Why you?' he asked. His tone was heavy with insinuation.

Farrell shrugged and then laughed nervously.

'I was just as surprised as anyone, Inspector,' he replied. 'It's one great story, though, isn't it? Ireland's second serial killer. And I'm right there on the inside track.'

'These people are dead, Mr Farrell,' said the superintendent pointing a finger at the names Ryan and Williams. 'Who are those others on the list, Inspector?'

Donegan nodded at Reidy.

'Give the name Gerry Feeney to Fox and McGrath, Sergeant,' he said. 'It was on one of the sheets that they gave me this morning. We'll check out this Lilly Carey ourselves.'

Reidy nodded, gave a final glance of disdain at Farrell and left the room. Donegan turned his attention back.

'You can write whatever crap you want about this, and we can't stop you doing it,' he said. 'But before you put pen to paper, I would ask you to consider the consequences.'

He moved around the desk to the front and sat on the edge with his arms folded.

'It's obvious that this maniac is *using* you.' He nodded his head for emphasis. 'You can see that, can't you?'

Farrell did not respond.

'Do not become his accomplice on paper,' warned Donegan. 'Write what you want, but if you bollocks up my investigation, *you* will answer for it. Do you understand what I'm telling you?'

Farrell stood up and extended his hand.

'Thank you for your time, Inspector,' he smiled. 'I'd love to stay and chat, but I have an article to write. We'll talk again, Superintendent.'

Donegan did not take his hand, choosing instead to brush gently past him and walk to the door. He held it open and removed a small card with his mobile number from his shirt pocket, then held it out between his fingers.

Farrell stopped in the doorway and nodded gently at him as he took it.

'I'll be as helpful as I can, Inspector,' he promised.

'Good day, Mr Farrell,' replied an irate Donegan.

CHAPTER NINE

Beano stood on the top step outside the station door for a moment and then slung on his suede jacket. He grinned as he gave the thumbs up to the car that was parked below him near the kerb.

'Elvis has left the building,' said Fox, as he hurriedly wound down the passenger window and beckoned to him.

Beano glanced left and right and walked casually down the steps, at the same time removing a dented green tin of cigarette tobacco from his jacket pocket. He did not approach the window of the car, choosing instead to seat himself opposite it against the railings of the station.

'Thanks for gettin' me outta there,' he muttered as he looked down and began to roll a cigarette. He did not look at them as he spoke. Instead he glanced left and right again and squinted up at the building in front of him. 'I won't let yez down,' he promised, his lips barely moving. 'I'm on to it right away.'

Fox quickly grew tired of the cloak-and-dagger charade. He leaned out the open window and jerked his thumb to the back door.

'Get in the car, Bond,' he snapped. 'We have some serious talking to do.'

McGrath smiled to himself as he watched Beano rise slowly from the low wall and approach the car. He sat in quickly and lowered himself down out of sight.

'You once told me when you were high, that you wanted to be a guard, isn't that right, Beano?' said Fox. 'Well, this is your lucky day, because you've just joined the Metropolitan Crime Squad.'

Beano, who had been hunched down in the back, sat up quickly and leaned between the two front seats.

'What do you mean?' he asked nervously.

'I'll tell you what I mean,' snapped Fox. 'Detective Bob McGrath, I would like to introduce you to Detective Beano the Tout, the newest member of our squad.'

McGrath turned. 'You're very welcome,' he smiled. 'I hope that we'll have a lot of success.'

'What the Jaysus are yez talking about?' asked a confused Beano.

Fox rested his head back against the seat and gave a heavy sigh.

'Beano,' he began in a friendly tone. 'There was

never a truer saying than "A policeman's lot is not a happy one". And do you know why that is?'

'No.'

'Because he has to account for every move that he makes. Has to contact the station every few minutes to tell them what he's doing. Can't even go for a cup of coffee without telling someone. Reporting on the hour, every hour. Basically, he's accountable for every minute of his day's work.'

Beano was slowly but surely beginning to get the picture.

'My phonecard is nearly out,' he mumbled.

'Not a problem, Detective,' said Fox cheerfully. 'We'll go on a bit of a shopping spree and get you a stack of them.'

He turned around in the seat and faced him.

'I want you to phone me every hour, do you understand?'

Beano nodded dumbly and then swallowed hard. 'Every hour,' he agreed.

Fox raised a cautioning finger.

'There's going to be no more bullshitting us,' he warned. 'You know a hell of a lot more about what's going on than you're telling us.'

Beano shook his head furiously. Fox paid little attention to the denial.

'Let me explain,' he said. 'We've got you out of a dealing charge, but your freedom is only temporary. That big detective you were talking to inside there is not one of your biggest fans. And if I don't tell him that you've come up trumps, then he'll personally see to it that you do a stretch.'

He gave a sympathetic smile.

'And let's be honest, Beano. You're not exactly suited to lifting weights and being the life and soul of the shower parties, even if you do have a ponytail.'

Fox was preying hard on the one thing that terrified Beano. He could see from his expression and the humbled nodding that it was working.

'Well, then, if you get us the slightest lead, I'll see to it that those charges go away. Am I being fair or what?'

'More than fair,' agreed Beano quickly.

'Good man.'

Fox turned back in the seat as his mobile phone rang on the dashboard.

'You don't have to ring me from there, Beano,' he joked as he picked it up to answer.

'Yeah.'

He listened for a minute and then jammed the phone between shoulder and chin, signalling to McGrath that he needed a pen and paper.

'Give me that again,' he said as he took the notebook and biro from McGrath, who watched him with interest. 'What number is it? Got it. We'll check it out straight away and get back to you.'

He threw the phone on the dashboard and leaned his head back.

'Looks like you're on the beat for the day,' he said to Beano. He struggled in the pocket of his jeans for a moment before pulling out a bundle of crumpled notes from which he took two twenties.

'Get those phonecards,' he instructed. 'Do not spend this money on the wicked weed.'

Beano reached forward and took the notes, his other hand opening the back door.

'Every hour,' warned Fox.

Beano closed the door and paused for a moment at the open passenger window.

'Mum's the word,' he whispered and then moved away.

Fox watched him go, silently hoping that Beano would get a lead, not alone for the success of the investigation, but also to save himself from jail. Finn had given him just three days' reprieve. Fox knew that the Drug Squad detective would stick to that bargain.

'Who is Gary Fenn... Gary Fff...?' asked McGrath beside him with a puzzled expression as he tried to read the name and address that Fox had scribbled in his notebook.

Fox snapped it from him and looked down, he too narrowing his eyes as he tried to decipher his own writing.

'Gerry Feeney, you eejit,' he said, as he suddenly remembered the name that Reidy had given him. 'We have to go and check it out. Something about a list of names that Donegan got from a reporter.'

'I know that name,' said McGrath as he started the car. 'Where did I see that before?'

He was still thinking as he pulled out into the lane of traffic.

'Fella who killed his wife,' he said suddenly. 'He was on the printouts that we got this morning.'

'Oh, yeah,' said Fox, pretending to remember. 'Anyway, Reidy seems to think that he might have been topped already by this Mercury Man headball.'

McGrath grimaced in disgust. 'You mean that we might be going to a corpse?'

'Well, that's very likely if he's dead, Guard,' grinned Fox.

The journey took just under half an hour. McGrath drove at his usual leisurely thirty miles an hour whenever the traffic permitted, Fox by his side muttering low curses under his breath whenever the car stopped at an amber light and jokingly accusing the driver of not wanting to get to the scene. By the time they reached Gerry Feeney's housing estate, he had run out of poor-driving put-downs.

'What number is it?' asked McGrath.

Fox looked out the window, his eyes darting from the house numbers on the doors to those on the outside pillars.

'That's the one,' he announced suddenly. 'Pull in.'

They stood outside for a moment, resting their arms on the warm roof.

'Fancy a game of tag?'

Fox nodded at the crowd of children who ran around the large play green in the middle of the estate, screaming and whooping, being followed by a lone youngster. The child stopped suddenly and then bent at the hips.

'I got ya, Mikey.' The child stood up and pointed an accusing finger.

The group stalled and looked back. One of them stepped forward cautiously.

'Ya did not, ya cheatin' shite ya,' he shouted and then retreated to the safety of the others.

The group fled as the chase began again, then

stopped suddenly, all heads turning to the woman who stood at the gate with a baby in her arms.

'Mikey O'Brien! What did I hear you say? You get in here right now!'

The youngster groaned as he moved away, nodding an apology to the others for the appearance of his mother, and whispering a guarantee for his prompt return.

Fox gave a soft whistle. 'Jesus, I know how that feels.' He smiled across the roof of the car.

McGrath nodded silently in agreement as he made his way to the rear of the car and opened the boot. He pulled two pairs of rubber gloves from a box of them and handed one pair to Fox.

They walked up the narrow path to the frosted glass door.

'Don't put those on yet,' McGrath whispered as Fox struggled to pull on one of the gloves.

'Why not?'

McGrath threw his eyes up.

'Supposing yer man is alive and he answers the door and there you are with a pair of crime-scene gloves on you to investigate his murder?'

'Point taken,' grinned Fox, and rapped with his knuckle on the glass, his other hand stuffing the gloves into his pocket. 'That'd be a fair shock all right.'

They looked at each other and waited for a short time before Fox rapped the door again.

'What do we do now?' asked McGrath finally.

Fox walked back down the path.

'Reidy said to give him a buzz if there was no answer,' he replied as he went to the car.

McGrath cupped his face with his hands and tried to look through the frosted glass. Unable to see anything, he moved along the wall to the front window. Fox stood outside by the car talking to Reidy.

'Anything?' he shouted.

McGrath turned from the window and shook his head. 'Can't see a thing.'

Fox listened to the instructions for a further minute and then beckoned to McGrath.

'He says that we're to check with the neighbours and if they haven't seen him then we're to try and gain access to the house.'

He looked at the houses on either side. 'Do you want to take the left or the right?'

McGrath thought about it for a moment. 'Eh, right,' he said.

They parted and went through the different gates, Fox disappearing out of view behind a thick hedge.

McGrath pressed the doorbell, at the same time fumbling for his ID card.

A small girl answered, rubbing the wisps of her white-blonde hair across her forehead. She looked up at him with piercing blue eyes and then pulled the door open fully.

'Ma, it's the rent man,' she shouted into the hall and then looked back up at him.

Before he could correct the mistake, a young woman appeared in the kitchen doorway, her face a mirror image of her daughter's, rubbing her wet hands down along her apron. She gave a pleasant smile and gently brushed her hand over the child's head.

'It's not the rent man, Andrea,' she said. 'Go on back to the front room.'

She looked up at McGrath and shrugged an apology.

'Kids,' she explained. 'They'll say anything, won't they?'

Not experienced enough in that particular field, McGrath smiled at her as he held out his ID.

'Detective Garda Bob McGrath,' he said. 'I was wondering if I could have a few minutes of your time? It's just a small inquiry.'

She looked down at the card and then stepped back.

'Come in,' she offered. 'I hope that you haven't any bad news for me.'

'No, no, not at all,' McGrath quickly dismissed the very mention. 'It's just an inquiry about your neighbour, Gerry Feeney.'

She made an O with her mouth, and tilted her head sideways.

'What has he done now?' she whispered.

'Nothing, nothing,' replied McGrath quickly. 'I was just wondering if you had seen him in the last few days.'

She raised a finger to her lips and thought for a moment. Suddenly she reached out and touched McGrath on the arm. 'I haven't seen him in a couple of days, now that you say it. But he's a very private man, after that business with his wife and all.'

McGrath looked over her shoulder and out through the kitchen window.

'Is there a way into his back garden from here?' he asked.

She suddenly became wary of him.

'Are you really a guard?' she asked nervously.

'Yes. Yes, I am.' He smiled to ease her worry. 'My

colleague, Detective Andy Fox, is talking with your neighbour on the other side of Mr Feeney's house at the moment. And he's asking the exact same questions. We only want to find Mr Feeney, you understand.'

Fox had drawn the short straw. He stood on the bottom step two doors down, looking up as he listened to the abuse from the unshaven Baluba in the vest.

'No I haven't seen the bollocks. I'm working nights. And if you do see him, tell him that if he looks at my wife again across the hedge, he'll need a gang of guards around to save him.'

Fox nodded and turned to go.

'Thank you very much,' he said politely. 'You've been most helpful. I'll pass on your good wishes to him. Go back to bed for yourself.'

He walked slowly to the car and rested against it for a moment. A rebellious cheer rose as Mikey returned to the game of tag. Fox turned to his left as McGrath appeared in the doorway and called to him.

'This is the other detective I was telling you about,' said McGrath, as they watched him approach. 'Show Caroline your identification, Andy.'

Fox kept his eyes on her as he took out his ID card. He extended his hand.

'Very nice to meet you, Caroline,' he smiled.

McGrath glared at him and then coughed suddenly.

'Caroline here is going to let us get into Mr Feeney's yard,' he said.

'That's very good of you,' said Fox.

'It's a fairly high wall,' she said turning from them and walking back into the kitchen.

'Behave yourself,' McGrath growled over his shoulder as they followed her.

'Tell me she's the daughter of the house, please tell me,' Fox whispered behind him.

McGrath ignored the pleadings as they went outside into the back garden.

Caroline pointed up at the wall as if they needed directions.

'Over there,' she said.

'You first.' Fox pushed McGrath in front of him. 'You're taller.'

McGrath scowled at him before jumping up on the wall and holding himself there by his elbows. 'There's a back window open,' he grunted and scraped his runners up along the dark-grey blocks. He sat astride the wall looking back down at them.

Fox raised his hand in a quick OK signal.

'Good man. I'll go around to the front and wait for you to open the door.'

He turned and grinned at Caroline.

'That's the price of being tall,' he said.

McGrath muttered something to himself before he lifted his leg to the other side of the wall and jumped from view.

'I hope that you guys are really guards,' she said mischievously.

Fox placed his hands in his pockets and looked at her. 'That's what the superintendent says to us every morning,' he joked.

They both laughed.

'I'm going in the window now, Detective. So why do I still hear you over there?' The voice shouted from the other side of the wall.

'Thank you, Caroline,' said Fox and made his way quickly through the back door.

CHAPTER TEN

Landers placed his briefcase on the marbled floor of the balcony and chose a table with a view of the front door of the coffee shop.

'Mineral water and tea, please,' he said to the waitress who approached.

He looked down at the box of painkillers he had bought and opened it quickly, releasing two of the oval tablets from the foil wrapping. Although the pain in his hand had abated somewhat, this simple exercise had set it throbbing again. The waitress returned with his order and set it down. He thanked her and waited until she had left before he reached out and clasped his injured hand around the ice-cold glass. His eyes closed for a moment as the relief set in. When he opened them, he glanced around at the tables beside him, and with all the finesse of a closet pill-popper, palmed the two painkillers to his mouth.

Below at the front door, Mr Doyle stood holding a small plastic carrier bag, his head moving slowly left and right as he scanned the crowded ground floor. He walked forward and up the wide marble stairway, a smile of acknowledgment appearing on his face when he saw Landers.

The heavy, cast-iron chair screeched along the floor as he sat down.

'You had me scared,' he said. 'I was expecting to see you surrounded by armed detectives when I arrived.'

Landers lowered the glass slowly on the table. 'You don't have to worry about me,' he said. 'Like I told you on the phone, it was a minor setback.'

He turned his hand over and showed the injury.

'Jesus, a *dog* did that,' gasped Doyle, looking at the palm that had turned a dark purple.

'It was the last bite of its career,' said Landers. 'It's gone to the great kennel in the sky. It's up there now with Mr Danby.'

Their eyes met for a moment before Doyle lifted the small plastic bag on to the table.

'Tetanus shot. You'll have to do it yourself. Some bandages and plasters. There's some heavy-duty prescription painkillers in there as well.'

'Yours?'

'Yes. Got them for a back injury a few months ago. Believe me, there's nothing stronger on the legal market. Or so my specialist told me. Tell me about this morning. I can't believe that you've done it so quickly,' he said.

Landers eased back on the chair as the waitress approached.

Doyle looked up at her. 'Just coffee for me, thank you.'

He turned back to Landers.

'It was stupid of me,' said Landers when she was gone.

Doyle became visibly nervous. 'What do you mean?'

'I mean that I did something I've never done before. I acted like an angry amateur.'

'But – but you did nothing to jeopardise the plan?' Doyle stuttered.

'No, Mr Doyle,' Landers reassured him. 'But I think you know me well enough now. I'm a man who likes to have planned to the last detail. Everything must be one hundred per cent certain.'

Doyle nodded, waiting for the bad news he felt sure was coming.

'That's why you're here,' he said.

Landers grimaced slightly as he rubbed his thumb slowly over the crusting puncture wounds.

'I don't think you really know who I am, Mr Doyle, do you? What were you doing when you were twenty?' he asked suddenly.

'Helping my father to run a chain of engineering workshops. Why do you ask?'

'Do you know what I was doing when I was that age, Mr Doyle?'

'I thought that we agreed not to discuss that.' Doyle shifted nervously on the chair. 'The less we know about each other, the better.'

Landers looked up as the waitress approached and put the white cup and saucer down on the table. He eyed the plastic bag beside the coffee. The sooner he took the tetanus shot the better.

'Yes,' he said when she was gone, 'you're probably right. It's better that way.'

Doyle leaned forward again, his elbows resting on the table, his fingers clasped.

'Mr Landers,' he whispered, 'I don't really want to know what you did in your previous life but, naturally, I have a fairly good idea. I have given you a task, and I hope that you will see it to fruition. How I got my money should be of little interest to you. What you did when you were twenty is of little interest to *me*. I am giving you a substantial amount of my money to see that justice is done. You are the instigator of this plan. I am merely the victim with the necessary information and the swelling bank account.'

Landers stared hard at him. He knew that this elderly cash-dispenser was right.

'My apologies,' he said. Then he smiled. 'I've had a tough day.'

Doyle relaxed and picked up his coffee cup.

'So that file I gave you upset you as much as it did me?' he said.

'Yes. Very much so,' Landers replied. 'It was foolish of the authorities to let an animal like him back on the streets.'

They sat in silence for a moment, Landers examining the contents of the plastic bag, the bandages, the rubber vial of anti-tetanus medicine, the hypodermic and the brown phial of painkillers prescribed for Doyle's back injury. No doubt from golf, he thought to himself.

Once he had finished his coffee, Doyle looked to his side and then leaned forward. 'The Metropolitan Crime Squad are on your tail,' he smiled.

'Should I be worried?'

'Should a rabbit be worried if a muzzled dog is following him?' Doyle grinned, then signalled to the waitress at the counter that he wanted a refill.

'I've heard of them,' Landers said. 'Ruthless but effective. Some might say the best squad of detectives in the country.'

Doyle looked down and shrugged. 'Well, that's the theory,' he replied casually. 'The main threat is not from the squad itself. The biggest threat comprises two young detectives.'

Landers leaned forward with interest. 'And – are they a *real* threat?' he asked.

'Well, my source tells me that they are a hit-and-miss outfit. But they have hit more than they have missed, if you know what I mean. The squad has *carte blanche* when something like this happens. And apparently, these two detectives stretch that privilege to the limit.'

'Who are they? What are their names?'

Doyle raised his eyes slowly and looked across the table. He knew that all he had to do was give the names, and this death-dealing puppet would solve the problem.

He looked down and rubbed at the grey hair on his knuckles before looking up.

'Mr Landers,' he said, 'I am paying you very well for doing what you are doing. Is that not so?' He did not wait for a reply. 'You have been given your assignments, but you can cease to be an employee any time that you wish.'

Landers sat in silence as he listened.

'We made one thing very clear to you from the beginning,' Doyle continued. 'Whatever happened, that no innocent person was to be touched. Correct?'

'Are you dissatisfied with my work?' Landers's irritation showed.

'No. Not at all. You have carried out your assignments without fault to date. But I want you to understand, you will stick to the plan. Or you can find employment elsewhere.'

Landers stared at him for a moment. He gave a thin smile and then nodded his understanding.

'The trick is to get away with it,' he agreed. 'That's why your contact devised the very clever plan that he did. Perhaps I can meet him when all this is over.'

'I'm afraid that's impossible,' said Doyle and sipped at his coffee.

Landers shrugged.

'In any case, it ensures that we *will* get away with it. That too, Mr Doyle, is one of my main objectives. That, and getting paid.'

Doyle smiled. 'You have shown yourself to be a worthy employee, Mr Landers,' he said. 'This morning has proved that beyond any doubt. You have one more killing to complete before the pinnacle. If you feel that it may in any way jeopardise your position, then so be it. Forget about it and concentrate all your efforts on the final deed.'

Landers picked up his cup of tea and sipped. He reached down to his side and then stood up, briefcase in hand.

'I like to see a job to the end.' He smiled down at Doyle. 'At my age, it takes more than a couple of enthusiastic young detectives to scare me away.'

Doyle looked up at him. 'I knew that I had been given the right man for the job,' he said with admiration. 'When will I hear from you again?'

Landers switched the briefcase from his left hand into the right and closed his swelling palm around the handle. His teeth clenched with the pain. He took a deep breath before replying.

'Deliver the money that you promised me last night to the hotel,' he said. 'Then, Mr Doyle, just sit back and relax.'

***

The small, wooden chair clattered to the ground as McGrath jumped down from the sink-top. He straightened himself up in the small kitchen and looked around, pulling the gloves tighter on his hands.

'C'mon, c'mon,' Fox rapped outside on the front door. 'What are you at?'

McGrath examined the floor as he walked cautiously along the narrow hall and opened the door.

'Jesus Christ,' muttered a clearly irritated Fox as

he brushed in past him, 'it's a good job that we're not in the house-breaking business. We'd spend most of our time in court.'

He stopped in the middle of the hallway and looked back. His face had paled. His nostrils opened and closed as he sniffed the air.

'Don't laugh at me,' he said quietly, 'but I can smell death.'

McGrath gave him an irritated glance and then held his gloved palms up.

'That's very interesting, Lassie,' he said. 'Now cover your paws, like a good collie.'

Fox took the gloves from his pocket. 'Don't tell me you can't smell it,' he said in a mixture of excitement and alarm, as he struggled to pull them on.

'The only thing that I can smell at the moment is bullshit,' replied McGrath, watching him. 'Now let's get this search done and get out of here. We'll look in there first.'

Fox moved towards the sitting-room door and turned the handle slowly. He felt the hairs on the back of his neck bristle as it creaked open a few inches. He stood upright and turned back. His face was now ashen.

'He's in there,' he said and pushed the door open with his finger.

McGrath stood behind him looking over his shoulder, his anxiety increasing. He sensed now that Fox was probably right.

The smell of lifeless flesh wafted out at them from the room, confirming Fox's assertion.

They stayed where they were, in the hallway, peering in at the body. They could see the calling card resting on Gerry Feeney's chest.

'Get "scenes of crime" down here,' said Fox quietly, his eyes still fixed on the body.

McGrath backed away slowly and then turned for the door. 'Yeah, right,' he panted nervously.

Fox looked down at the carpet and pushed the door open wider to look into the room. Much as he wanted to step inside, he stopped himself, knowing that the carpet might hold a vital clue.

His heart jumped as the mobile phone on his belt rang. He swallowed hard and cursed to himself before answering.

It was Beano reporting in as ordered.

'I should have something within the next couple of hours, I just got the word on someone that was looking for the Wolfman's girl a few weeks back. I'm going to check it out.' He spoke quickly, as if he had urgent business to attend to and this unnecessary telephone call was delaying him. 'Where are you now?'

Fox moved outside the front door and sat down on the step.

'Ah, we're dealing with this and that,' he said casually. 'Just another boring inquiry. We can't all have a life as exciting as yours, you know.'

Beano laughed. Fox could sense that his confidence was high.

'So tell me. What's this about the Wolfman's girl?' he asked. He could hear the traffic roar past in the background and he smiled to himself as Beano shouted in reply, his breath labouring as he walked and talked.

'I can't say for sure at the moment. It might be nothing. I want to check it out first.'

'Good man, Beano. You're even beginning to sound like a cautious detective,' said Fox.

'I'll ring yez later.'

'Do that. Mind yourself.'

The conversation ended. Fox remained sitting on the step, tossing the phone pensively from one hand to the other.

McGrath returned, snapping off the gloves and shoving them in the pocket of his denims.

'They'll be here shortly. Donegan and Reidy as well,' he said. 'This whole thing just took a twist in a different direction.' He fixed a stare beyond the open front door.

Fox stood up and clipped the phone back on his belt.

'It sure has,' he agreed. 'Looks like we're on the trail of a very interesting killer.'

'What did the old guy die of?' asked McGrath looking at him.

Fox shrugged.

'What the fuck difference does that make?' he said. 'He's dead. Doesn't look like there was a struggle, though. Room seems tidy enough.'

'How did he get in?'

'Well, there's no sign of forced entry, although the back window was open. The old guy must have let him in the front door. Same way that the Wolfman must have let him in. And let's be honest, whatever about this fella, you can be sure that he was well quizzed before he was allowed into the Wolfman's kip.'

'Both were tricked then,' said McGrath.

'Must have been. In this day and age, people are

wary about letting a stranger stand in their hall, let alone into the house itself. Unless the killer produced a gun at the door.'

McGrath pressed on.

'Why kill Williams in the open? Out on a city street in broad daylight.'

Fox squinted up at him. 'What have these two in common that Williams hasn't?' he asked. McGrath thought about it for a moment.

'He doesn't live alone,' he answered finally.

'Exactly. That computer printout that you got this morning just became our best lead. This fella has killed three already, and he's not going to stop there. The only way we're going to catch our man is to second-guess him to the next victim. How many are on that list who live alone?'

'Six, seven maybe.'

McGrath stretched himself up and looked across the tall hedge along the row of houses.

'I wonder what kind of help we'll get from the neighbours?' he mused. 'I mean, this ould lad mustn't have had many visitors. A caller would have been spotted quick enough by anyone.' His voice lowered. 'Then again, if he was as popular as the Wolfman, we're not going to get much.'

Fox wasn't listening. He moved slowly down the path, his eyes fixed on the group of children who swarmed around the green, Mikey now the lone hunter.

McGrath remained at the step and folded his arms as he watched Fox cross the road and jump the kerb on to the green.

'I'll just wait here then,' he muttered. He shook his head and leaned back against the wall.

Fox moved almost to the middle of the green and stood squinting up at the sun with his hands in his pockets. The group moved *en masse* past him, some of the heads turning with puzzled expressions, before racing on again.

'You're not very good at this are you, Mikey?' he said as the youngster approached.

The youngster stopped suddenly and looked at him.

'How do you know my name?' he panted in surprise.

'I know everything, Mikey,' replied Fox. 'I'm a detective. That's my job.'

The others had stopped and were looking back. Mikey's breathing softened as he examined the man who grinned back at him.

'You are in your shite,' he exclaimed. 'You don't look like a detective.'

Fox reached into his back pocket and took out his badge.

'What do you think of that?' He smiled as he held it out, the gold crest sparkling, the glare throwing a fleck of light on the youngster's face. The others moved back cautiously in a semi-circle at a safe distance behind Mikey, the taller ones moving closer to the front.

'Are you a cop?' asked one.

'He's a detective,' Mikey corrected him. 'And he says he knows everything.'

There was a low murmur amongst the group.

'Who knows Gerry Feeney?' Fox asked as he replaced his ID card in his pocket.

A pretty child raised her hand as she edged her way to the front of the group.

'Sir, sir, he's the old man who lives over there,' she said quickly and pointed.

'That's right,' Fox smiled down at her. 'Who else knows that?' he asked looking around at the others.

The hands raised slowly, the faces furrowed with worry.

'We never did anything to him,' Mikey blurted out. 'It was the older fellas.'

Fox rubbed his hand slowly across his mouth as he pretended to be carefully considering whether to arrest them all or not.

'Mmmm,' he said, and all eyes widened.

'Do you all play here every day?' he asked.

The heads nodded together, glad now that the subject was changing.

'Every day since the holidays,' said Mikey.

'Well, I'm looking for Mr Feeney at the moment, and I can't find him. I wonder if someone called to him and maybe took him away for his holidays.'

'I saw him at the shop on Monday,' said one youngster. The rest looked at him and hurriedly began to volunteer information about the sightings of Gerry Feeney as far back as Christmas. Fox called the excited group to order.

'Did anyone call to Mr Feeney's house in the last few days?' he asked.

There was silence for a moment. A hand raised at the back, and the group parted as the chubby, red-faced youngster stepped forward.

'The other morning,' he started. Fox patted his

trouser pocket for the notebook. There was none.

'What morning?' he asked, then turned and whistled loudly through his teeth at McGrath, who stood idly beside the front door of Feeney's house.

The youngster counted on his fingers and looked up.

'Tuesday,' he said with conviction. 'A man called to his house.'

'Was there anyone else here with you? Any of the rest of this group?' asked Fox.

'Yeah, nearly all of us. Frankie, you were here, you saw him as well.' He pointed into the group.

Fox's heart soared as the tall youngster Frankie nodded from the middle of the crowd. He guessed that he was at least twelve, not old enough to have the black facial hair that sprouted from his chin, still young enough to play tag.

McGrath jogged up to them and Fox held out his hand for the notebook and pen.

'What did he look like?' he asked. 'Old, young?'

'Oldish,' replied Frankie. 'He had a small suitcase.'

'Like a businessman carries?'

'Yeah. It was black.'

'What was he wearing?'

'He had a shirt and tie and a jacket.'

'What colour was the jacket?'

'Brown. His trousers were darker.'

Fox racked his brains for the preliminary questions. The important ones would take more time.

Some of the others in the group added to and contradicted the answers given by Frankie until all were in agreement. And then Fox began. Hair colour, style, build, face, all the way from top to bottom. The contradictions amongst the group were minor this time.

And finally the most important part of the puzzle.

'Age?' he asked.

The group looked at one another. A small grubby-faced youngster pointed.

'The same as Mikey's dad,' he announced, and the group around him nodded.

Fox turned around quickly to see the same unshaven Baluba in the vest who he had spoken to earlier, cross the road and approach with menace.

'Who's this tulip?' asked McGrath beside him.

Mikey's dad looked from Fox to McGrath and then down at the children.

'What the fuck is goin' on here?' he mumbled, his eyes heavy from lack of sleep.

Fox jotted 'late forties' in the notebook and smiled as he clicked the pen.

'Thanks very much, lads,' he said and walked away to the verge of the grass.

Mikey's father followed and edged himself in front.

'I asked you a question,' he said as he stood blocking the way. 'What were you talking to the kids about?'

Fox swallowed his anger as he looked up.

'Do you really want to know?' he asked.

'Yeah, fuckin' right I want to know,' the reply came in a mixture of agitation and spittle.

Fox brushed past him. 'C'mon then.'

Before McGrath could stop him, Fox was leading Mikey's father up the path.

'Don't touch anything,' he warned.

McGrath cursed and whispered in protest behind them.

'Have a look at that, tough guy,' growled Fox as he pointed into the sitting room.

Mikey's father glanced nervously at Fox and then edged his face around the door.

Two bluebottles tangled noisily in the dried saliva on Gerry Feeney's cheek.

'Love thy neighbour,' said Fox. His tone was accusing.

Mikey's father raised his hand to his mouth and raced out past McGrath at the door.

'Have a good sleep now,' shouted Fox after him.

CHAPTER ELEVEN

Tom Farrell cracked his knuckles and then spread his hands at either side of the keyboard. His wife of twenty years stood behind him, nervously caressing a mug of coffee, her eyes fixed on the six words on the computer screen.

'What do you think of the title?' he asked without looking back.

'It's – eh – yes, Tom, it's – definitely catchy.'

His hand reached over his shoulder, open to receive the mug.

'This is the big one, Anne,' he said excitedly, as he took it from her and sipped at the coffee. 'This is the one to put us on the map.'

She had heard the line so many times before. Heard him promise holidays in the sun, payment of their mortgage, which was three months in arrears, replacement of their twelve-year-old car. How many times had he said 'This is the big one'?

He placed the mug on the table and sat back from the screen with his hands outstretched in a gesture of introduction.

'"Mercury Man – Divine Justice At Last",' he announced. 'Welcome to the big time.'

He turned and looked up at her, his face gleaming with anticipation.

'Did you hear it, Anne?'

'Hear what, Tom?' she asked gently.

'The phone, love. The phone. It hasn't stopped ringing all day. They all want the story.'

She tried to smile.

'Yes, it's been very busy. They're all very interested.'

As if by divine coincidence, the telephone on his desk rang. He looked back at her and laughed. 'I think I'll let it ring for a while,' he said, 'just to annoy them.'

She looked at the phone and waited anxiously for him to answer.

Farrell reached out and placed his hand on the receiver, allowing the ring to continue. She nudged him on the shoulder. He picked up the receiver slowly and eased back on the chair.

'Yes... Speaking.'

After listening for a minute, he selected a pencil from the mug in front of him and scribbled a number on the pad beside the phone.

'How much did you say?' he asked, lifting the pad

to show to his wife. 'I'm afraid that if you want the exclusive, we really must talk a hell of a lot more. You're trailing the pack at the moment. And trailing badly, if I may say so.'

His head nodded as he listened, trying to keep calm in his voice. All his financial worries were about to be swept away by one story. A story that had yet to be written.

'Yes,' he said, 'I spoke to the men in charge of the MCS this morning, in the inner sanctum, so to speak. Detective Inspector Frank Donegan is in charge of the case,' he added with authority. 'Yes, speak with your editor. I'll hold on.'

He removed the phone from his ear and rested it on his chest. He smiled at his wife who leaned over his shoulder and checked the number on the writing-pad.

'I'm going for double that,' he said. 'This is the first time that I've had control over these arseholes, and I'm going to squeeze them for every cent.'

'That's a lot of money, Tom,' said his wife, clearly distressed at his devil-may-care attitude to the figure. 'We could sort out everything with it.'

He dismissed her anxiety with a casual wave of his hand. 'Leave it to me, love,' he assured her. 'I know who I'm dealing with here.'

He lifted the receiver and jammed it between ear and shoulder, the beginnings of the story tingling at his fingertips. He leaned forward and began to type:

There are those of us who place their ultimate trust in the power of our judicial system and those infallible men of legal wisdom who sit high on Anglo-Saxon benches.

He smiled as his wife gasped behind him.

'My God, Tom, you can't say that.'

He shook his head and continued to type.

'The public love this shit,' he muttered.

Then, there are those amongst us who believe that justice is as the word is defined – upright, fair, equitable. Law and justice. How wide the ravine has grown between these plains.

And it grows ever wider. That is, until now. Now from the sands of injustice rises one known only as 'The Mercury Man'.

'How can you write that?' she protested. 'This person is a killer. He killed a young boy.'

Farrell let the phone drop from his shoulder into his hand.

'Do you want this money, or don't you?' he snapped. He remained looking at the screen as he awaited her answer.

'Well, Tom,' she started, 'it seems – well it just seems wrong, that's all.'

'For Christ's sake, it's just a story,' he raised his voice. 'This is the only time in my life that I've been first to the finishing line, and all you can do is stand there behind me and throw obstacles in my way. Give me some support, why don't you?'

She moved around in front of the table and looked directly at him.

'I'm worried about you,' she explained. 'What have you gotten yourself into?'

His casual laugh spurred her on.

'Why did these people pick you? Out of all the crime journalists in the country, they picked Tom Farrell. Why was that?'

Her question echoed the words of Inspector Donegan in his mind.

Farrell had not thought about it before. At least, he tried not to.

'All those top journalists are in cahoots with the guards.' He knew that his explanation was weak, but continued nonetheless. 'These people, whoever they are, they knew that I'd tell the full story, no watering down because some chief asked me to hold off for a while.'

She wrung her hands, her head shaking in disagreement.

'Tom, this is...'

His hand rose to halt her as the voice crackled on the receiver. Farrell waited, his face breaking into a wide grin. He looked up at his wife.

'How much did you say?' he asked as he reached for the writing-pad. 'Yes, I can now announce that you are the pride of this auction. What's your fax number there?'

He tried unsuccessfully to hide his delight as he scribbled the number on the pad.

'I'll send it at seven this evening,' he said, his voice rising with excitement.

He replaced the receiver and rested his arms on the table, a smug grin on his face.

He nodded at the writing pad.

'Remember the first number you saw?' he asked.

His wife raised her eyebrows in thought.

'Yes.'

Farrell lowered his head and shuddered.

'Well – double it,' he shouted and then laughed aloud.

She raised her hand to her mouth and hid her smile. 'That's unbelievable.' She spoke through her fingers.

He pointed to the door.

'Let me get this done, and then we're rich,' he said excitedly. 'Go on, woman. Pack your bags for a holiday.'

She smiled at him and left the room in a fluster. Farrell gazed back at the screen and then down at the photocopy of names and the message from the Mercury Man. He knew the circumstances of the Wolfman and Henry Williams's demise. He could wing it with the other two. He now believed that this was the story that would make him. The story that he had been waiting for all of his life. He thought about the money. No more sucking up for the leftovers. Buying drink with his hard-come-by cash for the established bastards in the hope of getting the tail of a story. Now, the tables were turned and they would be the ones buying the drink.

He sat back for almost ten minutes and thought about it, rehearsing in his mind what to say and do when he would meet the ones who had shunned him in the past.

He smiled as the telephone rang again. He answered it and waited as he heard the sound of a coin box beeping, and then the voice.

'Mr Farrell?'

'Yes.'

'I wonder if you might be good enough to add the name "Ivor Danby" to your article.'

'Who is this?'

'Never mind. Just do what you're told,' the voice growled.

The line went dead.

Farrell slammed down the receiver as if it was white-hot. He searched through the papers on his desk for a moment and then stood up in panic. Outside in the hall, he searched through the pockets of his jacket, his urgency abating as his hand closed around the small card that Donegan had given him. He returned to the room and dialled the number, drumming his fingers on the table as he waited.

'Inspector,' he panted, 'I've been contacted, and I've been given the name Ivor Danby. Does that mean anything to you? No, I didn't get anything else. I think he was calling from a phone box. It sounded like it anyway.'

He listened for a couple of minutes, then his expression changed and he banged his fist on the table.

'Yes, Inspector,' he shouted, 'I damn well *am* going to write this story.'

***

The steel gurney carrying Gerry Feeney rattled along the narrow, uneven path towards the waiting van, the body shuddering beneath the white plastic cover. A uniformed garda moved along outside the low wall, releasing lengths of crime-scene tape from a large roll and threading it between the steel railings. The men from the Technical Bureau, dressed from head to toe in white and armed with cameras and suitcases, moved in a group towards the house, looking more like the Wehrmacht Alpine Corps than Irish policemen on a hot summer's evening.

An unmarked car drove into the estate and parked at the end of the line. Donegan appeared from the back door in his shirtsleeves. He spoke and pointed at the detective who appeared from the other side of the car, as if taking his ire out on him.

'I want the surveillance squad on that journalist prick night and day,' he said. 'And I want his phone tapped. I want a record of all calls to him. Every move he makes, I want to know about it.'

The detective held his hands out in question, but Donegan was already walking away.

The detective shook his head and looked across the roof at Reidy, who scribbled something in his notebook and snapped the page off. He held it out to the bewildered detective.

'Get on to the sergeant in surveillance,' Reidy said hurriedly. 'This is the number of the man who deals with the phone taps.'

The detective took the small page and looked down. 'Don't I need a bit more paperwork than this for...'

He looked up as Reidy took his arm and shook it. His eyes flashed.

'Just do what you're told, Detective. And less of the stupid questions, OK?' he snapped and moved away.

Fox and McGrath remained seated on the kerb of

the green as they watched Donegan approach. He muttered something to a scenes-of-crime man who pointed over at them.

'I'd say he's in great form now,' whispered Fox.

'Right, let's hear it,' said Donegan as he walked across the road to them.

'There's not much to hear,' said McGrath standing up and brushing at the seat of his denims. 'We got in through the back window, and there was yer man in the sitting room. Doesn't look like a struggle. I'd say choked or poisoned. There was a lot of gunge around his mouth.'

Donegan placed his hands in his pockets and rested his foot on the kerb beside Fox. He looked with a tired and strained expression at the group of children in the middle of the green, who stared back at him from a distance.

'We have a description,' said Fox. 'Well, at least we think we have.'

Donegan stood back quickly and removed his hands from his pockets.

Fox held up the notebook. 'It's the best we have at the moment.'

Donegan took it and narrowed his eyes at the page. 'Jesus, read it,' he said in frustration as he held it out to McGrath. He took his own notebook from his shirt pocket and wrote as McGrath slowly dictated the description of the visitor to Feeney's house.

Donegan replaced the notebook in his pocket.

'Great stuff, lads,' he said with genuine admiration.

Fox clapped his hands together and eased himself up from the kerb.

'Well, that's our quota up for the day,' he grinned. 'Time to get into a nose-bag. What kept ye anyway? I bet you and Reidy didn't miss lunch.'

'There's been another one,' said Donegan. 'Lilly Carey. An oulwan. Did you ever hear of her?'

'Christ,' gasped Fox. He shook his head.

McGrath did likewise.

'That's what kept us, Detective.' Donegan eyed Fox. 'We found her hanging from a pair of nylons in her wardrobe. The calling card pinned on her face. She'd been there for more than four days.' He swallowed as the image returned. 'Not a pretty sight.'

'And what did she do to deserve that?' asked McGrath.

'Stabbed two of her grandchildren to death. Too old to put in jail. Too mad to keep in the jigsaw factory. Just like our friend Mr Feeney there,' replied Donegan, removing the crumpled sheet of paper from his pocket and flattening it.

Fox shrugged and turned to walk away. 'This whole thing is getting better and better,' he said in disgust.

Donegan glared after him.

'Please don't voice that type of opinion in public, Detective,' he said. 'There's a – a journalist, if I can use the term, by the name of Tom Farrell. And it looks like this maniac is using him to tell the world.'

He beckoned to Reidy, who was giving instructions to the uniformed man outside the gate of the house.

'Sergeant, get this description to the lads,' he said, holding out his notebook.

Reidy looked down and read it, dialling the mobile phone with his free hand.

'I take it that this Lilly Carey lived alone, Kig?' said Fox.

'Yeah, just like the rest of them.'

'All except Williams,' McGrath corrected. 'Why was that different from the others? I mean, he was following a pattern, and then changed. Why take the risk?'

'To show us,' Fox said in a low voice, then leaned down and pulled at a long blade of grass at the kerb.

Donegan and McGrath looked at him.

'To show us *what*?' asked Donegan.

Fox chewed on the grass and squinted at them. 'To show us that he can,' he said. 'To show us that he's an expert, and that we're never going to catch him. He's acting the clown with us.'

Donegan narrowed his eyes. 'Less of that pessimistic shit talk,' he growled. 'He's going to slip up. Even experts have a bad day.'

Fox scowled at him for a moment, then laughed and slapped him on the shoulder. 'Just testing your mettle, Kig,' he smiled. 'Course we're going to get him.'

He strolled towards the car. 'We just have to get something to eat first.'

'One minute,' Donegan called as he followed quickly. 'The entire squad is tied up at the moment. You two are the only ones with a free run.'

'Yeah. So?'

'So I want you to get to this address. Ivor Danby. The local uniforms are already on the way to the scene. Our eminent journalist gave me the name. He says that it's added to the list. Says that he got an anonymous call.'

'I take it this journalist is being watched, Kig?' said McGrath.

'Yes, yes. I've just gotten the surveillance lads on to him.'

'What about potential victims?' asked Fox. 'Should they not be warned?'

Donegan sighed. 'We're doing our best about that. We're trying to keep this as low a profile as we can for the time being. No point in causing a major panic. Anyway, it would take the entire force to cover them all.'

'There surely can't be that many in the last five years, Kig,' McGrath objected.

Donegan shook his head. 'Forget that five-year crack,' he said wearily. 'Lilly Carey killed those children in 1978.'

CHAPTER TWELVE

The lift doors slid open and Landers stepped out, looking fresh and relaxed from his afternoon rest, although his stomach churned slightly from the tetanus shot he had given himself three hours earlier. The porter behind him wheeled out the steel trolley containing his two briefcases, a large black Samsonite and four suit covers. The assistant manager approached and held his hands out in a gesture of disappointment.

'You're not leaving us, Mr Landers,' he said, his tone that of a distressed relative.

'I'm afraid so,' he replied. 'Some urgent business has come up.'

The assistant manager smiled. 'Well I hope that you've enjoyed your stay with us. And that it will be the first of many.'

'It's been absolutely marvellous,' Landers beamed. 'I shall be sure to recommend your wonderful hotel to all my associates.'

The assistant manager's expression changed and he immediately assumed the pose of taskmaster, his fingers snapping quickly at the doorman. He turned back to Landers.

'I take it you require a taxi?' he said.

'To the airport.'

The young doorman walked smartly across the marble foyer and stood almost to attention in front of them.

'A taxi for Mr Landers, Jeremy,' said the assistant manager. He extended his hand to Landers and they shook. 'Have a safe trip.'

'I will. Thank you again.'

The assistant manager smiled and then turned his attention to an elderly couple who were coming down the stairs. Landers made his way to the reception area where he listened for a further minute as the two receptionists prattled on with the same mock distress at his departure.

'I believe there's a message for me,' he said when they had finished. One of them reached back and placed the large white envelope on the counter. He took it, signed the bill and paid in cash, then thanked them and went outside to where the taxi man was putting his luggage in the boot. He handed the doorman a twenty-euro note and gave another to the porter.

'Keep up the good work,' he smiled back at them as he sat in.

He looked out at the city as the taxi struggled through the traffic towards the airport. He would be sorry to leave. Dublin was indeed a fascinating place. All that he had read about it was true. A city full of exuberance and youth. And he felt that he had in some way contributed to its wellbeing, ridding it of a few impurities.

'That'll be twenty-three euro,' said the taxi man over his shoulder when they arrived at their destination. Landers paid him and waited while the driver went for an airport trolley. He stood at the rear of the car, listening to the tannoy and to the deafening roar of approaching and departing flights. The taxi man loaded the trolley and grunted a nod of departure.

Inside the door, the uniformed airport security guard moved the hand-held explosive detector across each person as they passed. Landers pushed the trolley in front of him and waited.

'Go ahead,' said the security guard after a scant wave of the useless implement.

Landers sniffed a laugh of contempt to himself as he made his way into the main lobby of the airport, his eyes lifting to read the digital screens of arrivals and departures.

How he would love to take the first flight to Antigua! Or perhaps the Bahamas. Yes, the Bahamas. Oh, to sit back and bake in the sun for a week or two, and drink exotic cocktails!

He pushed the trolley slowly, contemplating the idea, the wheels beating a dull rhythm across the large tiles. He promised himself a refreshing holiday when his business was finished. But it wasn't to catch a plane that he was here today.

The car-rental reps stood in crisp and various coloured blazers inside the line of booths.

Landers wheeled his trolley up to a young man who looked like a student on a summer job, his buttoned shirt collar much too large for his neck.

'I would like a car for two weeks,' he said. 'Something roomy, but not too garish. And two-litre of course. I've heard about your Irish roads.'

The young man laughed nervously and then began to tap with obvious inexperience on the keyboard. He apologised after a moment and started again.

'A Rover,' he announced after a minute, in surprise at his own ability. 'I can have it delivered to exit number four.'

'Excellent choice, young man,' smiled Landers. 'The best cars in the world.'

'Well, you would say that,' the rep quipped, relaxing now with his success. 'If I can just have your driving licence particulars and – card, cash or cheque?' He read from the screen. 'If paying by cash, then we require an additional deposit of one hundred euro.'

'Cash,' said Landers. 'I can't abide those plastic abominations,' he added with faint disgust.

Preliminaries and payment complete, he made his way to exit door number four.

The dark-blue Rover gleamed outside, the attendant standing at the driver's door, rolling the keyring on his finger.

'Be careful with her,' he smiled, holding it out as

Landers approached. 'She's got a hell of a kick and loads of poke.'

Landers's face was expressionless.

'Don't worry about me,' he mumbled as he looked in at the white leather interior. 'I've driven faster cars than this in my time.'

The attendant helped to place the luggage in the boot, all except for one of the briefcases, which Landers placed beside him on the passenger seat. He gave a smile at the attendant and made his way to the airport exit, his free hand moving to his side and flicking the clasps of his briefcase open.

He drove on through the slow-moving traffic for a while until he joined the ring road and increased speed. Then he reached back and searched through the documents until he felt the mobile phone. He followed the evening traffic that left the city as he dialled the number and lifted the phone to his ear.

'Yes.'

'Ah, Mr Doyle,' he said.

'Everything is well, I take it.'

'Yes, fine, fine, thank you. Just to let you know that I'm heading down country as we speak.'

There was a short unnerving pause before Doyle spoke.

'I'm afraid that there has been something of a setback, Mr Landers,' he said.

'Oh?'

'Yes. I have just got word that your description has been circulated. It's nothing to get unduly worried about. It's a poor enough one, but a description nonetheless.'

'Was it from Danby's street?' Landers gritted his teeth.

'No. From Gerry Feeney's estate.'

'When you say "poor enough description", Mr Doyle, what exactly do you mean?'

'It could be one of fifty thousand men. But it shows that you have to be more careful from now on. I know that you won't see this as a major obstacle.'

Landers listened to the praise. Doyle was right. A scant description by the gardaí was not going to stop him. But he would just have to be more cautious.

'I take it that you'll make the necessary arrangements down the country as planned.'

'Yes, yes, of course,' replied Doyle. 'I'll tell him to expect you some time later this evening. I must say, I'm impressed with your determination.'

'It's like I told you today,' said Landers, 'when I take on a job, I see it through to the end.'

***

Inspector Frank Donegan slung his jacket over his shoulder and walked across the car park in the direction of the MCS building. He went directly to his office and phoned home, informing his youngest daughter that he would be late and assuring her that he had not forgotten the two passes for her and a friend to a concert in the Point Depot.

'No problem, I'm looking at them now,' he tried to laugh through the lie, but the panic was evident in his voice. 'I'll leave them on the kitchen table.' He dug the hole deeper.

He rummaged through the desk drawers for his telephone diary as she giggled through the story of a humorous incident at school. He laughed at the end with her, although he had not heard one word she had said.

He hurriedly replaced the receiver and flicked through the pages. Two phone calls later he had secured the passes from a retired superintendent who was head of security for the concert. They would be delivered to his office later that night.

He slumped back on the chair with relief for a moment before leaning forward and stacking the heavy pile of questionnaires between his hands. The two detectives in the outer office had already put them in order of importance, along with the up-to-date reports from the forensics lab, computer printouts of the victims and, finally, the statement of the car-park attendant, who had been the last to see Henry Williams alive.

He began with this, running his finger down quickly through the preliminaries until he reached the description of the man the attendant had seen: dark suit, briefcase, middle-aged, five-foot eleven to six foot, average build, with lots more information, but nothing that would narrow the field down.

He turned the sheet over on its face and picked up the report from Malley in forensics. A human hand had not lit the fire in the Wolfman's house. Petrol was the accelerator, and the device found had a timed sparking mechanism, which meant that the killer had been long gone when the wide-eyed victim watched as the room mushroomed into an inferno. No prints on the cash box or on any of the other correspondence from the Mercury Man.

The pieces of Henry Williams's mobile phone contained elements of a high-grade, home-made plastic explosive. There was no trace of the detonator.

'Thanks a million, Malley,' he muttered, as he slapped the sheets down on the desk.

He sat back and groaned, rubbing his face vigorously. A middle-aged vigilante in a suit carrying a briefcase. Where would they start?

He was stirred from his misery by the sound of a knock on his office door, and a busy-looking detective entered carrying yet another stack of sheets.

'Tell me that you have good news, Pat,' said Donegan.

The detective smiled as he thudded the pile down on the desk.

'Nothing worthwhile in that lot,' he replied, 'but if you want to hear some *really* good news...'

Donegan looked up. 'Yeah?' he said eagerly.

'I just heard that Maurice Fitz is back for the All-Ireland.'

Donegan shook his head with a half-laugh. 'You're forgetting that I'm a Corkman, Pat,' he smiled.

The detective turned for the door.

'I know you are, Kig. I didn't say the news was good for *you*,' he said and left.

Donegan looked down in dismay at the useless pile of questionnaires and statements, knowing that he would have to double-check them himself. Not out of distrust for the detectives under him but because what one man won't see, another man might.

He pulled the computer sheets towards him and lifted the top one.

'Well now, Jimbo,' he whispered as he looked at the photograph of the Wolfman.

He pulled another sheet and scanned it quickly.

'And Henry.'

Then Gerry Feeney's. And finally Lilly Carey's.

He fanned the sheets between his hands and looked at the photographs of the victims. Typical Garda station poses. Blank eyes staring into the distance. The shock of being caught and the fear of the consequences evident on the faces of all four.

A rapist, a drug-dealer, a wife-killer and a child-killer.

Apart from the obvious, there had to be another common denominator. Something that bonded them together. Why was this Mercury Man so random in choosing his victims?

He placed the sheets side by side on the table and leaned over them, his head moving slowly left and right from one to the other and back across. Addresses, crimes, court dates, acquittal dates. He stared at them until his eyes hurt and his mind began to wander from the task at hand. He sat back and tilted his head upwards, his eyes closed, as the sheets and photos still flashed one after another through his mind.

Search three of three.

He sat up quickly and ran his finger across the bottom of the four pages, then gazed out across the desk.

'Search three of three,' he said out loud. 'That can't be right.'

He scrunched the sheets together and stood up quickly.

Outside in the corridor, the detective was putting on his jacket. The other detective was still in the office, cursing his lost pen.

'Time for the grub, Kig,' he said as he straightened his collar.

Donegan hid the urgency in his voice.

'Tell me, Pat,' he said calmly. 'You know a bit more than most of us about this computer crack, don't you?'

The detective shrugged. 'A fair bit, yeah. What do you want to know?'

Donegan held out the sheet on Lilly Carey and pointed at the bottom.

'What does that mean?' he asked, and handed the sheet over.

'Search three of three,' replied the detective casually. 'It just means that there were three searches made for her on computer.

'Aw, right, gotcha,' said Donegan slowly, like a man who was the last to get a joke.

'Well, one of those searches is ours anyway,' said the detective. 'We did it for the file you have on your desk.'

'Can you find out when the others were done?' asked Donegan, knowing that McGrath had done one of the remaining two the previous day.

'No bother, Kig. I'll do it after the grub.'

Donegan smiled as he put his arm around the detective's shoulder and squeezed.

'Pat, me ould charm. You'll enjoy the grub a lot more knowing that I'm not waiting for you to be back here on time. Am I right?'

The detective folded the sheet and shouted through the open door of the office.

'Give me a few minutes, Mick. I have to do a quick job.'

Donegan slapped him on the back. 'That's the stuff.'

He paced up and down the corridor and examined the other sheets as he waited.

'You haven't seen a silver Parker around anywhere, Kig?' asked the detective from the office. 'You can't leave a thing out of your hand in this place. They'd take the eye out of your shaggin' head,' he continued angrily without waiting for an answer.

The door of the superintendent's office opened and he appeared in the corridor, craning his neck as he tightened his tie.

'Frank,' he said with surprise, 'any developments?'

He rummaged in his pocket for the key of his door as Donegan approached.

'I want to speak to you for a minute, Kieran,' he said.

The superintendent frowned as he flicked his sleeve back from his watch.

'I'm a bit caught for time, Frank,' he said as he put the key in the lock. 'I have a meeting with you-know-who in ten minutes.'

Donegan reached out and placed his hand on the superintendent's outstretched arm.

There was a low warning in his tone as he spoke slowly.

'I think – that it would be in your own best interest to give me that minute,' he said.

It was a line that always worked with officers who

had their eyes set on higher plains.

'Very well, Frank,' he said, his displeasure evident. 'But this better be good.'

CHAPTER THIRTEEN

The two Garda cars were parked and empty on either side of the steps that led up to Danby's open front door, their flickering blue beacons just about visible amidst the strong rays of the evening sun. A young, uniformed garda in shirtsleeves stood at the foot of the steps, a folder held in one hand, his other hand adjusting the cap across the sweat on his forehead. His sergeant appeared in the doorway above and stood there for a moment taking deep breaths, before walking slowly down the steps and patting the young guard on the back.

McGrath watched from the car, drumming his fingers gently on the steering wheel.

'Ever get the feeling that we're turning into death-collectors?' he said dryly.

Fox nodded silently in agreement as he opened the passenger door. He crossed the path and lifted his foot onto the low brick wall to tie his lace.

The sergeant narrowed his eyes with suspicion for a moment and then relaxed the expression to a faint smile.

'Well, now, if it isn't the great gun-fighter himself,' he joked.

Fox laughed as he stood up.

'So, you've heard the story too, have you?' he said as he approached them.

The young guard tried to smile with them as the men shook hands, his sergeant slapping the unshaven arrival on the arm.

'I was his skipper when he came fresh from Templemore,' the sergeant told him. ''Twas like trying to put a leash on a mink. What's that you said your family motto was again, Andy?' he asked.

Fox extended his hand to the young guard.

'Kill 'em all,' he replied as they shook, and the young guard managed to laugh with them.

McGrath approached, his eyes searching the street, watching as the uniforms moved from one house to the next. 'Can we take it that this Danby character is no more?' he asked.

The question sobered the others, the smiles fading from their faces.

'Yeah,' said the sergeant. 'He's in the hallway. The burn marks on his neck suggest that he was strangled. Done with a rope of some kind.'

He turned back to the steps. 'C'mon,' he said. 'Take a look.'

'Detective Gardaí Andy Fox and Bob McGrath,' said Fox to the young guard who noted their names and the time of their entry to the scene on his folder.

'Was the door closed when you arrived?' asked Fox as he followed the sergeant.

'Yeah, the door was sound. Had to pinch-bar it open.'

'Allowed in again,' muttered McGrath behind them.

The three of them stood on the step outside looking in at Danby on the hall floor.

Fox took a step forward. The sergeant held out his arm to block his way.

'And just what do you think you're doing, young Foxy?' he said looking at him in surprise. 'This is my crime scene, boy. The Bureau lads haven't been here yet. No one is going to make a stones of any vital evidence.'

Fox pulled a rubber glove from his pocket and smiled as he held it up.

'I won't touch anything, I swear,' he said as he peeled it on.

The sergeant lowered his arm. 'So you're a real-life detective now.'

'Something like that, Sarge,' replied Fox, and took three steps into the hallway.

'Let me hear your theory then,' said the sergeant.

Fox looked around and then back at the two of them.

'He was taken by surprise at the door. Not like the others,' he said as if to himself. 'This was a real rush job.'

McGrath lifted his eyebrows. 'What happened here, Poirot?' he asked sarcastically.

'Poirot my hole,' snarled the sergeant. 'Clouseau more like. Fox, get out of my crime scene and stop your bluffing.'

'What makes you think that it was a rush job this time?' asked McGrath.

'Well, firstly, he's in the hall,' replied Fox.

'So what?'

Fox took a further step in and looked down at the body. 'The other three were killed inside their houses, in the sitting rooms – and Lilly got it in the bedroom.' He pointed at Danby. 'This old guy got it the minute he opened the door.'

The sergeant frowned. 'What others?' he asked.

McGrath coughed and quickly changed the subject.

'Why do you say that?' he asked.

Fox pointed with his gloved hand to the book on the floor.

'Since when have people started reading in the hall?' he replied. 'Pal here was reading that book – not in the hall we can take it. He came to the door with the book in his hand – and bam.'

McGrath thought about it for a moment and then pursed his lips in agreement.

The sergeant placed his hands in his pockets and leaned against the jamb of the door.

'Bullshit,' he said forcefully.

'I think you'll find that it's not bullshit, Sarge,' Fox corrected.

'Yeah, well who killed his dog then, smart guy?' asked the sergeant.

Both of them looked at him.

'What dog?' asked McGrath.

The sergeant removed one of his hands from his pocket and pointed to the end of the hallway.

'The big, fat, dead dog in the kitchen,' he replied. He raised his eyebrows at Fox. 'Or maybe the poor animal died of a broken heart.'

Fox moved quickly along the hallway towards the kitchen door amidst the protests of the sergeant. He pushed it open gently and looked down at the dog lying on its side on the floor, one of the eyes open in wonder, the long, pink tongue hanging limply from its mouth on to the black and red tiles.

'Yeah, that is unusual,' muttered Fox silently.

'Looks like the dog was choked to death as well. No sign of blood.' The sergeant's voice echoed in the hall behind him.

Fox closed his eyes to drown out the sound.

'Danby answers the door,' he muttered. 'The killer strikes. The book falls from Danby's hand. The dog appears and attacks the killer. Dead dog.' He paused and opened his eyes. 'Why put the dog in the kitchen?' he asked.

McGrath and the sergeant looked at each other and shrugged.

Fox snapped the glove from his hand as he made his way back to the door. He stood for a moment with his back to them, blocking their view of the hallway, then turned around and looked at them.

'Why put the dog in the kitchen?' he repeated.

The sergeant tossed his head back in annoyance.

'What difference does it make?' he grunted. 'I've

got a dead body on the floor there, and all you can think about is what happened to the shaggin' dog. So with all due respect, Andy, if you can't tell me *who* killed this child molester, then you're really just wasting my time.'

With that, the sergeant left them in the doorway and went down the steps where he began to give instructions to the crew of another patrol car that had just arrived.

'What the hell is all this talk about the dog?' whispered McGrath.

'Do you agree that Danby was taken by surprise?' asked Fox ignoring the question.

'Yeah, fair enough.'

'Right, doorbell rings. Danby is reading his book in the – in the sitting room, say. Danby answers the door and our man pounces, book falls to the ground, right so far?'

McGrath nodded.

'OK,' continued Fox. 'So take it that the dog appears during the attack. How would our man have time to kill it and put it in the kitchen without Danby escaping? And if Danby was already dead, then why kill the dog?'

McGrath shook his head in confusion and began to step away.

'I haven't the faintest idea what you're driving at,' he said. He stopped at the sound of Fox's mobile phone ringing and looked back, waiting.

'Beano,' Fox smiled and his head nodded as he listened. 'You're a good one, Beano,' he said. 'We'll meet you there in fifteen minutes. Who? Never mind. Keep her entertained.'

He clipped the phone back on his belt and moved quickly down the steps past McGrath.

'C'mon,' he urged. 'Our man Detective Beano is hot on the trail. He's with the Wolfman's bird.'

They sat into the car and McGrath paused for a moment.

'So we've dispensed with the dog problem for the moment then?' he asked.

Fox shook his head pensively as he spoke. 'I don't think he meant to kill the dog,' he replied softly.

McGrath threw his eyes up as he started the car.

'Great news,' he said sarcastically. 'He's an animal lover.'

***

The superintendent stood looking out the window of his office with his hands behind his back, tapping one gently into the other. Donegan sat outside the desk, waiting for the reaction to his theory.

'Let me get this straight in my mind, Frank,' said the super without turning around. 'You now have reason to believe that this – 'Mercury Man' has either hacked into our computer system...' He paused and blew gently through his pursed lips. 'Or else, he has been given the information on his victims – by one of our own.'

Donegan remained silent.

The superintendent turned slowly and stared hard at him.

'Is that what you're telling me, Inspector, is it?'

'That's what I'm telling you,' replied Donegan without emotion.

The superintendent muttered something incoherent as he pulled his chair towards the desk and sat down. This was not the type of lead in the case that he wanted to hear about.

'Which one is it then?' he asked gruffly.

'Which one would you like?' Donegan was unruffled. 'At the moment, you have the choice between a useless computer system costing millions and a man on the inside.'

'I'll take the useless computer system any day, Frank,' said the super, his voice softening. 'That can be blamed on someone else. This "man on the inside" falls back into my lap.'

Donegan nodded. Career first, crime a poor second, he thought.

There was a gentle tap on the door. It opened and a detective put his head around.

'I got that for you, Kig,' he said, and crossed the office with the sheet held out. He nodded at the superintendent and left.

Donegan looked down at the page for moment. 'Yes indeed,' he said with disgust.

The superintendent stood up. 'What? What is it?'

Donegan held out the sheet to him. 'Lilly Carey's file was pulled three times from the computer in the last year.'

The superintendent shrugged as he read. 'So?'

'So,' Donegan answered in a sigh. 'It was pulled yesterday by McGrath, today by our man there – and the time before that?'

The superintendent looked at the date and then raised his head as he calculated.

'Six months ago,' he said casually. He gave a nervous laugh and placed the sheet down on the desk in front of Donegan. He shrugged again as he walked behind him to the middle of the office.

'This means nothing, Frank,' he said. 'Just because someone checks her on the computer doesn't necessarily mean that we have a mole. I really thought that you had something stronger than this.'

Donegan closed his eyes and gritted his teeth.

Any policeman with half a brain and his mind on the case and not on the dizzy heights of promotion would have made the connection, thought it unusual, suspicious even. But not the superintendent.

'There are thousands of checks made on our computers every day, Frank,' said the superintendent as he took his jacket from the grey coatstand. 'Person checks, car checks, crime... The list goes on. Lads are checking on that Wolfman fella every day. There must be a hundred entries on him every month.'

Donegan swiped the sheet from the desk and stood up.

'What if the searches on the other victims were done around the same time? Would that satisfy you that the information on them is coming from a source within the job?' His irritation was evident.

The superintendent straightened the front of his jacket and eyed him with caution as he removed a comb from his trouser pocket.

'I really don't see where you're taking this, Frank,' he said, rubbing his hand back through his hair. 'I suppose, if you wish to make some remote connection...'

Donegan exploded in rage.

'For Christ's sake, Kieran,' he almost shouted, 'have you been listening to a word I've said?'

The loud protest echoed around the office as the two men looked at one another. Donegan was breathing heavily. The superintendent gazed at him scornfully.

'You really haven't seen the danger yet, have you?' said Donegan, lowering his voice to a whisper. 'Someone is giving information on the victims to the killer. A policeman is assisting in the murder of these people. Can I make it any clearer for you?'

His grooming complete, the superintendent replaced the comb in his pocket.

'Let's look at what you have so far, Inspector,' he said. 'You believe that we have a mole who has given the computer files on these victims to our Mercury Man, and you are basing this theory on the fact that they were previously checked on computer. Why not go the whole hog, Frank. Why not say that this Mercury Man *is* a policeman?'

Donegan crumpled the sheet in his hand and started for the door.

'What do you intend to do now?' asked the superintendent.

Donegan paused with his hand on the doorknob. 'Well, Superintendent. I'm going to have a check on all the searches done on the victims in the last year. I'm going to collate the times of these searches, find the terminal that they were done from and catch the man who did them. What are *you* going to do?'

'I'm going to wait and see what you come up with, Inspector.' The superintendent was unruffled. 'I take it your theory that the computer was hacked is out the window then?'

'Impossible,' said Donegan, 'unless he had someone's private code.'

The superintendent gave a derisive laugh and shook his head.

'Tell that to the FBI and the teenager who did it,' he said.

Donegan left the office, slamming the door behind him.

***

Beano stood outside the pub with his hands in his pockets, jigging nervously from side to side on his toes as he waited. He pulled his hand free and checked his watch, his lips moving in a series of mumbled curses. His expression changed to a weak smile of greeting as he watched Fox and McGrath approach. He moved towards them, immediately taking control, his hands held out.

'She's inside,' he said. 'She's frightened, nervous and confused.'

Fox glared at him.

'Cut the social worker horseshit, Beano,' he snapped. 'First things first. Who's *she*?'

Beano stepped back and leaned against the outside wall of the pub. They stood on either side of him, waiting.

'The Wolfman's girlfriend,' he whispered.

Fox sniggered. 'Who's that now, Beano? Vampirella maybe?'

Beano looked at him. 'No. She's Tweety-Bird,' he confirmed.

'Tweety-Bird,' repeated McGrath in surprise. 'Is she a bit of a looker or what?' he asked.

Beano shook his head. His expression remained serious. 'Nah. It's because her head is the shape of a fuckin' peanut. Some sort of an operation she got when she...'

'Get to the point,' said Fox interrupting him. 'What does she know?'

'Right, right,' said Beano. 'I think that she might have met this fella that you're looking for.'

McGrath looked across at Fox.

'What makes you think that, Beano?' he asked

'I'm not sure. It's just the way she tells it. Some sort of weird English fella. Look it, come in and she'll tell you herself. Just take it easy that's all. She's been through a rough time of it.'

'Yeah, yeah, Beano,' said Fox as he pushed him towards the door.

Tweety-Bird sat beside the bar at a low, black table, nursing a half-finished pint of cider. Fox noted that she did, indeed, have a head shaped like a peanut, although the long, black hair on her forehead disguised the severity of its size. Her face was pale and her eyes reddened from crying. Then again, he thought, she had spent the afternoon with Beano. The bar was smoke-filled, and Fox noted the large, black Alsatian that wandered aimlessly amongst the customers.

Beano smiled at Tweety-Bird and spoke in a soft

voice, as if he was introducing two bishops.

'These are the men I was telling you about, love,' he said.

She looked up at them and said nothing. She knew that they were the law, although their appearance made her feel more comfortable. Beano, acting as maître d', motioned them towards two vacant stools and went to get the drink.

'I'm Bob and he's Andy,' said McGrath. 'You don't have to give us your name if you don't want to.'

'I won't so,' she said and looked up at the bar, waiting for Beano to return.

'How long did you know the Wolfman?' asked Fox.

'His name was Jimbo,' she corrected him. 'And why should that matter anyway?'

Fox shrugged. 'Just trying to make conversation,' he said.

'I'm sure that yous fellas were fierce upset that he was done in,' she sharply. 'Well, he's gone now.' Her voice cracked as a tear fell from her eye.

McGrath looked at the ground and then up at the bar. 'What's keeping you, Beano?' he growled.

'We're trying to catch the man who killed Jimbo,' said Fox. 'What we thought of him doesn't matter. Our job is to get the person responsible.'

'Was he dead when he was burned?' she asked, sniffing and wiping at the tear on her face. 'They wouldn't tell me anything at the hospital.'

'Yes, yes, he was dead,' Fox lied immediately. 'I'm afraid that I can't tell you anything else, except to say that he felt nothing.'

She looked at him, searching his face for a sign of

deception. Fox looked back at her with a poker face. Suddenly her lips cracked to a faint smile.

'Well, at least that's something,' she said, and Fox and McGrath nodded solemnly in agreement.

Beano returned with the drinks and placed the glasses down slowly in front of them. He took his seat beside Tweety-Bird and Fox immediately noticed that he placed a comforting arm around her waist and gave her a squeeze.

The fast bastard, he thought. Obviously the shape of her head was not going to be a deterrent.

'Beano here tells us that you may have some information.' McGrath leaned forward in a confidential whisper. 'Something about a strange Englishman.'

She looked at Beano, who gave her an encouraging nod.

'Go ahead, love,' he said. 'I know these two. Tell them what you told me.'

'He had a sort of an English accent,' she started. 'But sometimes he sounded a bit Irish, if you know what I mean.'

'When and where did you first meet him?' Fox asked.

'It was about six weeks ago,' she replied. 'It was here in this pub.' She pointed to the side of the bar. 'I was sitting up at the counter there with Jimbo.'

All heads turned to look and then back at her to listen.

'He looked out of place,' she continued. 'Fairly well dressed and clean. He looked like a fella on holidays. He had a bit of a colour.'

'Describe him for us as best you can,' said McGrath.

She picked up the glass of cider and took a gentle sip. It was then that Fox noticed the darkened puncture holes on her upper arm.

'I'd say he was nearly fifty,' she said as she put the glass back down. 'His hair was full and dark, but it was going a bit grey in places.'

'That's very good,' Fox said encouragingly.

'He had a scar here,' she rubbed her finger across her forehead just beneath her scalp-line. 'Not a big one. About two inches. I only noticed it because the rest of his face was kinda brown and it stood out.'

McGrath pictured the description in his mind. This was not the place to take out an official notebook and begin scribbling.

She narrowed her eyes in thought.

'He was fairly fit looking for a fella his age,' her hands shook as she reached for her tattered, black-leather bag and took out her cigarettes. 'About five ten or maybe a bit more.'

'Can you remember what he was wearing?' asked Fox.

She held the cigarette delicately between her two, brown-stained fingers and took a thoughtful drag.

'A blue tracksuit,' she answered, through a cloud of smoke. 'Like I said, he was very clean looking.'

'You say that he had an English *and* Irish accent,' said Fox, shaking his head in confusion.

'Yeah,' she said with enthusiasm. 'That was kinda weird. One minute he was talking away like a Brit, and the next minute, his accent was gone. He sounded like a culchie or something. Or maybe from the North.'

'Do you think that he was English or Irish then?' asked McGrath.

She looked at him and shrugged.

'English, I'd say,' she replied. She was not really sure.

Fox took a long gulp of his pint and leaned forward as he placed it back on the table. 'OK,' he said, 'let's get a clear picture of what happened. You and Wol... Jimbo were in this pub about six weeks ago. The fella you describe walks in and – what next?'

She gave a short sigh. 'He sat up at the bar next to us and just started talking about how great Dublin was and how he was really enjoying himself on the town. He talked about everything from the weather to soccer. Jimbo was a big United fan.'

'So Jimbo talked to him then?' said McGrath.

She nodded. 'Only a bit. Jimbo doesn't... didn't like the English for what they did to our country.'

Fox looked at the floor in disgust. The irony of it all. A patriot who sold drugs to kids.

'When they did talk, what did they discuss?' he asked. 'Did they talk about drugs?'

McGrath winced inwardly. Fox was rushing things.

She stared hard at them through the wafting cigarette smoke.

Beano gave a nervous cough. 'I told her there'd be no talk about that business, lads,' he said.

McGrath tried to smile. 'You're right, Beano,' he said. 'Andy here is just a little anxious. He wants to make sure that someone in the drugs trade isn't responsible.' He turned to Fox. 'Why don't you get us another round?'

Fox stood up from his stool and went to the bar. He leaned sideways with his elbow on the counter looking around. The Alsatian sat beside one of the low tables where three men were playing poker, resting its black wolf-like head on the edge, watching the game.

If *he* had been there to greet the Mercury Man when he entered Danby's hall instead of the small, fat spaniel, thought Fox to himself, that would have been some contest.

He stiffened as the Alsatian lifted its head from the table, scratched for a moment at its black-studded collar, and then approached him in an arrogant saunter.

Fox straightened up against the counter, and the Alsatian, as if sensing the fear, stopped to show who was master of the establishment. Fox took a deep breath and held it. The elderly man on the stool beside him smiled.

'Don't mind him, young fella,' he laughed. 'He's only a big eejit of a puppy. He won't go near ya.'

The remark did nothing for his confidence, coming as it did from an old man who was drunk and smelt like a urinal.

'Ross, get outta there *now*,' shouted the barman. Fox flinched.

The dog paid no heed to the command, remaining where he was and raising his eyebrows in contempt at the frightened customer. The barman slammed the empty glass down inside the counter.

'Right. That's it. You're gone,' he yelled, as he made his way out from inside the bar.

Fox watched in relief as the barman grabbed the dog by the head and collar and dragged him like a stubborn calf towards the side door that led to the yard.

'You'll come back when you've manners,' he shouted, slamming the door shut.

A few protests rose from a number of the customers.

'He had his chance.' The barman reduced them all to silence.

'Now,' he said when he returned behind the bar, 'what can I get ya?'

'Em, three pints and a cider,' replied Fox, his train of thought taking him elsewhere. 'No wait,' he said suddenly, 'make that just two pints and a cider, and drop them over to that table there.' He pointed with the rolled twenty before putting it on the counter.

He approached the hushed conversation and snapped his fingers at McGrath.

'Keys,' he said. 'I've got the drink in. I'll be back shortly.'

McGrath struggled in his pocket for the keys and held them up. He winked at Fox.

'She's just been telling us that she left Jimbo and our man alone that evening,' he said.

'Yeah, very good.' Fox appeared uninterested as he took the keys. 'See you in a while.'

He ran back to the car and sat in, muttering loudly as he adjusted the seat.

'The big, lanky...' he grunted in protest as he jerked at the handle.

He pulled out of the parking space at speed, almost colliding with a passing car, which blew its horn loudly. He ran his hand clumsily along the centre console until he felt the siren switch and turned it on. It wailed around him as he drove through the traffic with gritted teeth, his heart jumping with every near miss. By the time he arrived at Danby's street, he was a nervous wreck. The street was lined with cars now, the on-scene Bureau van parked directly below the steps, the white suits moving away from it.

He jumped from the car and shouted as he slammed the door. 'Wait! Stop there!'

The heads turned and watched as he jogged in exhaustion towards them.

'What the hell is wrong with *you*?' Malley stepped forward from the small group.

'Have you just arrived?' Fox stood in front of him, panting.

Malley nodded. 'Just this minute. What's the problem, eh, Detective Fox?' he snapped.

'The dog,' said Fox. 'There's a collar on the dog in there.'

The sergeant, who had been leaning against the side of a patrol car, stood up and moved beside Malley.

'In the name of God, Fox,' he snarled. 'Will you give over about the shaggin' dog.'

Malley frowned with annoyance at the sergeant as he held his finger up to silence the objection.

'What's so important about the collar, Detective?' he asked quietly.

Fox struggled for a reasonable answer.

'Just bag it for printing, that's all,' he said finally.

Malley looked him up and down for a moment.

'Fair enough,' he said and turned away with the others.

Fox sighed as he walked back towards the car.

'How did they *ever* make a detective out of you?'

the sergeant shouted from behind him.

Fox stopped and looked back at him from the open car door.

'Aw, kiss my arse, flatfoot,' he muttered to himself as he sat in.

CHAPTER FOURTEEN

The wide tyres of the Rover crunched to a halt on the gravel driveway. Landers stepped out and arched his back, looking across the wide billiard-table lawn and then up at the greyish brown stone front of the country house hotel. He removed his luggage from the car, then, feeling that he was being watched, turned and looked back at the line of granite steps that led up to the front door.

'Mr Landers, would I be correct?' said the elderly man in the green, sleeveless fishing jacket, who stood at the front door, leaning in Fred Astaire pose against a polished briar walking stick complete with brass handle. He had the appearance of an aristocrat – tweed waistcoat and matching trousers, check shirt with fully knotted green tie and polished brown brogues. Landers did not reply at first, choosing instead to pick up his luggage and move towards the steps.

'I'm Robert Haskard.' The elderly man straightened and moved down towards him. He extended his hand. 'I'm a *very* good friend of Mitchell Doyle. I've been expecting you.'

Landers placed the suitcase awkwardly on the steps and shook the outstretched hand.

'How much has Mr Doyle told you?' he asked as he picked up the case and moved up the steps.

Haskard placed his hand on Landers's shoulder as they went inside.

'Just enough,' he replied. 'You don't have to worry.'

He beckoned to the porter at reception by lifting the briar walking stick.

'Room number 24, Paul,' he said. 'Good lad.'

He turned to Landers. 'We must have a drink before you freshen up.' He smiled and pointed with the stick towards the open door of the large sitting room. 'Don't be concerned. The only guests staying here at present are three Frenchmen. They're out fishing and won't be back until late tonight. We have the entire building to ourselves.'

They sat opposite each other in oversize armchairs as the waiter in a white jacket brought them two brandies.

Landers looked around and then gazed up at the ornate ceiling.

'This is quite a place you have here,' he said as he swirled the brandy inside the heavy crystal glass.

Haskard looked around with him as if he, too, was seeing the room for the first time.

'Yes,' he said with satisfaction. 'Been in the family for over two hundred years.'

'Why change it to a hotel then?' Landers was genuinely curious.

Haskard smiled at him, tapping the stick on the toe of his polished brogue.

'Boredom mainly. And of course money,' he replied with a smile. 'One doesn't keep oneself in surroundings like this without it. Wouldn't you agree?'

Landers paused before answering, trying to sense any accusation in Haskard's tone.

'No, I suppose not,' he said finally.

Haskard looked at him for a moment before leaning on the cane and rising awkwardly to his feet. He walked slowly to the door and closed it.

'Mitchell has told me about your purpose in coming here,' he said as he returned. 'I will assist you in any way that I can.'

'I think that was very foolish of Mr Doyle,' said Landers. 'Foolish, that is, to involve a third party. Can you tell me why he would do such a thing?'

Haskard sat back down and picked up his glass.

'I have lived in this country for most of my life,' he said. 'Except for the war, of course, when we all had to do our bit for queen and country.' He looked over his shoulder at the black-and-white photograph high on the marble mantelpiece. 'My two brothers were killed, unfortunately. Both of them lieutenants. Damn brave soldiers.'

He leaned forward and spoke as if sharing a confidence.

'Strange thing is, Mr Landers, I wouldn't give you one sod of Irish peat for the whole bloody empire. I love this country and its people as if it were my own.'

He relaxed back in the armchair and waited for a reaction.

Landers cupped the glass between his hands.

'I'm afraid that I fail to see the connection,' he said. 'What has all this got to do with the business that I'm involved in?'

Haskard placed his glass down carefully on a silver coaster.

'When Mitchell first approached me with the idea, I thought that he was quite mad. I pleaded with him to reconsider. Why should a man take these risks? But he was determined. There was no stopping him. You yourself must know what a driven man he is after the time you've spent with him?'

'Yes, yes I do.' Landers nodded.

'I must admit that it took some time and convincing for me to see the light,' Haskard went on. 'To see that justice no longer exists in this lovely country of mine. And then, of course, to agree that a *little* justice is better than none at all. That's where you come in.'

Landers sipped from his glass and put it down. 'Can I take it, then, that my business here is directly related to you?' he asked.

'Yes, you may. I felt it important that I "muck in" with Mitchell, so to speak. I can tell you all you need to know about the person in question. I can even tell you where he will be tonight.'

'May I ask, what is your relationship to Mr Doyle?' asked Landers.

Haskard shrugged casually.

'Well, if Mitchell did not see fit to tell you, then I think it's best that I keep it to myself for the time being,' he said. 'I hope that my secrecy doesn't offend you?'

'Not at all,' Landers assured him. 'And I hope that, in turn, mine does not offend you.'

Haskard tapped the tip of the stick on the marble floor.

'You're quite right of course, Mr Landers,' he smiled. 'It was foolish of Mitchell to give so much information. But you must forgive him. He's not ex-service. What's that old saying from the war? Loose tongues cost lives.'

He laughed suddenly. 'Forgive me,' he said. 'What am I saying? You were still a twinkle in your father's eye back then.'

Landers smiled at him. 'Only just.'

'Loose tongues cost lives,' Haskard repeated. 'Yes, yes indeed. That was it. And nothing has changed one bit. Not one bit.'

He picked up the white porcelain bell from the table beside him and gave it a single ring.

'Will you have another?' he asked.

'Perhaps later,' replied Landers as he put his glass down. 'I'd like to shower and take a short walk to check out a number of things. We can talk again after dinner this evening if you like.'

Haskard stood up as the waiter entered.

'I'd like that very much,' he smiled. 'What is chef rewarding us with this evening? Oh, never mind. I'm sure it's wonderful.'

He patted Landers gently on the back again.

'If there's anything that you need, let me know.'

The waiter held the door open as the men left the room.

Although it was still bright outside, the entrance hall was tastefully lit by a collection of strategically placed antique lamps.

'Your room is ready, sir,' said the porter holding out the key.

'After dinner, then,' said Haskard and turned to the front door.

Landers climbed the winding stairway to his room. Ex-service or not, he was irritated that Doyle had been so free with information about him to the war veteran.

He brushed these doubts aside as he showered and changed, choosing instead to focus on the task at hand.

He opened the briefcase and removed only the equipment necessary for the job. According to the file, his victim was less than three miles away. Walking distance through the fields. Maybe Haskard could come in useful after all. Almost immediately he changed his mind. This would not be a rushed job ending with him fleeing the scene like a hunted rabbit, voices shouting behind him.

He lay down on the bed and closed his eyes. The pieces of the plan were there. It was just a matter of putting the jigsaw together.

***

It was almost nine o'clock by the time the entire MCS squad had gathered for the final conference. Donegan looked around for a moment at the men who talked amongst each other, notebooks held out as information was exchanged. Low mutterings and shrugging shoulders. Fox sat on the edge of McGrath's desk, his hands moving in explanation of some action or other. McGrath shook his head in defeat.

The stack of paper on the top table had grown considerably since early morning.

Donegan scraped his chair purposely beneath him to get attention.

'We have a lead,' he announced.

The room fell silent and chairs clattered to a halt.

Fox winked across the desk at McGrath.

'You were all given a summary description earlier today. We can now improve on it.'

He looked down at the sheet in front of him. Pens clicked into action.

'Late forties, five eleven to six foot, average build, full, dark hair greying at the temples, slightly tanned complexion, two-inch scar just below scalp above right eyc, speaks with a false Irish accent, more than likely English – but don't take that as iron-clad.'

He allowed the detectives to mutter amongst themselves for a moment. He knew that the fact an Englishman could be involved would fuel their curiosity.

'This description has been drawn up from four sources,' he continued. 'Our attendant at the multistorey. A child from Feeney's estate. An elderly woman from Danby's road. Isn't that right, Tom?'

The heads turned and looked at the detective who nodded with a smug grin.

'And someone that Fox and McGrath were talking to. For God's sake don't ask...'

Muted laughter crossed the room. Fox clasped his hands and raised them above his head.

McGrath did likewise.

'Thank you, gentlemen,' said Donegan. 'Now, as regards clothing, we have this fella in a dark-blue tracksuit, no make.' He cued McGrath with a pointed finger.

McGrath swiveled in his chair as he spoke. 'Jimbo and our man met downtown about six weeks ago. Our source left them alone for the evening, so we don't know what was discussed. What we *do* know is that an arrangement was made for another meeting some time later. Maybe Jimbo thought he had a new customer, who knows. Our source never saw our man again with him. But I think we can safely assume that it's how he got easy access to the house before he torched him.'

Donegan nodded.

'We also have him in a dark, double-breasted suit at the multi-storey and smartly dressed in a shirt and tie outfit at Feeney's estate. All the information is here on the sheets.'

A hand rose from the back.

'What about forensics, Kig? Have they come up with anything?'

Reidy picked up one of the papers in front of him.

'It's very threadbare,' he started. 'Malley has two staff working round the clock to find the source of the detonator. They have no prints from any of the scenes. And the devices that were found – well he's never seen anything like them before. All home-made.'

Donegan stood up.

'It's going to be footwork that catches this fella,' he

said. 'Whoever this Mercury Man is, we know one thing for sure. He's careful, methodical and he doesn't want to be caught like a lot of other psychos we've seen in the past. All the killings have been planned to the last detail. I've been...'

The telephone on Fox's desk rang.

'Yeah,' he answered, then grimaced up at Donegan as the call was put through.

'Detective Fox?'

'That's me.'

'Dan Malley from forensics. Are you some sort of policeman or are you just lucky?'

The question was followed by an excited laugh.

Fox leaned back on his chair and lifted his feet onto the desk.

'Yes,' he said casually. 'As a matter of fact, a bit of both. What can I do for you?'

Apart from a few whispers between two detectives at the back of the office, the room was silent with all eyes on Fox.

'This famous dog of yours may have just become the best witness that we have.'

Fox threw his feet from the desk and sat bolt upright.

'What do you mean?' he asked quickly.

McGrath leaned across the desk in a futile effort to hear what was being said. Donegan left the top table and moved silently towards him.

'I'm in the scene-van at the moment. I've just examined this collar.'

'And?' Fox breathed rapidly.

'And I've found two of the finest fingerprints I've ever laid eyes on.'

Fox clenched his fist and then relaxed it as the realisation dawned.

'What about the victim?' he asked. 'Could they be Danby's?'

'Nope,' said Malley. 'I did a preliminary with his prints and they're way out. Anyway, these are fresh.'

Fox held the receiver with an outstretched arm to Donegan.

'It's Malley,' he smiled. 'He's got prints.'

He leaned across the desk and spoke to McGrath, the excited chattering between Donegan and the forensics man a faint distance.

'Told you the dog was the puzzler in this,' he grinned.

'What do you mean?'

Fox ignored the question, choosing instead to lean back on his chair and hold his hands out.

'Gentlemen,' he announced, 'I am the greatest. From now on, to save time, assume that I know everything.'

'Yeah, yeah, you're brilliant,' the crowd muttered back and jeered.

Donegan pointed around the room to silence them, but he could not hide the smile.

'That's great stuff, Dan,' Donegan gushed into the phone. 'Two definites and a partial. And just when the lads here were saying what a useless shower of wasters ye were.'

He laughed as he listened to the rebuttal and then replaced the receiver. He looked down at Fox and McGrath. 'Good work, lads,' he said with sincerity.

He returned to the table, sat down beside Reidy

and waited for the excited chattering to abate.

'Now, gentlemen,' he said, 'let's just pretend for the moment that we don't have a print. Let's pretend that we don't get a match for this print. I don't want any of you going away from here and thinking that this case is a walk in the park just because forensics have finally come up with something. It's no good knowing *who* he is. We still have to catch the bastard.'

He scanned the room.

'How are things going with the local lads? No problems I hope,' he said.

Heads shook.

'Not a bother, Kig.'

'Sound out.'

'Decent fellas.'

'Good. Let's keep it that way. Take what information we have here and go through it tonight. Back here tomorrow morning at six sharp.'

The tired detectives stood up and slouched behind one another towards the table, each one of them taking a sheet. Fox and McGrath followed in the queue.

'Who knows what tomorrow will bring?' grinned Fox. 'I can feel my hand on the back of his neck already.'

McGrath looked back at him with weary eyes. Indeed, the news of the prints had put a spur into the proceedings. Still, it was not enough.

'Don't tell me you're not tired,' he said.

Fox rubbed his hands together. 'Four pints at my local, and then a quick snore in the scratcher.' He slapped McGrath on the shoulder, grinning. 'How can you be tired at a time like this? Why the big, sad head?'

McGrath turned around and looked down at him. He struggled to smile. 'Can your girlfriend divorce you?' he asked.

Fox took one of the sheets from the desk and winked at Reidy. 'Of course she can,' he replied. 'It's when she says that she wants to "break it off" that you should *really* get worried. Remember that fella in America who woke up and found that his wife had cut off his lower brain.'

McGrath took the sheet and folded it in half. 'It's at times like this that I wish we'd been confined to barracks,' he moaned.

'Cheer up for Jesus' sake,' urged Fox. 'C'mon. We'll go to Scanlon's for a few scoops and you can forget all about her. What about you, Sergeant Reidy?' He looked down at him. 'You've been a good boy all day. You surely deserve a Lucozade and a packet of Taytos.'

Reidy lifted his eyebrows at Fox and spoke as he picked up the loose sheets of paper.

'Whatever I've learned about this case today, Detective Fox, I'm not going to donate it to the oblivion of alcohol and fatigue,' he said as he shuffled the remaining papers and stacked them neatly on the corner of the desk.

Fox threw his eyes up in disgust as he left the office. 'This job is getting weirder by the day,' he protested loudly. 'One fella married to it and the other fella can't find a wan to marry.'

Reidy watched them go.

Fox glanced down at the sheet on his way to the exit door and then crumpled it into his pocket. The sense of achievement he had felt at the news of the fingerprints was beginning to fade. The thought that it had brought them closer to catching the Mercury Man warmed him again as he crossed the tarmac and sat into his car.

He laughed to himself as he thought about Beano and his newfound love. The pressure he had put him under had paid off. Fair dues to Beano, he thought, as he waited for the barrier at the gate to be lifted. Under different circumstances, he'd have made a great policeman.

He reached for the mobile phone on the passenger seat and dialled.

His call was answered by a loud, thudding noise, as if the receiver had been lifted and dropped accidentally on the desk.

'Drug Squad.'

'Is Brian Finn around?' he asked.

'Hold on.'

The musical interlude jingled annoyingly for nearly a minute.

'Yeah, this is Brian Finn.'

'Did anyone ever tell you that you're the best drug man in the country?' he asked.

Fox listened to the hiss of disgust.

'What do ya want Fox?' snapped Finn.

'Are you busy?'

'Why?'

'I'll see you in Scanlon's for a couple of pints. Ten minutes. I'm buying.'

'So now even your other half doesn't want to drink with you?'

'I'm a very lonesome detective,' said Fox and faked a sniffle.

'I'm not a bit surprised,' Finn retorted. 'A pint in Scanlon's, eh? Fair enough. I take it this means that my lovely case against your tout just went down the shitter.'

Fox trapped the surging laughter and brought it under control.

'Yes, Detective Finn,' he replied, 'something like that.'

CHAPTER FIFTEEN

Dressed in his Sunday best, Pat Doherty stood up on the foot bar of the counter and swung a clenched fist at the television, his loosened tie sweeping across the head of his full pint. He stumbled backwards as he lost his balance and then, having regained as much of it as his alcohol intake would allow, began to shadow box at the nervous customers around him.

'Come on, ya boy ya, ya have him... *ya have him,*' he shouted at the screen. The others turned and looked up at the heavily muscled, sweating boxers as they slugged it out for the heavyweight championship of the world. 'Hit him, ya fucker.'

Doherty pulled his large bulk against the counter,

his mouth hanging open, his body swaying involuntarily as he watched the remaining seconds of the final round with glazed eyes.

The silence of the customers changed to a loud cheer as the bell rang.

Doherty lifted his hands in the air and did an ungraceful victory dance between the stools, his wide frame and expansive stomach jostling the men around him as they gave him the expected congratulatory pats on the back before moving away.

He pulled his full pint from the counter and held it aloft, the frothy head and half the contents spilling from it on the shirt of a man beside him. He slapped roughly at it and then pulled the man towards him by gripping at the back of his neck.

'Don't worry, baby,' he slurred. 'I'll get ya a new wan.'

The others laughed with apprehension.

'Fair dues, Pat,' said one. 'How did ya pick the winner out of those two?'

Doherty frowned for a moment before taking two clumsy steps towards him. He wiped the sweat from his forehead and then tapped with his finger at his temple and winked.

'Mind yer own fucking business,' he warned, the spittle from his mouth peppering the smaller man's face.

'Take it easy now, Pat,' the elderly barman urged.

Doherty glared at him and then back at the smaller man. 'I'll take it easy all right,' he growled. Without warning, he slammed his forehead down onto the smaller man's cheek.

'Ya nosy little fucker,' he said, as he turned for the bar and took a staggering gulp from the remainder of his pint. 'All belongin' to him were nosy fuckers.'

He knew that there would be no retaliation. No one had ever messed with Pat Doherty, least of all a wimp who was six stone lighter. He fumbled in the pocket of his suit jacket for a moment and pulled out the yellow betting slip, his brain struggling to calculate the amount won.

The man he had struck moved to a table near the front door and sat down, nursing his cheek.

'Gimme a double for the road,' said Doherty, as he put the slip back in his pocket and then withdrew a handful of notes from his trouser pocket. He awkwardly selected one and threw it inside the counter.

'Keep the change,' he muttered, as he lifted the glass and finished it in a single gulp. As he placed the glass back on the counter, it slipped from his hand and rolled a short distance before the barman caught it.

'I'm away now,' said Doherty. 'But I might be back.'

He belched and moved towards the door, the others taking steps back. He stopped and slapped the man he had struck on the back.

'Sorry about that, Mick,' he slurred, as he groped for the door handle.

He stood outside, looking up the street, his eyes opening and closing slowly.

'Doherty,' called a voice from behind.

He turned and focused on the navy-blue Garda patrol-jacket, his eyes lifting to the scowling face of the sergeant. He grinned awkwardly as he lifted his hand and touched his forelock.

'Good evening to you now, Sergeant,' he said, and then snorted a laugh at a private joke.

The bones protruded angrily from the sergeant's jaw.

'You'll never learn, will you,' he said, looking directly at Doherty.

Doherty looked around in mock amazement.

'I'm minding my own business, amn't I?' he said. 'You should do the same.'

'You *are* my business, pal,' growled the sergeant.

The smile disappeared from Doherty's face and he took a step back. He raised his finger in warning.

'If you don't stop harassing me, I'm going to get my solicitor on to you. You're at me every time I come in to the village.' His voice rose, just enough to show his ire, but not enough to be threatening.

The sergeant smiled to annoy him.

'Go to your solicitor, boy,' he said. 'You can take the public order summons I'm going to send you to him the same day.'

He stepped forward and pressed his finger into Doherty's fleshy chest.

'This was a nice, quiet place before you came home with your navvy money from the buildings,' he said. 'Well, let me tell you this, Doherty. You're still the gouger you always were. Money or no money.'

Doherty looked down at the spot where the sergeant had prodded him.

'That's an assault. You're for it now,' he promised.

The sergeant smiled and nodded at the two men who passed them quickly on the path.

'Boys, oh, boys,' he said when they were out of earshot. 'If only it were the good old days I'd be kicking your fat, idle arse up and down the village. Ah, well, sure,' he added happily, 'maybe some night when 'tis nice and quiet.'

Doherty pulled his stained jacket closed and buttoned it, his stomach creating a large V at the front. 'I just won eight hundred,' he announced with a stupid grin. It was the only rebuttal he could think of. 'You'd be a long time walking the beat for that.'

The sergeant pulled at the end of his patrol-jacket and straightened up.

'Leave that car where you parked it,' he warned as he walked away. 'I don't want any more children killed.'

Doherty fumed inside. He wanted to lash a right hook at the departing sergeant, but he knew better.

As a younger and fitter man in his twenties, he had tested the fighting skills of the sergeant one night at the chip shop and had paid a heavy price. Not alone had he ended up in court on a charge of assaulting an on-duty garda, but he had also been beaten to a pulp with ease.

Now, almost twenty years later, the sergeant looked as fit as ever, whereas he himself had changed from a muscular builder to an overweight and out-of-breath slob who contented himself with beating smaller men. It was his reputation alone that kept them from retaliating.

'Behave yourself,' the sergeant warned.

Doherty shoved his hands in his pockets and looked down the village street to where he had parked his white, rusting Jaguar XJS. He decided to have a pint across the street and wait for the sergeant to go. If the coast was clear, then he would drive it home.

Inside the bar he had just left, a number of men consoled the man he had struck.

'Forget it, Mick,' one said. 'No point making a complaint about it. It'll only make things worse.'

The barman nodded in agreement as he put a head on the pint of Guinness beneath the tap and then placed it on the counter in front of a stranger.

'Sorry about all that,' he said. 'I hope it hasn't spoiled your holiday. You seem to have taken a shine to our porter.'

'Yes, indeed,' smiled Landers. 'It has an unusually pleasant taste.'

***

Mitchell Doyle awoke from a comfortable snooze on the crimson leather armchair in his study. He remained motionless for a moment, his gold-rimmed reading glasses balancing on the end of his nose, the large volume on the rise and fall of the Roman Empire lay open on his chest. He closed his eyes again and tried to remember the dream.

His lapse back into pleasant sleep was halted by the sound of the study door opening. His wife Emily was standing there with his nightly mug of steaming hot chocolate.

'Will you just look at yourself, Mitchell Doyle,' she gently scolded and smiled. 'Retired for almost five years and more exhausted now than ever. You really should cut back on all the golf you're playing. You're just not a young man anymore.'

He smiled at her but did not answer, choosing instead to watch her as she placed the mug down on the coffee table and then set about the minor tasks of poking the reddened embers in the grate and tidying up the scattered array of daily newspapers.

'What a wonderful woman you are,' he said, as if to himself.

She pulled the back of her dress under her and sat down on the edge of the coffee table facing him.

'You should be taking life easier, Mitchell,' she said, as she took the book from his chest and closed it. 'I've never seen you as active, rushing here, rushing there. You should be enjoying yourself instead of tiring yourself out.'

She picked up the mug and held it out to him. 'What about that wonderful moulding hobby that I bought you?'

She looked up at the four statuettes on the mantelpiece. 'You haven't made half of them.'

He removed his glasses and sat bolt upright, looking at her with a boyish grin as he took the mug.

'But I *am* enjoying myself, darling,' he said. 'I enjoy making myself tired. Please stop fussing. I've never felt better.'

She stood up and spoke as she made her way to the glass book cabinet. 'That's not what Dr Thompson said the last time. I don't think that all this activity is going to do your blood pressure any good. He recommended two games of golf only a week. You should spend more time with your collection of books.'

He sipped at the chocolate and rested the mug on his chest as he looked up at the ceiling.

'What do these doctors know, anyway?' he fobbed her off. 'Everything is cell counts and blood pressure with them. If they had their way, we'd all spend our time in bed with a nurse standing over us.'

She laughed as she placed the book back in its space and turned around.

'Just slow down a bit, Mitchell, that's all,' she pleaded. 'Promise me.'

He held his arm outstretched to her and then closed it around her as she sat beside him.

'Yes, dear. I promise,' he said gently, as he hugged her.

He rested his head against her side and they sat for a minute in silence, their thoughts drifting in very different directions.

'Is Susan asleep?' he asked, raising his head and looking up at her.

She looked down at him and nodded fondly.

'What kind of a day did she have?' he asked.

She rubbed her hands together and then examined the rings on her wedding finger.

'Not very good,' she replied sadly. 'You know how she can be sometimes. There are days when everything annoys her.' She shrugged. 'Just gets on top of her, I suppose.'

Doyle gazed into his mug. 'Yes,' he agreed softly. 'We can't begin to imagine.'

She placed her arm around him and rubbed gently at his shoulder.

'Are you coming to bed?' she asked.

He looked up at her and smiled. 'In a little while,' he replied. 'I'm waiting for a call. Terence is looking for a partner in the fourball on Sunday,' he lied.

'Mitchell Doyle,' she scolded.

'Just one game,' he promised. 'Go on. I'll be up shortly.' He pulled his arm free to encourage her to go.

She collected the newspapers from the coffee table and waited while he finished the chocolate. 'You've got half an hour, old boy,' she said, and left the room.

Doyle rose stiffly from the armchair and stood for a moment in front of the fireplace. Only when he heard the creaking of the floorboards overhead did he move. He locked the door, went to his leather-topped study desk and took the key of the drawer from his pocket.

Shortly, everything was in readiness. He pulled on the surgical gloves and removed one of the sheets of paper from the fresh bale. He sat back and unscrewed the top of the fountain pen as he prepared the words in his mind. And then he began.

'Pat Doherty RIP.

This road safety campaign has been sponsored by the Mercury Man.'

He folded the paper and placed it in the self-seal envelope that he had taken from the middle of the pack. Even though it was his own idea to send these taunting notes to the gardaí, Mr Landers had given him the full rundown on how it should be done.

'No prints on the paper. And no DNA left by saliva on the envelope.' And he should print in block capitals.

He placed the sealed message back in the drawer with the paper and unused envelopes and pulled the rubber gloves from his hands. He went to the fireplace and threw them in on top of the dying embers. They sizzled for a moment before bursting into a purple-green flame.

The telephone on his desk rang as he stirred the burning embers with the brass poker. He straightened up and walked slowly back to the desk. It was the call that he had been expecting.

'Mitchell?' said the voice. A bip punctuated the question. The call was from a public phone. Glasses clinked amidst the loud voices in the background.

'Yes.'

'Mitchell, there's a problem.'

'Yes?'

'We have prints from Danby's house. Your employee left them on the collar of his dog.'

'Impossible,' Doyle protested, and immediately lowered his voice. 'That couldn't have happened.'

'Well, it has, Mitchell. Fingerprint section are trying for a match as we speak.'

Doyle pinched the bridge of his nose and tightened his eyes.

'What position does that put us in?' he asked, already knowing the answer.

'A very dangerous one. I suggest that your employee abandons his work as of now and gets the hell out of here. The risk is too great. Where is he?'

'Down the country.'

'Well, that's good news at least. We have a full description of him, down to his accent. You have to stop it. If he's caught, we're all caught.'

The voice softened.

'Mitchell, you know this meant as much to me as it did to you. But we can't take the chance. Call him off for now.'

Doyle rested his head in his hand as he struggled to get the words out.

'So much planning. How can we waste it? All that work.'

'Mitchell, you have to see the sense in this.'

He straightened behind the desk and gave a purposeful cough. It all should not end like this. All that killing and still the main purpose had yet to be achieved.

'I will consult Mr Landers,' he said firmly. 'I will tell him what you've told me and let him decide for himself. Are you agreeable to that?'

'Mitchell, you're not listening to me.' The tone quickened in urgency. 'The squad will have him within days. Get him out. Now.'

'I'll let Mr Landers decide his own fate,' said Doyle calmly.

'Ours as well?' the voice was raised.

'Calm yourself. Ring me tomorrow night.'

Doyle placed the phone down without waiting for a response and sat back on the chair.

He pulled the desk drawer open and looked down at the prepared message for the gardaí.

'So much time and effort,' he thought as he shut it again.

He stood at the door for a moment looking back into the room, switched the light off, and went to bed.

CHAPTER SIXTEEN

The detective eased back from the screen and moved his head slowly from side to side to stretch his tired neck muscles. He turned the watch on his wrist and glanced down. It was almost midnight. The modem crackled and the screen changed from white to blue and back again.

He tapped at the Page Down button and then leaned forward to check the search data.

'Nothing on this one either, Kig,' he said. 'File hasn't been opened since the acquittal.'

Donegan sat behind him, shuffling the two concert tickets that he had just been delivered.

'Fair enough, Pat,' he said casually. 'How many more have you to do?'

The detective put his hand on the stack of files and flicked at the corner like a deck of cards.

'At least fifteen,' he replied. 'Why do you want to know how many times they were searched anyway, Kig?'

Donegan put the tickets back in the small envelope and wheeled his chair towards the desk. He picked up the files that had already been checked and pretended to read through them. He could feel the detective's eyes on him, waiting for the answer.

His mind raced for a reasonable explanation that would satisfy the detective's curiosity, but none was forthcoming. Finally, he threw the files back on the desk in defeat and looked directly at him.

'Pat,' he began, and then paused. 'I think,' he went on, 'that all the information on the victims that the killer has – came from a source within the job.'

The detective looked at the screen. 'I see,' he said softly. 'Jesus.'

Donegan reached across and picked up the unchecked files.

'It's the one thing that all the victims have in common. All checked on the same day at the same time on our computer system.' He held the files out for the detective to take.

'What I want to know is how many more are in here. And I want the fella who checked them.'

The detective took the files without looking at him. 'I see,' he said again.

'Needless to mention, Pat,' said Donegan, 'we're going to keep this between ourselves for the time being.' He gave a nervous laugh. 'Just in case I'm wrong and I end up back on the beat. If I do, you're coming with me.'

The detective smiled as he leaned forward and lightly drummed his fingers on the keyboard for a moment without pressing the keys. And then, like a man hit with a sudden rush of inspiration, he began to tap at speed, giving a running commentary as he worked.

'First things first, Kig,' he said, the keyboard rattling beneath his hands. 'We find the terminal that was used. Pity you didn't tell me earlier,' he added. 'I could be in my bed now like the rest of them.'

'Sorry, Pat,' said Donegan. 'But as you can imagine, it's not something that happens in the job every day. I want to be sure.'

'Mmmm. Isn't trust a wonderful thing?' The detective smiled. He nudged Donegan with his elbow as he continued to type. 'Give me the numbers on the victims' files,' he said.

Donegan read them slowly, his eyes rising and falling from the screen.

They both sat back and waited.

'Where did you pick up so much about this crack anyway?' Donegan was genuinely curious.

'From the young lad at home,' the detective laughed. He rolled the mouse in a circular motion and then clicked on the cursor.

He saw it before Donegan did and he cursed softly.

'The searches were done... from one of the terminals in the building,' he said, pointing to the code on the top left corner of the screen.

'Could they be the ones that McGrath did?' asked Donegan, not wanting to believe what he was hearing.

The detective shook his head and then worked the keyboard for a moment, inwardly hoping that he had made a mistake. He shook his head again and looked at Donegan.

'No, Kig,' he said.

Donegan rubbed his hands down along his face. 'Check the other files,' he said. 'And when you've done that, find out who did them.'

He pushed himself back from the desk and wheeled towards the phone. 'Time to ring Mr Know-it-all for his opinion,' he muttered.

The telephone rang just as he reached for it. 'Yes,' he shouted, startled by the shock.

'God, aren't we very touchy,' said Malley.

'Sorry, Dan. What's the story?'

'Well, we have one print ready for checking. It's a beaut, Frank. A real beaut. We should have the others in about an hour or so. I'll drop them over to the print section in the morning. Unlike us, they have homes to go to.'

Donegan laughed. 'Thanks, Dan. Home to bed now.'

He replaced the receiver, lifted it again and dialled. The phone at the other end rang out. He dialled again. 'Wake up, you lazy bastard,' he muttered.

It was answered by a voice talking into a pillow.

'Superintendent,' he said cheerfully, 'I think that you better get in here now.'

'What? Who is this?'

Donegan was pleased with his timing.

'Frank Donegan, Super.'

'What's the problem, Inspector?' the tone was sleepy and uninterested.

'I'd rather not say over the phone.'

The superintendent groaned in dismay as he raised himself out of the bed.

'Give me twenty minutes,' he said.

Donegan replaced the phone and looked back at the detective. 'Well, Pat?' he asked expectantly.

'I have three more files checked. Nothing. This one is...' He stopped. 'What was our date again?' He leaned closer to the screen.

Donegan wheeled back beside him and looked curiously at the screen as the detective pointed.

'Jesus, that's it,' he whispered. 'Whose file is it?'

The detective scrolled back through the pages to the beginning.

'Pat Doherty,' he said slowly. 'Drunken driving causing death.'

Donegan took out his notebook and jotted down the address and other details.

'Disqualified for five years, one year's suspended sentence, four hundred pound fine. Nothing else.'

He punched the detective gently on the shoulder. 'Good stuff, Pat,' he said. 'Do the rest of them. Any sign who did the checks yet?'

'I can't do it,' replied the detective.

'What!' snapped Donegan.

'I can't do it, Kig,' he explained. 'There's some special keyword to get in. And I don't have it.'

'Then, who does?' asked Donegan with urgency.

The detective shrugged.

'Dunno. One of the top lads I suppose. Maybe the super.'

Donegan tossed his head back. 'Great,' he said with

sarcasm. 'I'll bet he's a real whizz kid on the oul' keyboard.'

The detective smiled as he picked up another file and typed in the code.

'Unless, of course, it was put on lockout when the checks were done,' he said casually.

'What does that mean? Lockout?'

The detective typed as he spoke. 'Means that we won't be able to find out who did them. Someone could have simply hacked into the system,' he said.

Donegan dropped his head and sighed, then looked down at his open notebook.

'Well, at least we have something,' he said wearily.

***

Fox opened one eye slowly and looked at the red glow of the digital clock on the bedside locker. It was just after 4am. He held his breath as he listened to the movement behind him in the room, the shuffling of feet and the rubbing of a hand along the wall as it searched for the switch. He sat up quickly in the bed and turned just as the light went on and remained in the same position as he struggled to focus through the haze of alcohol.

'This place looks like there was a riot in it,' said McGrath casually. 'Was it leaded or unleaded you were drinking?'

Fox looked at him, his jaw sagging, his eyes squinting.

'What are... How did...' He gave up and rolled himself out of the bed. He stood for a moment, wavering in his boxer shorts, looking around at his clothes on the floor as he tried to get his bearings.

'You're not still drunk, are you?' asked McGrath in a concerned voice.

Fox coughed loudly and rubbed his hands down his face. 'Let's say that I'm just about capable of having proper control of my brain in a public place. You should have seen me here last night. 'Twas like the Stations of the Cross, only I fell more times.'

'Well, get a grip on yourself,' snapped McGrath. 'Donegan wants to meet us at five. Have a shower and I'll put on the kettle. Have you anything to fry?'

Fox gulped and smacked his lips in an effort to regain his sense of taste.

'Yeah,' he nodded. 'There's something in the fridge. Rashers and a sausage.'

McGrath clapped his hands. 'Lovely. A big fry-up so.'

Fox pulled a towel from the back of a chair and shuffled past him. 'Don't cook anything for me,' he warned, 'unless you want me to vomit up on the inspector.'

McGrath flinched back with an expression of disgust.

'Eat a tube of toothpaste, will you,' he said. 'What the hell did you drink? I thought you said that you were only going for a few pints.'

Fox nodded as he went into the bathroom and left the door ajar.

'I met Brian Finn for a few and straightened things out for Beano,' he said, his hoarse voice breaking to a squeak. 'I tell you, that man should get himself some serious counselling.'

McGrath switched on the kettle in the small kitchen opposite.

'How many pints did ye have?' he called out.

Fox replied through a mouthful of foaming toothpaste. 'Just the two. Two pints of – Jack Daniels. And guess who was buying?'

McGrath sniggered. 'That was a fairly expensive square.'

'The man is a bottomless pit,' shouted Fox, then lowered his voice in self-doubt. 'Jesus, how did I get home?'

McGrath searched the presses beneath the sink and took out a small stainless steel frying pan. A quick visual inspection of the lone sausage suggested that the Ebola virus was alive and well in Fox's refrigerator. He tossed it into the nearby waste bin and to his surprise found that the pack of rashers resting beside a half-frozen bottle of tomato ketchup was still in date.

Fox gave a guttural cry as the cold water of the shower washed over him.

Two minutes later he appeared in the kitchen doorway with a towel wrapped around his waist.

'Well, it's not going to be the banquet that I hoped for,' said McGrath, as he rushed around the smoking kitchen. 'The bread is stale. Therefore toast. You have no milk or butter and you're basically a total fuckin' disaster.'

'How did you get in anyway?' Fox looked puzzled.

'Ah, now that's a new trick I learned,' smiled McGrath. 'Come on and I'll show you.'

He led Fox to the main door of the flat and removed a comb from his back pocket.

'Watch, and learn,' he instructed. He reached down and turned the handle and pulled the door open. 'Are you impressed? Go on. Give me your honest opinion.'

Fox turned away in disgust. 'It's too early for that smart shite,' he growled. 'So I left the door unlocked. Big deal.'

McGrath laughed as he followed him back along the narrow corridor. 'Go on,' he slapped him on the shoulder. 'We've to be at Donegan's house in half an hour.'

Fox stopped and looked back. 'Donegan's *house*,' he said. 'I thought that we were going into the office.'

McGrath shook his head. 'He just phoned and told me to collect you and meet him at his house at five.'

'Did he say why?'

'Nope. He just said to pack some clothes, surveillance gear and firearms. And we're to use one of our own cars. Do you want to drive your car?'

'Yeah, very funny,' Fox sneered and turned for the bedroom. 'I'd have to find it first.'

McGrath returned to the kitchen and put three rashers between slices of toast.

Fox shouted to him as he dressed. 'I'm seriously thinking of giving up drink.'

'Yeah. Good man,' McGrath replied with a full mouth. 'And I suppose that you'll start liking people as well.'

'Aw, now, let's not go the full circle.'

McGrath grimaced as he took a mouthful of black coffee.

He looked up to see Fox pull on a multicoloured woollen jumper in the doorway.

'Good Jaysus,' he said. 'Where did you get that thing?'

Fox patted down the front of it and turned around in a full circle. 'The mother knitted it in the Clare colours.' He smiled and then raised his arms. 'The West's awake, boy.'

McGrath nodded and resumed eating.

'So madness *is* hereditary,' he said with a full mouth.

'Right,' said Fox with enthusiasm, appearing to have found a new lease of life. 'Enough of the smart talk for the time being. Where are we off to?'

McGrath stood up and dusted his hands. 'Where's your gear?' he asked.

Fox bent down and lifted a rolled sleeping bag from behind him in the corridor.

'Packed and ready,' he grinned. 'Always travel light. That's my motto.'

'And your firearm?'

Fox slapped at his belt. 'Right here.'

'Let's go, then,' said McGrath. 'I've got everything else we need.' He walked out past Fox. 'And lock the door. 'Twould be a fright if anyone broke in and took all the great stuff you have.'

The outside light of Donegan's house at the end of the estate greeted their arrival. McGrath turned and gave Fox a quick and silent inspection before tapping on the window. The door was answered almost immediately.

'Come in, lads,' whispered an exhausted-looking

Donegan, who pointed to the open sitting-room door. 'Sit yerselves down. I've just put the kettle on.' He disappeared from view before either of them could refuse the hospitality.

Fox slumped down on the sofa and grinned as he looked around. The warmth of the room, the comfortable glow of the lamp on the corner table, it all looked very pleasant.

'Now this is what I call comfort,' he said.

McGrath hushed him to silence and pointed to the ceiling.

'People are sleeping,' he warned in a low whisper. 'Besides, a cell in the Joy would be the Gresham compared to your dive.'

Fox nodded in agreement as Donegan appeared in the doorway with a tray holding three mugs and a pot of tea. He lifted the heel of his shoe and pushed the door closed behind him. Fox moved the small envelope aside on the coffee table and then picked it up. McGrath and Donegan looked at one another as he opened it and pulled out the contents.

'Aw, you got us tickets for the Point,' Fox grinned. 'Kig, you're an oul' dote. But couldn't you have waited until later to surprise us?'

Donegan placed the tray down on the table and smiled as he took the tickets from Fox.

He sat down in the armchair and looked at the two of them.

Fox raised his eyebrows in expectation.

'Well, Kig?' he asked. 'Why all the secrecy?'

Donegan leaned forward resting his arms on his knees, his fingers interlocked. He looked tired. More worried than tired perhaps.

'I've got a special job for the two of you,' he said quietly.

'Excellent.' Fox turned and smiled at McGrath, who remained stony-faced.

Donegan sat back on the armchair and looked at them. 'All the information on the victims came from one of the computers in our building,' he said. 'So it came from someone within the job.'

The room fell silent.

'Who?' gasped McGrath, eventually.

Fox looked in turn at the two of them. He knew that he was about to be left out of the conversation for now. Computers were not his forte. Anyway, McGrath could explain it to him later.

'All the information was got on the same day at the same terminal. At the moment, we can't determine who used it. A quick job, done professionally.'

Fox did not appear as shocked as McGrath.

'Well, that's me off the list as a suspect,' he said casually. 'I'm a "lets break it dot.com man" myself.'

Donegan glared at him. 'Exactly,' he said forcefully. 'The thing is, all of those checked have been victims. All except one.'

He reached down beside the chair and picked up a computer printout. 'This fella,' he announced. 'Pat Doherty from Lishane village in Kerry.'

'What'd he do?' asked Fox sitting up, his interest growing.

'Killed a child,' said Donegan and held out the paper to McGrath. 'Drunken driving causing death.'

Fox puffed through his lips and threw himself back on the sofa.

'Jesus,' he said. 'Who's next on the list? Shoplifters? I've heard of zero tolerance, but this is ridiculous.'

'He's the last one,' said Donegan. His voice rose slightly. 'The last chance we have.'

He eyed both of them, waiting to see who would say it first. As expected, Fox straightened up in the chair. He was back in play, back where he belonged.

'He's bait, isn't he, Kig?' he grinned.

Donegan pretended to be confused.

'I wouldn't use that term exactly.'

'Has his local station been warned?' he asked.

Donegan shook his head slowly and looked at McGrath.

'So, let's cut the bullshit, Kig,' said Fox with a smile. 'You know – or you suspect – that he's going to hit this fella, em...' He snapped his fingers as he pointed to the sheet in McGrath's hand.

'Pat Doherty,' McGrath prompted.

'Yeah, Pat Doherty,' said Fox. 'So now, he's set up as bait.'

Donegan's voice rose. 'He's not bait,' he all but shouted. He winced then and looked up at the ceiling.

Fox nodded and lifted his hand to quell the inspector's anger.

'OK. OK.' He lowered his voice to a whisper. 'We'll call it "helping the guards with their enquiries – unknown to himself" for the moment. Would I be safe in thinking that you want myself and the lad here to go and wait for our man to bite?' he rested back in the chair. 'I can feel that medal on my chest already.'

McGrath lowered himself into the conversation. 'Is that it, Kig?' he asked.

The concern was evident on Donegan's face. He leaned forward and took one of the mugs from the tray and held it out to McGrath.

'That's it,' he replied. 'That's it in a nutshell.'

He scratched pensively at the stubble on his chin for a moment. 'Only the three of us know about what I'm doing,' he said. 'I've spent the last two hours with the super and, although he now agrees that the leak might be coming from inside the job, he doesn't want to carry it any higher until he has more proof.'

'Then, why don't *you* bring it higher?' asked McGrath.

'I'm taking a hell of a chance doing what I'm doing,' Donegan explained. 'If I'm wrong about this Pat Doherty, then so be it. But – if I'm wrong about the leak, then I might as well resign.'

He moved to the edge of his seat and became more enthusiastic, as if encouraging himself as he spoke.

'Get down there and get an eye on this Doherty fella. If nothing happens, then nothing happens and I was wrong. Contact me on my mobile only. No one knows that I've authorised this, so try and not let it go pear-shaped, for all our sakes.'

He raised a cautioning finger at Fox.

'If there's a sign – *any* sign – that this Mercury Man might be in the area, do nothing until you get the all-clear from me. Wait for a decision to be made, for once.'

He looked at them in turn. 'Do both of you understand?' he whispered.

'What about the local station?' asked Fox.

Donegan gave an indifferent shrug. 'I'll let that up

to yer own judgement,' he replied. 'It isn't that big an area that you can't find out where a fella lives. Don't involve them unless you have to.'

Fox took a mouthful of the tea and stood up. 'No time to waste then, Kig,' he said.

McGrath folded the computer printout and put it in his jacket pocket.

Donegan followed them to the door. They stood on the step looking in at him.

'I promise that I won't shoot anyone,' Fox grinned.

Donegan tried to smile as he blessed himself in the doorway.

'Don't worry, Kig,' McGrath assured him. 'We won't let you down.'

CHAPTER SEVENTEEN

Landers finished his breakfast and stood up from the table in the empty dining room. He took his cup of coffee and walked out through the tall glass doors into the bright morning sunshine and selected a chair at the edge of the wide patio where he could look down on the rose garden. Beneath him and to his right, in the parking area, he could see the group of Frenchmen as they joked and rattled their equipment into the personnel-carrier for another day's fishing. He smiled to himself, remembering their previous night's exuberance and the celebration at having caught four small, brown trout, each of them no more than a pound in weight.

'You slept well, I trust,' came a voice behind, and he turned to see Haskard standing in the doorway, dressed in the same clothes as on the previous evening.

'Yes, very well, thank you,' he replied. 'I was just surveying your rose garden. It's quite spectacular.'

Haskard pulled one of the cast-iron chairs beside him and sat down.

'You have an interest in gardening, then?' he seemed surprised.

Landers shook his head. 'Not in a very long time,' he said. 'I remember my father winning many awards for his roses, though. He had a great fondness for flowers and anything to do with rubbing his hands in the earth. Personally, I could never really see the point of it all. I suppose it was the fact that he came from an Irish farm.'

Haskard rested his palms on the handle of the cane and smiled as he looked out across the garden.

'It's all about creating something that no one else can, Mr Landers,' he explained. 'I'm sure that your father explained that to you.'

Landers sipped at his coffee for a moment, pausing intentionally with the cup to his lips. When he had finished he placed the cup down on the ornate concrete railing and looked back at Haskard.

'You were correct about Mr Doherty,' he said coldly. 'He needs killing.'

'You've seen him then?' Haskard was pleased.

Landers nodded in silence and turned back to the rose garden. Haskard rested the cane against the side of the chair and took his pipe out of his waistcoat pocket. There was silence between the two men for a moment as he removed his pipe-lighter and rose slowly to his feet. He spoke through the clouds of smoke as he joined Landers to survey the garden.

'As you have probably seen for yourself, Lishane is a very quiet and pleasant area. Except, of course, for our Mr Doherty,' he said with disgust. 'When he returned, he brought with him an element of violence and fear that the people in this law-abiding village were not used to.'

He rested on the cane and puffed contentedly on the pipe as he continued.

'Knocking down and killing a child is something that could happen to any of us,' he said. 'A few miles per hour too fast, a pint or a scotch too many here or there and we could easily find ourselves in the same boat. But, to do such a thing and to have no regret, no prick of conscience, no shame...' His voice growled in anger as he spoke. 'Quite the opposite in fact – when drunk, to boast about getting away with it, and to have grown men shake in their shoes at the very mention of his name, to have the same hard-working men leave a public house at the threat of his impending arrival... It just cannot go on.'

Landers lifted his cup from the wall and stared into it. His eyes narrowed as he spoke.

'It won't,' he said without emotion. 'I'll kill him today.' He pulled the sleeve of his jumper back from his watch. 'This very morning in fact.'

Haskard's eyes widened. Although he was pleased with the news, this sudden realisation that he was standing next to a cold-blooded killer unnerved him. No one would have taken Mr Landers for the assassin he was, standing there dressed in dark slacks and bright-yellow golf jumper, sipping his coffee and casually looking into the distance, like a man on a tee-box contemplating the difficulties of a long par five.

'This morning?' Haskard repeated. 'Will I see you when it's over?'

Landers shook his head.

Haskard sat back down slowly on his chair. His initial shock had now been replaced with interest. 'How do you intend to do it?' he asked.

'I've been thinking carefully about it,' Landers replied, turning to him. 'And I've decided not to make it too elaborate. I've got just the weapon. Basically, it's going to be quick. I don't believe in risking the entire operation and getting captured offing some alcoholic village bully.'

Haskard raised his eyebrows. 'You don't believe that this is worth while then, do you?' he said.

Landers gave a casual shrug. 'I do what I'm paid for,' he replied. 'My objective is money and I'm not ashamed to say it.'

'Of course not, of course not,' said Haskard. 'And just how exactly do you...'

'It will be straightforward,' said Landers before the question could finish.

He swallowed the last of the coffee and tapped gently at the cup.

'Now, if you'll excuse me,' he said. 'I have some last-minute preparations to make.'

Haskard watched him walk towards the patio doors. 'I'll see that you're not disturbed,' he called behind him.

***

Detective Sergeant Charlie Cooper of the Fingerprint Section picked up the brown envelope marked 'urgent' from the reception desk and whistled as he made his way to the Automated Fingerprint Identification System room of the Technical Bureau. He tapped the envelope against his thigh in time to his walk, smiling as he nodded greetings to those who passed him in the brightly lit corridor.

Charlie had been in the Fingerprint Section for twenty of his twenty-five years' service. A likable and cheerful character, he never outwardly appeared to take his work seriously, but beneath the wisecracks and the slagging was a policeman more dedicated than most. A graduate of fingerprint courses with the FBI in Langley and with Interpol, there was nothing that Charlie didn't know about the science of fingerprint identification.

He pushed through the glass office door of AFIS and shoved the envelope under his arm.

'Good morning, print-people,' he shouted, as he took the glass coffee pot from the warmer and poured himself a mug. The three detectives looked at one another and smiled. It was the same greeting every morning.

Charlie replaced the pot, sipped at his coffee and sat down at his desk with a stern expression.

'Jennifer,' he said firmly, 'question for you.'

The detective stopped typing and eased back on her chair. She eyed him with suspicion as a smile broke across his face.

'Charlie, I'm in the middle of a very difficult file at the moment so this better not be another one of your stupid women jokes,' she warned.

He put down the mug and pulled the seal back on the envelope.

'Not at all,' he corrected her. 'Simple question. It's always been something of a puzzle to me.'

He looked at her. She glared at him in warning. He immediately changed his mind.

'On second thoughts, forget it,' he said.

'Coward,' she muttered, and resumed typing.

He looked at the others. 'I'll tell ye later,' he pretended to whisper. 'Heard it last night. Couldn't get to sleep for an hour.'

He narrowed his eyes with interest as he removed the fingerprint cards from the envelope along with the note from Malley.

'Mmmm,' he said out loud as he switched on the AFIS system. He folded the note and threw it on the desk, then began examining the prints in turn. He was pleased to see that at least one of them was of excellent quality. The search would not take long.

He scanned the most promising card, enlarging it on the screen in front of him, and then, as the others expected, he began to talk to himself through the procedure, punctuating it with, 'Oh yes, my little beauty. You lovely, lovely girl.'

Jennifer took the pen from her desk and threw it at him. It struck him on the back.

'I'd bring you up for sexual harassment if you were a man,' she quipped.

Charlie glowered in concentration as he worked

the keyboard. 'Sexual harassment,' he grumbled absentmindedly. 'There was no such thing in my time. If you grabbed a girl by the arse, she'd kick you in the balls and that'd be the end of it.'

He hit the Enter key and sat back.

'And... away we go,' he said taking his mug from the desk and swivelling his chair around.

'Right,' he became serious. 'I want to hear some gossip. It doesn't have to be the truth, just so long as it involves the nabbing of anyone of high rank in an awkward situation.'

He glanced from the computer screen to his watch and pointed to Jennifer. 'You've got twelve minutes. Begin.'

She laughed at him and sat back on her chair. 'I just don't understand it,' she said shaking her head in confusion.

'What?'

'How you can be so upbeat every day?' she asked. 'What drugs are you on?'

Charlie rested his arms on either side of the chair and twiddled his thumbs.

'Simple,' he replied casually. 'I've got a good life, a good wife and when that door closes behind me every evening, the job stays right here. You've lost your turn as usual.' He pointed to the nearest detective. 'Tom, the clock is ticking.'

'Nothing to report, Sarge,' he grinned. 'It's like everyone got religious all of a sudden.'

Charlie drooped his shoulders in fake dismay. He was about to point again, when the monitor beeped behind him.

'What's this, what's this?' he said urgently as he turned and waited for the result. 'It's never been as quick before. Maybe the hacks in the technology section have speeded the process up.'

The others lowered their heads back to work. Charlie leaned closer to the screen as the result flashed.

'No match on file,' he muttered. 'I'll give *you* no match on file.'

He worked furiously at the keyboard for a few minutes and then sat back. He had seen this result many times before but knew that the database when put to the limit would include all prints from Ireland, the UK and a number of other European countries. He hummed a tune and then broke quietly into song.

'If you're Irish, come into the parlour. There's a welcome here for you...'

Again the screen flashed.

'Shitsticks,' he complained quietly and spun in the chair. 'Jennifer, I apologise for all the stupid jokes I've told and furthermore, I admit that you are the most intelligent person in this office. Help me quickly. This new program is giving me a severe pain.'

She wheeled her chair across beside him and nudged him from in front of the monitor.

'I told you that you should have attended the updating course. It only took an hour,' she said as she worked at the keyboard.

They both sat back and waited for the result.

'That can't be right,' she leaned closer and frowned.

Charlie raised an eyebrow to her and looked at the screen. 'Thank you, Detective. You got "no match on file" in a different colour. Get back to your saltmine.'

He picked up the note from Malley and read through it again. It stated that there might be an English connection. He snatched at the phone and dialled.

'Good morning. Scotland Yard Fingerprint Section. How may I help you?'

'DCI Hampton, please,' he said and waited.

He smiled when he heard the voice.

'Michael, any good fishing lately?' he said.

They talked for a moment about this and that before Charlie got to the point.

'I've got a print here,' he explained. 'Our own system has come up blank and I was wondering if you could give it the once-over for me. There's a mention that the culprit might be a fellow countryman of yours.'

He laughed out loud.

'Yeah. We're importing yours and you're importing ours. Listen, I can fax it over and it shouldn't take that long. It's a good lift.'

He squeezed the phone between ear and shoulder as he listened and gathered the print cards from the desk.

'Great stuff,' he said finally. 'When will you get back to me with a result, if any?'

He looked at his watch and smiled. 'That'd be mighty. There's a bit of a rush on with this fella. I'll get them to you right away. Sound. Thanks, Michael.'

He replaced the phone and stood up.

'I'll be back in a few minutes,' he said as he left the office. 'I just want to check something out.'

***

The village of Lishane looked like a picture postcard from the top of the hill. Flanked on both sides by sloping green hills, the tiny settlement nestled comfortably in the centre of the valley, the mid-morning sun glinting off the windows far below. McGrath stopped the car and wrenched violently at the handbrake. Fox stirred beside him and opened his eyes, groaning for a moment as he massaged his stiffened neck.

'Are we here? Tell me we're here.'

'Now, that's what I call a view,' McGrath said with enthusiasm and opened the door. 'C'mon. Get some fresh air. It'll help clear your head.'

Fox muttered in disapproval as he wound the seat to its upright position and released his seatbelt.

McGrath bounded onto a rock at the side of the road and smiled as he looked down. 'God's country,' he said.

Fox shuffled up behind him and stood there with his hands in his pockets, his face a grimace of discomfort, shivering as the cool mountain air cut through him.

'Can we go now, please?' he said and turned for the car.

McGrath jumped from the rock and slapped him hard on the back.

'C'mon, boy. Smarten yourself,' he shouted. 'We've got to find out where this Doherty fella lives. And we have to do it without arousing any suspicion. I think a pub would be a good start.'

Fox brightened.

'Marvellous idea,' he agreed. 'I could do with a

quick cure to get me back to my old self.'

They sat into the car together.

'You can't be that bad,' said McGrath, frowning at him. 'You snored all the way down here.'

Fox took several gasping breaths and rubbed his face hard.

'You're right,' he said. 'This is not the time to be sleepy. At least not if what Donegan says is true. Give me a quick look at the sheet on Doherty.'

'That's the spirit.' McGrath smiled as he pulled it from between the seats and handed it to him. 'Of course 'twould make our job a whole lot easier if we could liaise with the local lads. I don't understand all this secrecy stuff.

Fox nodded as he read. 'Yeah,' he said. 'But then, we'd look a right pair of gobshites if Donegan is wrong about all of this. I think we'll keep it low profile for the moment.'

'And if he's right, though, what then?'

Fox muttered as he read. 'Ex-navvy home from Birmingham... four years ago, knocks down and kills a child coming from school... drunken driving causing death.'

Satisfied that he had taken in enough, he crumpled the sheet and forced it back between the seats.

'If he's right, then we'll deal with it,' he answered casually.

McGrath flashed a worried glance at him.

'Hold your horses there a minute now,' he warned. 'You heard what Donegan said about making any rash moves without contacting him.'

'Yeah, yeah,' Fox cut him off quickly. 'Don't worry.

We're going to do this by the book.'

McGrath turned his attention back to the road. 'Mmmm,' he said quietly. 'His book or yours?'

The entrance to the village was lined on both sides with old stone troughs that overflowed with colourful arrangements of flowers.

'Pub! Open pub!' Fox pointed excitedly.

McGrath pulled the car to the kerb. He switched off the ignition and rested his hands on the steering wheel.

'Now,' he began. 'Let's get our story straight. We can't just walk in there and ask where Pat Doherty lives. We've got to do this without anyone suspecting anything, especially Doherty.'

Fox rubbed his hands together. 'Leave it to me,' he grinned. 'I've got a plan.'

'And the plan is?'

'Trust me,' Fox replied. 'Beneath this city cop exterior beats the heart of a country bullshitter. You just get the drink and I'll do the talking.'

McGrath was unconvinced. 'You understand that if we make a bollocks of this, we're back in uniform on Monday,' he warned. 'We're on our last legs with the super. You *do* understand that, don't you?'

'All is well,' Fox smiled to reassure him. 'Now c'mon. This Doherty fella will be dead ten times over if we keep talking.'

McGrath locked the car and followed him into the coolness of the village pub. It was empty, apart from the young barman and an elderly customer who leaned over the counter from both sides across a small plastic chess set.

The barman shook his head slowly in defeat.

'Ya have me again, Jimmy,' he sighed. 'Can I not move this one across like this?' he asked giving a demonstration of his intentions. The elderly man took his hand without replying and guided the piece back into place.

'You're very hard on me,' sighed the barman.

Fox pulled out a stool beside them and leaned over to examine the board with interest.

'This'll be seven straight games,' the barman said, looking at him. 'And he only learned to play it a month ago.'

Fox moved his head closer to the game, his eyes narrowed.

'You should castle your king before...' he started.

The old man sat upright on his stool and looked at him.

'Is it yourself I'm playing, is it?' he asked in angry wonder.

Fox immediately raised his hands. 'My mistake,' he apologised. He turned to McGrath and tapped the stool in front of him.'

'You're a Clareman anyway,' said the barman nodding at Fox's jumper. 'How do you think ye'll do in the hurling this year – or have ye a team at all?'

'Ah, we're good and ready this time,' replied Fox casually, and turned his attention back to the chessboard.

There was silence for a moment before McGrath broke it with a gentle cough.

'Can I've two pints, please,' he whispered, at this stage hoping that Fox's plan of action involved a little more than merely annoying the local grandmaster.

The barman backed towards the taps, his eyes still fixed on the board. The old man lifted his head.

'Yerra, c'mon will ya,' he grumbled. 'I'm waiting for the last ten minutes for you to move.'

When he got no reaction to the protest, he twisted the board on the counter to Fox. 'Right so,' he said. 'Play for him you if you're that good.'

'Go on,' the barman urged. 'Do. I can't see any way out of it myself.'

Fox rubbed slowly at the bristle on his chin. 'You've given in too easily,' he said

McGrath sat beside him in silent prayer. *Jesus, don't let him beat the old man. Come on now, Jesus.*

Fox castled his king in the move he had suggested moments earlier. The old man smiled to himself and slowly took out a gleaming-white handkerchief from his pocket. He examined it for a moment and then moved his queen into position.

'Checkmate,' he said quietly, and blew his nose.

Fox, McGrath and the young barman all hovered over the board, their heads moving left and right quickly as they checked on the validity of the claim just made.

'Ya didn't see that wan coming, did ya?' The elderly man was still smiling.

Fox patted him on the shoulder. 'I must bow to the expert.' He smiled back and tipped his king over.

The old man beamed with pleasure.

'Are ye working locally or what, lads?' he asked.

Fox shook his head as he reached out and took his pint.

'Believe it or not, we're on our holidays,' he replied. 'We're flat out for the past six months and we decided to take a weekend break from it.'

'What do ye work at?' the old man pressed on.

'Plastering.' Fox replied and took a gulp of his pint. 'Dublin full-time now. Big contracts.'

The old man shook his head with sympathy. 'A tough line of work,' he said. 'Tough, but well paid though,' he added quickly. He examined the droplet of whiskey in his glass before finishing it and smacking his lips.

'Can I get you another one?' asked Fox. 'Seeing as you're the champion and all.'

The old man held his glass out to the barman.

'I won't insult you by refusing,' he smiled. 'What made ye pick our small neck of the woods?'

McGrath braced himself.

'No reason. Just passing through,' Fox replied. 'I thought I recognised the name when I saw it, though.'

'Were ya here before maybe?' the barman asked casually as he turned from the optic.

Fox shook his head. 'Nah,' he said. 'But the name Lishane definitely rings a bell with me. Probably some fella I met from here when I was on the sites in England. You know what it's like over there. You meet lads from the length and breadth of Ireland.'

The old man frowned in thought and looked up at the barman.

'Who could that be now?' he asked softly. 'Young Shea was there for a while. And Gerry McCarthy until the scaffolding fell on him. I can't think of anyone else from around here who would have been...'

He paused.

'Except your man, eh, Doherty – but he's home these good few years.'

Fox snapped his fingers. 'You have him,' he said quickly. 'Em, Doherty – Paddy Doc. Is his first name Paddy?'

McGrath relaxed and lifted his pint. He could see where the line of questioning was going. 'I don't think Paddy Doc was from around here, though,' he said to fuel the search. 'I thought he was from Tralee.'

The old man leaned back on his stool to look at him.

'There's a Pat Doherty just out the road anyway,' he said. 'He mightn't be the man ye're thinking of. But he worked a good few years on the buildings in England.'

Fox rubbed his hands and smiled.

'Well, that's a good wan now. And he's living here?' he said. He turned to McGrath. 'Will we call to see if it's our old pal? Jaysus, he was some tulip. The stories we could tell about him.'

The old man nodded. 'It sounds like ye have the right man to be sure,' he said.

The barman looked at him and sighed in private agreement before he began to point and give directions.

'Out the road till ye come to a cross. Take a right, then past the small woodland and he's in the house just beyond it. He won't be up yet, though.'

'Grand job,' said Fox. 'We might give him a call. What do you say, Bob?'

McGrath knew that it was now the time to throw the plan into reverse.

'The Paddy Doc we knew would be in his late thirties now, I suppose,' he offered.

The old man closed his eyes and he and the barman shook their heads in unison.

'Ah, yerra, not at all,' he said. 'Pat Doherty is nearly fifty. Ye have the wrong man altogether.'

Fox tut-tutted with disappointment.

'That's a shame now,' he said.

The old man lifted his glass and toasted them.

''Tis a pity all right,' he agreed and sipped at it his drink. He lowered the glass slowly and leaned towards Fox with a confidential whisper. 'If ye're going to stay around, the daughter has a fine B+B just out the road, reasonable too.'

Fox smiled as he lifted his pint and gulped it back, then moved towards the door. 'We'll keep that in mind,' he said. 'But to tell you the truth, we haven't really made any definite plans yet. We might see ye later, though.'

He waited outside, stretching himself and extending his arms until McGrath appeared behind him and slapped him on the back.

'Very nicely done, Detective.' He grinned and moved to the driver's door. 'It's time to stock up for the great stakeout.'

Fox puffed as he sat in.

'Yeah,' he said. 'I knew there was a tougher part to all of this. Go on. Find a supermarket. I'm not going to make the same mistake that I made the last time.'

'You mean the time you went with nothing to eat and ended up sitting in the back of a Hiace on your own for twelve hours?'

Fox nodded. 'Yeah, that time. I nearly drank my own piss with the hunger.'

McGrath laughed. 'That's surveillance for you.'

Fox removed his wallet and counted through the notes. 'Well, this time I'm going prepared.'

The supermarket was a brightly lit money trap. Exorbitantly priced specialities included prepared sandwiches, a selection of foreign newspapers for the tourists in the nearby caravan and camping site, and a colourful collection of plastic animal flotation aids for their children.

The shopping spree took less than five minutes. Fox dropped five bags of crisps, five chocolate bars and a two-litre bottle of orange on the counter. He turned to the rack of papers and selected one. The elderly woman picked it up slowly and squinted at the price through the thick lenses of her glasses. She pressed at the buttons on the cash register awkwardly and then looked up at him.

'That'll be thirteen euro thirty,' she grinned.

'What?' Fox gasped and his head began to move across his supplies in an attempt to calculate. Defeated, he held out a twenty-euro note.

'Things have got shocking dear,' she said by way of an explanation as she turned to him with the change, massaging each note carefully before handing it over. 'Are ye going to the beach? It's a glorious day for it.'

'No, we're going on a picnic,' grunted Fox as he pulled a plastic bag from the bunch and began to fill it with his shopping.

'Ah, sure isn't that lovely too,' she said. 'I'd love to

be out in it but I told my daughter I'd fill in for the day so she could take the grandchildren out.'

McGrath approached with six prepared rolls and two packets of biscuits. Fox smiled at him as he watched him place them on the counter.

'Get another bottle of minerals, just in case,' he said and began to leave. 'I'll be in the car if you need any extra money.'

When McGrath returned to the car, he threw the two plastic bags in the back seat and slammed the rear door with all his might. Fox smothered a laugh as he waited for him to sit in.

''Twas a small bit pricey, I thought,' he said as seriously as he could.

'Pricey,' McGrath almost squealed. 'That oul' wan should be wearing a balaclava.'

'Well, we're properly prepared for the job now,' Fox said. 'Turn the car and head for the end of the village, then take a...'

'I know, I know,' snapped an irate McGrath. 'I was there as well, remember?'

The rest of the journey was undertaken in silence. Once McGrath saw Doherty's house, he turned the car into the wooded picnic area and drove up past the wooden benches and tables, up to the small cul-de-sac. Both of them saw it together and the mood in the car immediately changed.

'This is just perfect,' said Fox as he looked down at Doherty's house, two hundred yards away below them. McGrath nodded and smiled. 'We couldn't have asked for better. And here was I thinking that we'd be lying down on a bed of pine needles. This is going to be a real handy number after all.'

Fox picked up his mobile, dialled and waited.

'Kig, we're in position. Class one view of the front and rear of house. Looks like Doherty is home. Smoke coming from chimney and his car is in the driveway. And he travels in style by the looks if it,' he added casually.

He nodded absently as he received further instructions from Donegan.

'Got it, Kig,' he said, and ended the call. He turned to an interested McGrath.

'He says to keep eyes on Doherty when he appears. One of us will have to take him when he goes anywhere. The other stays here with the house. We'll take it in turns.'

'Fair enough. Did he give you any idea of how long we're going to be living in the woods?'

'Nah. But I'm sure he'll let us know soon enough.' He reached back to the rear seat and picked up the binoculars, talking slowly as he lifted them to his eyes and rolled the focus.

'Wouldn't it be great if Mr Mercury turned up and we caught him right in the act?' he said. 'I must say, I've got a very good feeling about this. Can I have one of your rolls?'

McGrath looked confused for a moment. 'Course you can,' he replied settling back comfortably in the seat and closing his eyes. 'You don't think that I bought them all for myself, do you? Only a mean, miserable bastard would buy stuff for just himself on a surveillance job.'

Fox coughed and lowered the binoculars. He glanced down at the plastic bag of chocolate and crisps at his feet. 'Dead right, Bob,' he agreed and slowly raised the glasses again.

CHAPTER EIGHTEEN

Donegan chose a quiet table in the corner of the canteen and sat down with his cling film-covered sandwich, mug of coffee and morning newspaper. The murders of Ivor Danby and Gerry Feeney were getting scant coverage, both the stories no more than a sidebar on the inside pages – Garda investigation, state pathologist carrying out postmortem, brief history of the victims, the usual. Any journalist guessing from behind a desk could have written the stories.

A young detective approached with his tray and a shadow fell across the page.

'Morning, Kig,' he said cheerfully.

Donegan did not look up. He lifted his palm and

held it there until the shadow was gone.

He was in no humour for company.

The sandwich and coffee were also ignored as he turned the pages slowly and read.

'Jesus Ch...rrist,' he whispered through gritted teeth, his eyes moving quickly across the bold letters.

> *'Is there a serial killer on the loose? Is there a connection between the murders we read about every day? The answer is yes. Read the exclusive truth, tomorrow in the Sunday edition.'*

'That little f...'

He patted at his jacket pocket for his cigarettes, then realised that he had left them behind in his office. He searched around him for a smoker and on locating one called out his name, indicating with quick puffs on his fingers that he had once again forgotten his cigarettes and was in desperate need of a stress-relieving nicotine boost.

The pack and lighter were tossed to him and he quickly lit one, drawing in the smoke and holding it there until his head began to spin. He exhaled slowly with closed eyes, his hand resting limply above the ashtray. Fox and McGrath were in position on his say-so. He had bickered with the superintendent, told him too much too quickly. And now he had strayed from the investigation and had started his own. But he knew he could trust Fox and McGrath. Beneath all the impulsiveness were two relatively responsible policemen.

He flicked the ash and took another drag. Never before had he doubted himself. Maybe it was just the lack of sleep. He lifted the mug of lukewarm coffee and sipped at it. From the corner of his eye he could see someone approaching quickly and he turned.

'Charlie, oul' stock.' He smiled. 'How are things in the world of fingerprints?'

Charlie pulled out a chair and sat down at the other side of the table. He waited while a passer-by slapped him on the back in greeting, then glanced around before leaning forward.

'Something very unusual about those prints from the Danby case.' He pointed his finger purposefully at Donegan.

'What are you talking about, Charlie?'

'I'm talking about the prints from the dog collar. The ones that Malley left in to me for checking.'

'Oh yeah,' said Donegan. 'Those prints. What about them?' He leaned across suddenly and gripped at Charlie's wrist. 'You've got a match for us, oul' stock, haven't you?'

Charlie pulled Donegan's hand free and glanced around again. 'No, Frank. I didn't get a match on our system. But things got fairly strange when I got my man in Scotland Yard to try it on his.'

Donegan took a long pull on the cigarette and twisted the remainder in the ashtray.

'Charlie, please get to the point like a good man,' he said.

Charlie pressed his palms together and whispered in explanation.

'There was no match on file in our system, so I got on to DCI Hampton in the Yard section. He told me that it would take a while. An hour later, he phones me back. He sounded shit-scared and he wanted to know what case the print came from.'

Donegan straightened.

'You didn't tell him of course, Charlie?' he shook his head.

'No. Just that it was a murder investigation. Nothing more.'

'Well, then... Did he have a match for our print or didn't he?'

Charlie drummed his fingers nervously on the table. 'Frank, I genuinely don't know what's going on over there. Hampton phoned me back about fifteen minutes ago from his own phone. All he said was to expect communication from a much higher authority than a detective chief inspector.'

'And?'

Charlie shrugged. He was relaxed now. The message had been passed on.

'And then, we planned a fishing trip for the summer.'

'So, they must have a match for the print then?' Donegan pressed him.

'If they have, they're not letting us know. Hampton wouldn't say if they had or not.'

Donegan sat back on the chair and rolled his thumbs.

'You've been sitting in front of a computer screen for too long, Charlie,' he said with a smile. 'The reason the shit has hit the spinner over there, is that they *have* found a match for the print. Tell me what else this Hampton fella said.'

Charlie shrugged again, more nervous this time.

'He just said that he had done the check, and that

an alarm bell rang in an office a few miles away. A much bigger office than his. He got a call ten minutes later and the computer system was temporarily shut down.'

'Who called him?'

'He wouldn't say.'

'What sort of a fella is this Hampton anyway?' said Donegan. 'Is he a policeman or not?'

It was evident from Charlie's expression that he disliked the question.

'He's been very helpful to us in the past,' he replied. 'As well as being a good friend of mine.'

Donegan rapped his knuckles on the table.

'Then why the fuck won't he tell you what's happening?' he snapped.

Charlie shook his head.

'Dunno, Kig,' he sighed. 'If he knew what was going on, he'd tell me. I know that for sure.'

'Can *I* talk to him?' asked Donegan.

'I'd prefer if you didn't, Kig. In any case, he won't tell you any more than he's told me.'

'I'd like to try, Charlie, if that's OK with you. If there's something going on behind the scenes that we don't know about, I'd like to get in the picture.'

Charlie stared hard at him. He wasn't going to be bullied.

'No, Kig. You can't do that. Hampton has been a great help to us in the past when we were still at the teething stage in this computer game. And everything done off the record. He gave us a lot of print matches that we would have never got ourselves. Solved a few MCS cases as well, if I recall correctly. I don't want to repay his friendship by dragging him into the middle of this.'

Donegan smiled.

'So that's where we got all our Northern boys' prints when we needed them. Why, you cunning little devil.'

'Desperate times called for desperate measures, Kig,' said Charlie, and leaned closer with a grin. 'Surely you haven't forgotten. That era when "extradition" meant being driven to the border in the dead of night in the back of a branch car and your arse being kicked across the line to the RUC. Do you remember the lack of paperwork on those ones, Frank?'

Donegan snorted with laughter as he picked up the packet of cigarettes and rolled one between his fingers. He held out the pack to Charlie who declined with a shake of his head, still smiling.

'Ah, yes,' said Donegan, as he exhaled the smoke, breaking into semi-song, 'I remember it well.'

Charlie became serious. 'It won't take long before you hear from across the water on this, Kig,' he said. 'That's the one thing that Hampton is sure of.'

Donegan nodded and closed the newspaper slowly. He took another gulp of the cold coffee and shoved the sandwich into his jacket pocket. The cigarette hanging from his mouth, he blinked through the smoke as he folded the newspaper.

'Just don't let me be the last one to hear anything, Charlie,' he said, and stood up. He turned and lobbed the packet of cigarettes back to the donor three tables away.

Charlie looked up at him.

'Don't worry, Frank,' he promised. 'If I'm the first, then you're the second.'

Donegan winked. 'Sound man. That's good enough for me.'

He started to move towards the door, then stopped and turned back. He bent down beside Charlie's ear.

'One other thing,' he whispered. 'Don't let those original fingerprints out of your sight.'

***

Mitchell Doyle's tee-shot set off skyward with a solid crack from the driver head. The words 'Fine shot' had barely sounded from the lips of his playing partner when the ball arced wickedly to the right and drummed a quick hollow beat amongst the tall oak trees.

'Bad luck, Mitchell. It started out like the best drive of the day.'

Doyle bent down and whipped the tee from the ground in disgust.

'It's in a hell of a lot of trouble over there, Terence.'

He put the tee in his pocket and took his stance again, balancing on his feet and swinging the club back, trying to picture in his mind what had gone wrong.

Terence smiled as he watched the perfectionist at work.

'C'mon,' he said, as he pulled his trolley along the gravel path. 'You're still four strokes ahead with three to play. You can afford to be generous.'

Doyle returned to his golf bag and pulled the towel from it. As he wiped the club and watched his golf buddy walk down the fairway, his thoughts turned to Landers.

He had not heard from him in almost twenty-four hours. He felt sure that nothing had gone wrong, for if it had then it would surely have been the headline on the one o'clock news. The mobile phone in his bag was tempting. What harm could a quick progress report do? His wayward drive into the middle of the trees had presented an ideal opportunity. Luckily, Terence, a poor seventeen handicapper, would also have to do some searching in the rough on the opposite side of the fairway.

He removed the mobile phone from his golf bag and put it in his pocket as he set off down the fairway. Just a ten-second call would satisfy his curiosity. Terence waited for him in the middle of the fairway, adjusting his white sun-visor and rubbing more sun-screen on his cheekbones.

'I feel like a piece of shrivelled toast,' he joked. 'Thank God we're almost finished.'

'Now, now, Judge,' Doyle scolded. 'It's much better than sitting in a courtroom listening to horror stories and dealing with criminals, isn't it?'

Terence smiled. 'I can't say I miss it one bit, Mitchell,' he said, and then frowned suddenly. 'Now, if only I could make a hand of this sport they call golf.'

He laughed as he dragged his trolley away towards the tall grass.

'I'll just have a quick look for my ball as well,' said Doyle as he set off in the opposite direction. 'It'll save us some time.'

He stopped his trolley at the edge of the wood and pulled out a club.

He looked across the wide fairway. The retired

judge was hacking the long grass with a three iron in a futile search that would keep him busy for a lot longer time than was required to make the call.

Doyle stepped into the cool shadows of the tall trees, the dried twigs crackling like toy bangers beneath his golf shoes. He pressed the button on the phone and flicked the trickle of sweat from his earlobe before listening.

The reply was almost immediate.

'James? Mitchell Doyle.'

'This is not a very good time,' came the curt reply.

Doyle could sense the panic in Landers's voice. He moved behind one of the oak trees and looked out. This was not the response he had hoped for.

'What's gone wrong?' he asked. His breathing grew faster, the blood thumped loud at his temples. He pressed the phone hard against his ear as Landers lowered his voice to a bare whisper.

'The police, Mr Doyle. It appears that they know a lot more about what's going on than we gave them credit for. For example, I am now observing two of them who have our fifth target's house under surveillance.'

Doyle felt his legs buckle. A sudden rush of fear chilled him to his bones. He leaned against the tree for support, the club falling from his hand.

'Get out of there now. Cancel the entire operation. Your full payment will be organised as arranged.'

The words had a sudden calming effect. He was happier now that he had made the final decision.

'How do you know that they're guards?' he asked.

'Because I've trained my eyes to see,' Landers

replied. 'Not that I needed any training this time. They've been sitting in their car in a picnic area for the last two hours watching the target's house. Good job I checked before I moved, or I'd have fallen right into their lap. I'm going to have to wait until...'

The dried twigs snapped behind him and Doyle turned quickly.

'I found my one, Mitchell,' Terence declared with a smile, and then covered his mouth in apology. 'Sorry. Didn't realise you were on a call.'

Doyle dismissed the apology with a casual wave.

'So, I'll see you tomorrow sometime then,' he spoke cheerfully. 'Yes, that will all be fixed up. No need to worry yourself. Of course. Of course. Take care now.'

He looked at the phone and then threw his eyes up. 'These things can be a curse at times,' he complained and put it in his pocket. 'Never a moment's peace.'

'Then just don't carry one, Mitchell,' advised the judge and began to move away slowly, his three iron waving above the ground like some magical golf-ball detector. 'I had to chip mine back on the fairway,' he said forlornly. 'It looks like you're favourite to win our usual bet for the umpteenth time.'

Doyle walked around with his hands in his pockets, his eyes down, his thoughts a million miles from the search for the lost ball. His emotion was a mixture of anger and relief. Anger that he would have to wait to see justice finally done, and relief that he himself would not have to face it.

'Here you are, Mitchell,' Terence smiled and then clucked gently. 'MaxFli four, wasn't it?'

'Yes, that was it,' Doyle replied as he moved towards

the pointing three iron. He looked down to see the golf ball nestled deep in the twigs and leaves. He turned and marched angrily towards his golf bag.

'Shit,' he bellowed. 'There's no way I'm going to get out of this. I'm taking a penalty drop to be safe.'

***

Detective Sergeant Reidy stood looking at the piles of evidence bags strewn along the wall, containing clothes, blankets, large segments of carpet, pieces of timber. The other contents became so boring that he gave up and turned back to Malley, who sat on a high stool, his glasses perched on his head as he squinted through the microscope.

'Mmmm... Verree interessting,' he said to himself and removed the slide, marked it and selected another.

'What? What have you found?' asked Reidy anxiously. He moved towards him and looked at the tray of slides.

Malley turned with a frown. He pulled his glasses from his head and pointed with them at Reidy. 'Don't interrupt me when I'm working, young fella,' he snapped angrily. 'Why don't you go and do... go and...' He stuttered in frustration. 'If you want to stay here – then, then fuckin' shut up,' he said finally. 'I know that Donegan has you here to carry every detail back straightaway like some... some pony express rider. This is an exact science, boy. Not guesswork. So don't be rushing me now.'

Reidy looked at him for a moment. Malley turned quickly from the stare.

'I was only asking,' said Reidy. 'Maybe you haven't noticed, pal, but we're both playing for the same team.'

Malley threw his glasses on the lab-top and leaned down to examine the next slide. He turned the focus slowly and then sat upright. He changed the slide again and double-checked. 'Just as we thought, Dr Malley,' he whispered to himself.

Reidy leaned against the back wall with folded arms. He was not going to entertain this childish behaviour. Malley sat with his back to him, drumming his fingers impatiently. Finally he turned.

'Well?' he asked. 'Do you want to know what I've found here or don't you, Sergeant?'

'Jesus, make up your mind will you?' Reidy approached casually and glared at him. He was growing tired of being polite. 'Well, what is it?'

Malley smiled.

'Blood, Detective. And not the victim's.' He held up the first slide. 'This is blood from the late Mr Danby – and that slide there has the very minute traces of blood that we found on the tiles of his hall floor... and it isn't Danby's.' He looked at the detective for a moment and threw his hands out. 'So, do you want it sent for a DNA test or not?'

'Prints and DNA from the Danby scene,' said Reidy. 'And fibre evidence from Feeney's house.'

'Yeah, isn't that just marvellous?' said Malley sarcastically, as he leaned down again to the microscope. 'Now all you have to do is go out and catch the fella who matches them, Detective.'

Reidy did not appreciate the humour. He knew that Malley didn't really like him, certainly didn't enjoy having him constantly by his side in the lab.

'I'd better get the all-clear from the kig for the DNA check,' he said and turned for the door.

'Wait up there, Detective,' said Malley as he closed his folder. 'I'll go with you. I could do with the air.'

CHAPTER NINETEEN

It was almost three hours before Donegan had finally got around to finishing the last of his sandwich. He balled the plastic clingfilm in his fist, took aim at the wastebasket and prepared to throw it when the ringing of the phone on his desk halted him.

'Yes,' he answered with a full mouth.

'Frank.' It was the superintendent. 'Will you come up here a minute. I want you to hear this. It's... well, it's urgent.'

Reidy and Malley stood in the open doorway and he waved them away.

'We'll call back in half an hour,' said Malley and pulled the door closed.

Donegan tightened his tie as he left the office and walked along the corridor, stopping when an approaching detective held out a photo-fit.

'First print of the Pro-Fit from the description given by the car-park attendant, Kig,' he said.

Donegan took it and looked down at the grotesque jigsaw.

'Good Christ on a donkey,' he muttered. 'Who's this fella? He looks like something out of a leper colony. C'mon, man. Surely the computer can do better than that.'

The detective blurted out a stifled laugh. 'Well, it *is* the first attempt, Kig,' he said.

Donegan handed back the sheet.

'For God's sake try and make him look some bit human,' he said, as he went to the superintendent's door.

The super sat with his fingers interlocked beneath his chin. He looked up as Donegan entered. He tried to smile in greeting, but his face was pale with obvious concern.

'Frank, come in, come in,' he said hurriedly. 'There's something very important I want you to hear.'

Donegan nodded and looked at the other two men, who sat at either side of the desk, both of them dressed smartly in dark suits. The younger one stood up and nervously stretched out his hand. The older one remained seated, his head lowered to the file on his lap, pushing his steel-rimmed glasses up on his nose.

'Frank,' said the super, 'this is Stephen Jacobs from the Department of Foreign Affairs.'

'Pleased to meet you, Inspector,' said Jacobs.

Donegan took his hand and shook it cautiously, then looked down at the man who had remained seated.

The superintendent gestured with his hand towards him.

'And this is Ian Harris from the British Ministry of Defence.'

Harris removed his spectacles and stood up, but did not extend his hand. He snapped the spectacles shut and dropped them into the breast pocket of his suit.

'What's all this about?' asked Donegan, his eyes fixed on the superintendent.

'Sit down, Inspector, please,' said Harris calmly as he motioned to the chair he had just vacated. He closed the file and rested his rear against the front of the desk, tapping his signet ring on the edge of the file cover as he waited for Donegan to be seated.

Donegan sat down and looked again at the superintendent, who took a deep breath and appeared to hold it.

'So, what's the problem here?' asked Donegan.

Harris rose from the desk.

'Have you ever heard of 14 Intelligence Company, Inspector?' he asked.

'No,' Donegan replied with apparent lack of interest. 'What is it?'

Harris pursed his lips and looked up studiously like a professor in a lecture hall.

'14 Intelligence Company,' he began. 'A secret military unit of the British army formed in 1974, its sole purpose being to combat terrorism in Northern Ireland. Ring any bells?'

His tone was condescending. Donegan shrugged to annoy him.

'The very elite of the army,' Harris continued, unruffled. 'Forget the SAS, Inspector. The SAS are first-formers by comparison. The men and women of 14 Intelligence are the most highly skilled soldiers in the world. Undercover operatives with top knowledge of firearms, explosives and surveillance, counter-surveillance. You name it, they can do it.'

Donegan folded his arms and sat back.

'Well now Mr – eh – Harris, this is all very impressive,' he said with obvious sarcasm. 'Please let me know when you're going bring us all to the point.'

The superintendent shut his eyes.

Harris tapped the file on his chin and nodded wisely. He took his spectacles out again and flicked them open. Donegan looked across at Jacobs who had remained silent and motionless throughout. Clearly an escort from the Department of Foreign Affairs who had been told to bring Harris to the MCS office and to keep his own mouth shut at all times. He was doing well so far.

Harris cleared his throat before continuing.

'When the men and women of 14 Intelligence Company finished their tours of duty, thanks to the current climate of peace, they went back to their respective units, back to their families. Back to normality, so to speak.'

He placed the glasses on the rim of his nose and opened the file.

'All except this one – the man you are looking for, Inspector. He has obviously decided to use his skills and training for another purpose. Earlier today, a check was done by Scotland Yard on a fingerprint that turned out to be his and, naturally, our curiosity was aroused.'

Donegan sat up with interest, his hand reaching involuntarily for the file.

Harris gave a thin smile as he handed it over.

'Unfortunately, as you can see, our Official Secrets Act forbids us from giving any details, or his real name,' he said. 'In any case, he has many names, including John Sommers, aka Paul Winters, aka Richard Faul and, of course, George Spring. He's a very imaginative fellow, don't you think?'

Donegan looked down at the photograph of the man in the smart officer's tunic, down into the dark eyes of James Landers. He turned the remaining four sheets over in turn. They were blank.

He clenched his jaw. The sudden realisation of what had been said slowly dawned on him. Shit. Fox and McGrath.

'Where's the rest of this?'

Harris gave him a look of indifference. 'Come now, Inspector, you must appreciate...'

Donegan stood up quickly to the surprise of all present.

'Listen, you arrogant prick,' he spat through clenched teeth. 'If what you say is true about this soldier of yours, then I have two men in immediate danger. So cut the "secret-agent" bullshit and give me all the details.'

The superintendent glanced in puzzlement at Donegan.

'Now, now, Inspector,' said Harris calmly. 'Surely a photograph is enough for a squad of able policemen like the MCS.'

Donegan closed the file and rolled it between his hands. He moved closer and poked Harris in the chest with it. The superintendent and Jacobs stood.

Donegan's eyes narrowed. Suddenly his face relaxed.

'How come the British Ministry of Defence have suddenly become so helpful?' he asked. 'Why are you here at all? I mean – why even give a photograph? You could have buried any fingerprint search, denied that there was any match. Yet here you are. Just off a fast government jet from Heathrow, no doubt. Here to stop the rot. That's what fellas like you do, isn't it? Suits with power they shouldn't have.'

For the first time, Harris looked uncomfortable. The superintendent had been easy opposition. This inspector, however, was different.

'C'mon,' Donegan pressed him. 'What's the *real* reason?'

The superintendent moved around the desk.

'I think that's quite enough, Inspector.'

Donegan cut the objection with a glare of warning and turned back.

'I'm still waiting for your answer, Mr Harris,' he said.

Harris removed his glasses slowly and swung them gently between his middle fingers.

'You're obviously not a politician, Inspector,' he said. 'Otherwise, you would have seen the reason long before now.'

'Humour me,' said Donegan abruptly, his voice deepening. 'Pretend that I'm just a thick Paddy policeman from Cork.'

Harris folded his arms and stared hard at him.

'There is peace on this island after many years of needless killing,' he explained. 'A tentative peace, but a peace nonetheless.'

He smacked his lips. His mouth had gone dry.

'If it were to be found out that an Englishman, nay, an Irishman trained in England, an ex-British army operative, was now killing Irish citizens, be they the dregs of humanity or no, how do you think the public would react?'

Donegan eased himself back into the chair.

'Well, my first thought is that they'd be fairly cheesed off,' he said with obvious unconcern. 'So, we're into the *cover-up* scenario, are we?'

Harris sat back on the edge of the desk. He took a deep breath, as if composing himself, and exhaled slowly through his nose.

'Inspector,' he said, 'this goes much further than the killing of a drug-dealer or a child molester – not forgetting, of course, that Danby was, after all, British.'

'I see that you've been brought up to date on all our affairs, Mr Harris.'

Donegan gave the superintendent an accusing glance as he spoke.

'Well, as you can imagine, Inspector, any such publicity would be detrimental to the good relations that exists between the two governments at present. And you wouldn't want to jeopardise that, would you?'

He did not wait for a response.

'All we ask, Inspector, is that if you capture our man alive, you turn him over to us. Warn your own men of the dangerous individual they are dealing with. There is little likelihood that he will give up easily, so I suggest that you prepare them for a violent engagement when the time comes.'

Donegan looked at him for a moment. He had heard of people like Harris, but never really believed in their existence. Seen fictional characters like him on television and read about them in spy novels. Men who sat in plush government offices with a portrait of the Queen hanging behind them, puffing on King Edward cigars and using words like 'terminate' and 'liquidate'.

He shook his head in disbelief and gave a contemptuous laugh.

'You'd like that, wouldn't you?' he said. 'Unknown killer slain in shoot-out with gardaí.'

Harris pursed his lips. 'Well, Inspector, I believe that it would be the most appropriate ending to this tragic sequence of events. I get the feeling that you disagree?'

The office remained silent for a moment as the others waited for Donegan to answer.

He looked down and opened the file. He studied the photograph for a moment before folding it and putting it in his jacket pocket. He closed the file and held it out to Harris.

'Peace process, my arse,' he said quietly. 'You're here because this Winters or Faul, or whatever the hell you call him, has done this type of thing before. Trained by the British government. And now he's what's known as a "smoking gun". Isn't that right, Mr

Harris? Well now, let me make myself very clear. I'm giving you one hour to fill this with the information that I need before any of my men get hurt. If I don't get what I want, then you can watch the story you've told me on the six o'clock news.'

Harris did not take the file. Donegan released his grip on it and the cover and blank sheets fell to the floor.

The superintendent stood up quickly and placed his clenched fists, knuckles down, on the desk.

Donegan nodded at Harris and started to move.

'Frank,' said the superintendent, 'all Mr Harris has done is to warn us how dangerous this person is. Nothing more. I think you've misread the situation.'

Donegan stopped and looked back. 'It's a bit late for putting the shit back in the horse now, Superintendent,' he said disdainfully.

He turned to Harris.

'If I ever join a death-squad, I'll give you a buzz,' he said. 'In the meantime, I intend to catch this Irishman and march him up the steps of the courts. By the way, as my superintendent here can confirm, I have just become very good friends with an enthusiastic journalist,' he warned. 'You've got one hour, Mr Harris.'

He pulled the door closed and walked quickly down the corridor. Inside his office, he searched frantically through the laminated phone list for Fox's mobile number.

'Oh sweet Jesus,' he whispered as he searched.

***

McGrath yawned loudly as he rubbed his eyes and ran his hand across the bristle on his chin. He straightened up in the seat and looked at Fox, who was munching pensively on a handful of crisps.

'Anything?' he asked.

Fox shook his head slowly. 'Now *this* is what I call boring,' he said.

McGrath turned and looked down at the picnic area below. Two small children ran around a rough wooden table as their mother fussed over the large basket and their father struggled in vain to light the portable barbecue. An elderly couple sat on folding chairs in the shade at the open boot of their car, the man pouring steaming hot tea from a large, tartan flask. At the entrance to the picnic area, a man stretched himself on the long bench beside the table, his hand hanging over the side and holding a can of beer. He was middle-aged, wearing an American T-shirt and bright shorts, his red baseball cap turned back to front, his large sunglasses concealing whether he was snoozing or looking up at the trees.

'Do you want to go and stretch your legs or something?' asked McGrath. 'I'll take over for a couple of hours.'

Again Fox gave a shake of his head. 'Nah,' he said quietly. 'My body is gone kinda numb. And that suits me fine. I'll stay here and try not to be brain dead when you get back.'

'Did you see any sign of Doherty yet?' asked McGrath looking at the house.

'Yeah, he's in there. One of the curtains opened and that was it. The lazy bastard probably went back to bed. He's a real nightlifer I'd say.'

McGrath reached back and picked up the half-empty bottle of orange. He spat the first mouthful through the open window. 'Jesus, it's boiling,' he said with disgust.

'Yeah, the sun'll do that,' said Fox as he raised the binoculars. He searched left and right and then dropped them back on his lap. 'Now I know what it's like to be a wildlife cameraman,' he said. 'Sitting on your arse for hours in the scalding heat beside a water hole, waiting for Mrs Lion to come and bite off Mrs Wildebeest's head. The only difference with us is that we have to shoot Mrs Lion when she arrives.'

'Ahem. I think you'll find that the word is "arrest", Detective,' corrected McGrath.

'Yeah. Whatever.'

'I wonder if they're making much progress back at base,' said McGrath. 'A match for the print maybe?'

'Yeah,' grumbled Fox. 'You'd think that they'd keep us informed, wouldn't you? Just because we've been handed this shit tour doesn't mean that we're off the panel. I'm beginning to wonder if it was the super's idea instead of Donegan's to send the two of us down here. It's like something that he'd come up with to keep us out of the game.'

McGrath looked at him. 'C'mon, you don't mean that. If you think that's what happened it means that you doubt Donegan.'

'Course I don't doubt him,' snapped Fox. 'I'm getting a little anxious, that's all. Here we are like Hansel and fuckin' Gretel in the middle of the woods, burning up with the heat, nobody telling us anything and nothing left but half a bottle of hot orange and a toasted roll.'

McGrath took in what had been said for a moment, then swivelled his head around and searched the back seat.

'Jesus Christ,' he protested. 'You don't mean to tell me that you ate...'

Fox's mobile rang. He lifted his hand to pacify McGrath.

'It's Donegan,' he confirmed as he looked at the screen.

'Kig,' he said cheerfully, into the phone. 'Yes, I can hear you loud and clear.'

His eyebrows narrowed as he listened intently.

'Do we go there straightaway?' he asked, then flinched at the answer.

'And what about Doherty, Kig?' he asked sheepishly.

Even McGrath could hear the inspector's loud response from where he was sitting.

'Do what you're told, Fox.'

'Gotcha,' he said and threw the phone up on the dashboard. 'We're free to go,' he said pointing ahead. 'He wants us to go to the local station and contact him from there. Says he's sending down a fax and that he's giving the local sergeant the full rundown.'

McGrath started the car and began to drive away. 'Well, did they get our man or didn't they?' he asked.

Fox shrugged. 'He didn't say.'

'Well, it seems a bit stupid if they haven't, doesn't it,' McGrath said, surprised. 'I mean there was so much importance placed on this Doherty fella. And now we just drive away and leave everything to chance. Is that the plan?'

Fox tapped his hand on the open window ledge.

'Yeah, seems a bit ridiculous all right,' he agreed. 'Donegan did say something at the start about the two of us not being enough, just before he started roaring at me.'

'Not being enough for what?'

'Dunno,' said Fox and motioned with his hands towards the road. 'The quicker we get down there the sooner we'll find out.'

McGrath increased speed along the narrow country road until he reached the junction, then slowed as they drove into the village. A tall, grey-haired sergeant stood waiting outside the low wrought-iron gate of the station. McGrath pulled the car alongside.

Fox stepped out quickly and extended his hand.

'Detectives Fox and McGrath of the MCS.' He smiled.

The sergeant nodded solemnly and gestured with his hand towards the door of the station, shaking McGrath's hand as he passed.

'I've been expecting ye, lads,' he said. 'I was just talking with your Inspector Donegan.'

He followed them in the door of the station to the small day room and pointed to the fax machine. 'He said he'll be sending a message in the next few minutes.'

'Thanks for the help,' said McGrath.

'Sit down there for yerselves,' he said. 'I just put the kettle on. That's an awful job ye had today, stuck out in that place. Reminds me of the time I spent up on the border.'

And with that he disappeared into the hallway.

'What kind of a fax is that?' enquired McGrath.

'A one from the Middle Ages by the look of it,' replied Fox.

The sergeant returned a few minutes later, smiling. He clapped his large hands together as he strolled around the counter.

'Tea is just drawing,' he said. 'So, someone has come all the way down here to kill Pat Doherty,' he said. He boomed a short laugh as he sat down behind his desk. 'Now, who in their right mind would waste their time and energy killing a big, useless gobshite like that fella?'

It was evident that Donegan had not revealed everything to the jovial sergeant.

'Well, he must have enemies,' said Fox innocently.

'Enemies?' the sergeant repeated in mock surprise and laughed again. 'Not counting myself, I'd say about three hundred. He's an awful gouger and a bully. But I doubt if anyone would kill him for that.'

He picked up a plastic biro from his desk and tapped it annoyingly on the edge as he spoke. 'I remember one night a couple of years back, a few of the local men decided that they had put up with his carry on long enough. They formed a gang of five and, being big GAA fans, they decided that they'd get him walking home, jump him and beat the shit out of him with hurleys.'

McGrath laughed. 'And?'

'And nothing,' smiled the sergeant. 'Ye're in Kerry now, lads. Hurleys are scarce, and drunken late-night co-operation even more so.'

The fax machine buzzed and all turned to it.

'It can be very slow when it wants to,' the sergeant warned. 'But the print is good.'

He wasn't lying. For every fifteen seconds of buzzing a millimetre of paper appeared. Fox grew tired of watching it and leaned down on the counter.

'How is it that one fella can cause so much hassle in a small place like this?' he mused.

The sergeant eyed him.

'I know what you're thinking, young fella,' he said. 'That the local guards don't do anything about him and let him do what he wants. Well, you're wrong. You're in the job long enough to know that if we don't have a complaint in writing, there's not a damn thing we can do about him. And no one ever makes one. Personally speaking, I annoy and harass the bastard every chance I get. Maybe I'm getting a bit sadistic in my old age. Only last night I made it my business to see that he walked the couple of miles home and left his car. Drunk as a skunk and not a peck of insurance on it. God forgive me, I suppose I was silently hoping that he'd get knocked down or fall into a drain and that'd be the end of it.'

Fox looked at McGrath and shook his head.

'Well, I'm afraid you didn't do a very good job there, Sarge,' he smiled.

The sergeant threw the biro on the desk and looked at the two detectives in turn. 'What do you mean by that now, young fella?' he asked.

'I mean that he *did* drive home. Or someone drove it for him,' replied Fox. 'His car is parked right outside his door. And I have to say, she's a fine-looking bus.'

The sergeant swallowed hard and looked back at the fax machine. 'Ah, there's a lot of rust on it,' he muttered and then changed to a snarl. 'Jaysus, the fat, sneaky bastard must have collected it some time this evening.'

'No, no,' Fox pressed on. 'It's been there all day.'

The sergeant looked at him with a furrowed brow.

'Well, you're the one who's wrong now, Detective!' he said. 'Doherty's white Jaguar is parked in the village all day. I made it my business to put a ticket for no tax on it after I had the dinner. Things like that are good for a man's digestion.'

McGrath's face sagged as he looked at Fox, who in turn paled to a light cream as he moved slowly from the counter to the desk.

'Doherty doesn't drive a zero one, dark-blue Rover 750 then?' he ventured, his heart beginning to race.

The sergeant eased back on his chair and gave a sarcastic laugh. 'Yerra, not at all. What put that into yer heads?'

Fox pulled at McGrath's jacket and headed for the door.

'Get back on to Inspector Donegan and explain what's happened,' he shouted at the sergeant. 'Tell him we're on our way back to Doherty's house. Notify the local detective branch and tell them to get everyone who is working here as quick as they can.'

They had both gone before the sergeant could voice a question. He picked up the phone and dialled Donegan's number.

'Yes, Inspector Donegan, Sergeant Power back to you again. Yes, I had the two of them in here just a minute ago, nice lads...' He began to explain the mix-up of vehicles and how both detectives were heading back to Doherty's house. He listened to further instructions from a clearly panicking Inspector Donegan and nodded in the emptiness of the day room.

'I understand exactly, Inspector,' he said calmly, then added, ''Tis a pity – all this confusion could have been avoided if only ye had contacted the local men.'

CHAPTER TWENTY

Pat Doherty was dead. And he didn't even know it.

Landers had shot him from point-blank range through the temple with a silenced .22 calibre wax-coated bullet while he snored on his stomach like a blubbery suckling sow. It was a bullet that served a very specific purpose. Hard enough to penetrate soft human bone and do severe internal damage. Soft enough to lose its coating and remove any chance of identifying the weapon that had fired it.

Landers had fired the fatal shot at 10.45am that morning. It was now 5.50pm, and Landers was driving the Rover away from Doherty's cottage.

He pulled at his loosened tie, lifted it over his head

and threw it on the back seat. Although he cursed through his teeth, a wave of relief rushed over him. He had spent the better part of the past seven hours in the small, revolting kitchen, sitting in the shadow of a tall press, squinting his eyes through a gap in the curtains as he watched the activities of the two undercover policemen sitting in their car in the cul-de-sac of the picnic area. He had expected the doors to crash in at any moment from all sides, followed by a burst of gunfire and loud roars demanding surrender.

But these policemen were amateurs even at surveillance. If they had done their job properly, then he would never have seen them and would have walked out into certain capture, or maybe even death.

And then, for no particular reason, they had gone. Why?

He had to be sure that a more elaborate trap had not been set. He checked his rear mirror every ten seconds for almost half an hour, settling the car in the shelter of an articulated lorry just in case there was a checkpoint ahead and he needed to turn in a hurry.

Eighty miles and an hour and a half later, he turned off the main road onto a country lane that divided two expansive wheatfields, and drove on until he had a clear view of the road in both directions. The only house visible was a black speck in the distance. He stopped the car and stepped out, gasping, holding his head back to let the rivulets of sweat run through his hair. He opened the boot and checked both empty briefcases. He had burned the incriminating file in the fireplace of the large sitting room that morning he left, before bidding Haskard a casual farewell.

There was nothing to connect him to the killing. Nothing except the hand-sized .22 with which he had killed Doherty. And it was too early in the game to dispose of that.

He pulled his shirt over his head and used it to wipe the sweat from his armpits, then stood there for a moment to let the cool evening breeze calm him before removing a fresh, white T-shirt from the suitcase. He pondered his predicament as he put it on, then sat on the open ledge of the car boot and folded his arms. After a moment, he reached back and took a folded map from the suitcase, examining it to find the next large town. Returning directly to the city to pick up his carefully stashed money, packed in piles of fifty-pound notes in a cardboard box in his locker at the health club, would involve an element of risk in light of recent events. The police had a vague description of him, and the car had been spotted. And Doyle, his employer, had become unusually nervous for some reason or other. For the first time since he had taken the assignment, Landers felt that he was becoming the hunted. He wondered if he should cut his losses and forget about the money for the time being. After all, his locker wasn't going anywhere. His health-club membership was good for another nine months – enough time for the heat to die down. He had enough for the moment in the payment that Doyle had given him for Danby.

He stood up suddenly and threw the map back in the boot. It wasn't worth the risk. The money was over a hundred miles away. The first thing that would have to be done now was to change his mode of transport.

At the next town he would abandon the car, stay in a low-key hotel for the night and get out of the country through a southern port the following morning. A tractor chugged away in the distance and Landers waited until the sound had lowered to a faint ticking on the horizon.

He drove back onto the main road, headed for the next town and made his way to the centre. He drove through the streets a number of times, his eyes picking out the hotels and side-alleys. Within ten minutes he had parked in a derelict side street, wiped the car and the empty briefcases of prints, and was carrying his suitcase through the doors of a hotel.

***

The enthusiastic recruit on the beat sixty miles back the road had done his job well. He had listened intently to the message over his walkie-talkie. The make and number of the car, the description of the driver, followed by an instruction that any sighting should be reported immediately. A murder had been committed in the small village of Lishane in Kerry earlier that evening and the suspect was possibly headed in his direction. A guard for less than four months, it was for excitement just like this that he had joined. The only disappointment came with the order that under no circumstances should the driver be approached.

He had abandoned the menial task of issuing parking tickets and positioned himself in a doorway that gave a clear view of the main street. His meal-break had come and gone unnoticed. He was determined to be the one who started the ball rolling.

His dedication paid off as the blue Rover with Landers at the wheel drove slowly through the evening traffic. He steadied his hand and pressed the mike on the collar of his shirt.

'Two two four to base. That car has just passed.' He could barely contain the excitement in his voice.

Moments later, he stepped from the shadows as the unmarked Garda car pulled up.

'Headed that way,' he said, pointing.

'Good work, young fella.'

The tyres squeaked in protest as the car pulled away.

***

Donegan had immediately summoned the assistance of the Emergency Response Unit as well as the surveillance squad. He knew that once he kept Landers in sight, he could choose where and when he would close the net. The Garda helicopter joined the operation and had spotted the car ten miles from the town. It kept all units informed of his movements. The observer had given their final message as Landers entered the hotel, and repeated it once more before it veered back towards the city.

Things were beginning to come together.

Still, there would be a lot of answering to do after the Doherty fiasco. Donegan had made arrangements to meet Fox and McGrath in the town station. The three of them could start preparing their defence then.

He rubbed the tips of his fingers wearily across his forehead. Reidy, in the driver's seat, looked at him, reading his thoughts.

'Why should you worry, Kig?' he said. 'You did everything you could.'

Donegan shook his head as if he didn't have much faith in Reidy's assessment.

'How much longer?' he asked looking at his watch.

'We'll be there in twenty minutes. The surveillance team is in place. Have you decided how you're going to work it?'

Donegan swallowed.

'The shit's really going to fly over Doherty,' he whispered, ignoring the question. 'What in the name of God was I thinking? Jesus Christ! When it gets out that two of the squad were actually watching the house...'

'He could have been dead long before Fox and McGrath got there,' Reidy offered. 'This fella is some sort of ghost. No one could second guess him.'

'But we did,' Donegan cut him short. 'The car was parked in front of the house. And Landers was inside.' He rubbed his fingers across his forehead again. 'Jesus Christ!' He almost laughed at how crazy it all sounded. 'The super's going to have a field day.'

A faint smile cracked on Reidy's lips as he looked back at the darkening road. He flicked on the parking lights. 'You took a risk, Kig,' he said. 'If you'd stuck to the rules, we'd never have this fella cornered like a rat. So with all due respect, fuck the superintendent, and the rules as well. We're going to get a result.'

Donegan looked at him and smiled. In all the time he had been in the squad, he had never heard Reidy use the F-word before.

'Yeah,' he half laughed. 'Dead right, Sergeant.'

Reidy looked at him and turned back to the road. 'Dead right,' he repeated and waited for a moment before asking. 'So who's going to take the capture?'

'We are,' said Donegan firmly. 'It might work in our favour when it comes to the public inquiry. You know: Guards make a balls of it but then do something good.'

'So the ERU don't get near him then?' Reidy sounded pleased.

'The Emergency lads are here strictly as backup. It's just you, me, Fox and McGrath going in and...' He stopped as he realised the relevance of Reidy's question. 'You'll be the one to charge him, Alan, if that's what you're asking.' He smiled. 'It should look good on your promotion CV.'

'I appreciate that,' said Reidy without emotion.

***

'We're fucked, we're gonna be sacked.' McGrath thumped his head back on the passenger seat. 'The laughing stock of the job.'

His stomach churned. He was glad that he had turned over the job of driving. Fox drummed his hands on the steering wheel and whistled the William Tell overture as they approached the town from the opposite side. The report from the Garda helicopter over the walkie-talkie to the surveillance unit had given him a new lease of life. McGrath, however, had resigned himself to the possibility that they, along with Donegan, would face a kangaroo court, be dismissed on the spot and he would lose girlfriend and house in that order.

'Ah! Give over your whingeing,' Fox snapped as he pulled the car across the road, skidded to a halt and wound down the window.

A man walking two fawn-coloured greyhounds pulled on their leads like a farmer halting two plough horses.

'Where's the Garda station here?' asked Fox, and then listened to the directions.

'Thanks,' he said and began to drive away. 'They're fine-looking dogs you have.'

The man was visibly pleased by the compliment.

The big Garda station yard was surrounded by a sixteen-foot high stone wall. Fox drove in and nodded his head in the direction of the three high-powered cars parked side by side. A group of ten stood at the rear of the cars as the black kit bags were handed out.

'Looks like the heavy hitters have arrived,' he said dryly. 'I hope they don't think that they're going to steal our thunder.'

McGrath cursed them under his breath. 'Do you think they know about our little adventure in the woods?'

His question was to be answered.

One of the ERU squad laughed as he dropped his kit bag and took a few steps forward. He smiled as he leaned down beside the window.

Fox knew him. 'Oh, please no,' he whispered.

'Well, well, Andy. Tell us, now, is there any truth in the rumour that you two sleuths are going to become lecturers in surveillance at the Garda College?'

The others behind him roared with laughter.

Fox pushed the door open purposely ramming it against the ERU man's legs.

He stood out and stretched as he looked at them.

'Why don't you airheads do something useful for a change? Like go and spit-shine your sergeant,' he said.

The entire group laughed. McGrath got out and attempted a smile. The banter continued for a minute, Fox giving as good as he got. McGrath refused to get into the spirit of things as the other members of the unit ganged up on Fox with the verbals.

He was glad when he saw Donegan's car drive into the yard with Reidy at the wheel. The relief was to be short-lived.

Donegan stood out and looked across at some of the ERU men who were still laughing at one of Fox's put-downs. Even in the fading light, his face looked flushed. He slammed the door and walked directly up to one of the younger men, who looked down at him.

'Do you think this is some kind of joke, do you?'

The ERU man dropped the smile. 'Yeah. As a matter of fact it was a joke that was cracked. And exactly who might you be now?'

Those present who knew Donegan looked at the ground, Fox and McGrath included.

'I'm Inspector Frank Donegan, the man in charge of this operation. And the last thing I need in my way is a gorilla with a sense of humour. Do you understand me? Nod if you have English, boy.'

The ERU man nodded. 'I get it. You're the man in charge of this entire operation.'

Donegan turned and walked slowly away.

'Jaysus, Inspector, you must be *fierce* proud of developments so far.'

Donegan turned and sprang on the ERU man.

'Why you fu–'

They were separated quickly, men from both sides looking around quickly to check for any outside witnesses. Donegan shrugged Fox's arm from his shoulder and stepped forward as he straightened his tie back into place.

'Get one thing straight here and now,' he panted. 'I've had a tough few days and 'twould be a fierce mistake to upset me any more than I am. Bring whatever shit it is that you fellas carry and follow me inside. A room has been set up.'

He walked back and stopped in front of Fox and McGrath.

'Let's get this circus over with,' he said.

Fox lifted his hands.

'I know we bollocksed it up, Kig. He was in the house when we arrived. We never went near the local lads and the car threw us out. Christ, if only we had waited, we'd have had him cold.'

Donegan slapped him on the shoulder and pulled him away from the leaning ears of the ERU. McGrath followed and a huddle formed at the rear of the car.

'I doubt if ye'd have outwitted him, boy. He's about five lifetimes of training and discipline out of our league. He's an ex-British army operative in his mid-forties. And, according to the rest of the file I got on him, he makes that group over there look like a bunch of nancy-boys with spud-guns. I've even considered calling in the Rangers, just to be safe.'

'And who's with him now?' The urgency was apparent in Fox's tone.

'Don't worry. I've got the three best surveillance men in the job watching him. They took his shadow as soon as the chopper left. All I know is that they won't lose or spook him.'

'Yeah. Thanks, Kig. Vote of confidence badly needed there.' McGrath dropped his head. The blood had drained from his face.

Donegan moved into the centre of the huddle.

'Listen, McGrath. I haven't the time right now to be taking you aside and massaging your ego. Find a woman to do that for you. The Doherty problem is mine and mine alone. So straighten that long back and try and take a little example from Fox here, who, quite obviously, doesn't give a shit about that small mishap.'

'The inspector is right, Bob,' smiled Fox. 'All we should be thinking about now is snapping the cuffs closed on this fucker.'

'How do you intend to do it, Inspector?' asked Reidy calmly, from where he stood at the car door.

'According to surveillance, he's checked into the hotel. Room 16. We have one man inside. The other two covering front and rear.'

'Excuse me, Inspector,' Reidy interrupted. 'But should we not save all this until we have the ERU and local detectives at the briefing?'

'The ERU will be nothing but a perimeter fence,'

Donegan snapped at him. 'I want to take this bastard alive to answer a few questions. This arrest belongs to the MCS.'

His words made Fox strain at the leash.

'When do we take him, Kig?' he asked.

'First things first. We get our personnel into position and the civilians out of the danger area. Then we can sit back and pick our time.'

The radio crackled on the dashboard and Reidy stretched in for the mike.

'Go ahead.'

'Put me on to Inspector Donegan.'

Reidy strained the coiled flex and handed the mike to Donegan. 'It's the super.'

'Great. Donegan here. Go ahead.'

'I'll be with you in fifteen minutes, Inspector.' The irritation was tangible.

Donegan's jaw clenched shut.

'We'll be waiting for you,' he replied through his teeth.

CHAPTER TWENTY-ONE

Mitchell Doyle placed his knife and fork side by side on the half-empty plate. 'That was just wonderful.'

His wife touched the side of her mouth with a napkin and craned her neck like a bird to inspect what he had left.

'You haven't eaten your broccoli,' she scolded. 'It's so good for you.'

'No, it isn't,' Doyle smiled. 'Broccoli tastes like... well, it doesn't taste of anything at all. If there was a taste for green, then it would be broccoli.'

She smiled and resumed eating.

'How was your round of golf?' she asked. 'I hope you didn't overdo it.'

Doyle swiped the napkin from his lap and laid it beside the plate. He struggled to appear calm. He had developed a slight ache on his cheekbones from straining to smile, appear content and hide the anxiety that trembled inside him. He hoped that his efforts weren't too obvious.

'It was the usual hundred-euro bet,' he replied. 'Terence is the worst golfer I've ever seen. The man has no co-ordination whatsoever. A golf club in his hands? He may as well have a club with a big nail through it.'

He was pleased when she laughed.

'So you won again?'

'Yes, but I didn't have the heart to take his money so we went double or quits on a three-foot putt at the eighteenth.'

'And he beat you?'

'I let him win, my love,' Doyle corrected her.

She gave a coy smile and rose from the table, taking her own plate and walking around until she was standing beside him.

'That was very nice of you.'

She laughed softly as she placed her plate on his and took them into the kitchen.

Doyle sat alone at the end of the polished dining table, resting his face in the palms of his hands. It greatly disturbed him – the vengeance he had longed for would have to wait for another day. How often he had pictured it in his mind. The day of their release. A release that would not even warrant a mention on the early news bulletin.

But they would have made the evening news. Oh

yes. No doubt. The very first headline.

He stirred from his misery as his wife returned and put the coffee-pot on the table. As she left, his thoughts returned to the task in hand.

It was obvious that his contact had been correct. The gardaí were on to Landers. Now, every tie would have to be severed. Landers would return when the time was right and finish the job. Even if it took a year. Even ten years. He relaxed back on the chair as he consoled himself with that fact. They would never get away with it.

There was still some cleaning up to do. After his phone conversation with Landers from the golf club, a nervous chill had run through him. Although the worry had subsided, it stung to the bone now and then without warning.

He glanced at his watch. There was still an hour before they closed and there was no time like the present.

His wife returned and they chatted casually for nearly ten minutes. At the end, Doyle tactfully brought up an incident, mentioned a friend and then cursed at his watch as he claimed that he had promised a meeting for a quick drink that very night.

'You should write these things down, Mitchell,' she said as she watched him fuss in the hallway. 'You're getting very forgetful lately.'

He pecked her on the cheek and made his way quickly to the door. He stopped with his hand on the latch and turned back.

'Almost forgot.' He brushed past her into the sitting room.

The soft warm lighting of the room was matched by the soothing music of Handel.

He moved in front of the chair, looked at his daughter and smiled. He moved around her and knelt down. She looked back at him with her dark-brown eyes, and for a fleeting moment he could have sworn that she had returned the smile. He kissed her gently on the forehead. 'Good night, Princess,' he whispered.

'Don't be long,' his wife called after him, as he left.

His mind checked through every detail as he drove through the almost empty streets. He convinced himself that he was about to dispose of the only thing that could link him to Landers. It was the emergency plan. If in doubt, cut all ties with Landers. And right now, he was in doubt. He faintly regretted the fact that he had not listened to the advice of his contact who knew the system so well. Still, beneath the faint regret was a quiet confidence that *he* would not be the one to pay the piper if it all went wrong.

He pulled in beside the kerb and stopped. The lights were still on in the building and people were chatting in the lobby. He pushed through the glass doors and nodded a greeting at a man in the group who was barely known to him.

'Mr Doyle!' The receptionist's shrill voice called behind him.

He turned and tried to smile.

'Mr Doyle, the gym is closed for cleaning, but you can use the sauna and jacuzzi.'

He walked towards her and rested his hands on the counter.

'Don't worry yourself, young lady,' he promised.

'I'm just here to pick up some of my tennis gear. My last doubles partner told me it was time I had it washed, if you get my meaning.'

'I didn't know you played tennis, Mr Doyle.' She smiled as she pictured the sixty-something in his usual pose on the exercise bike. And, even then, he only stayed there for ten minutes before retreating to the steam-room.

'I've suddenly got a new lease of life,' he said and headed for the locker-room door.

He checked the room before removing his keys and searching for the one he had had cut to deliver all payments to Landers's locker as he had been instructed. He moved three lockers down from his own and unlocked number 240. He worked quickly, taking an empty black sportsbag from the back of the locker and pulling the contents of the locker into it, first a sellotaped cardboard box, then a bundle of copied files, and finally a layer of tracksuits and running shoes. He had no idea that the cardboard box contained Landers's stash of notes, assumed it was just more files.

Wipe your prints, his subconscious whispered.

He worked quicker now, swallowing hard as he rubbed the inside of the locker with one of Landers's flannel cloths, slammed the door with his elbow and picked up the sportsbag.

It was heavier than he had expected. His arm muscles strained as he crossed the lobby.

'Amazing how heavy a couple of rackets and a few wet towels can get,' he remarked as he passed the desk.

'Good night, Mr Doyle,' said the receptionist.

The bag crashed like a battering ram against the door.

'Yes, yes, my dear, good night,' he puffed, and swayed out onto the street.

He heaved the bag onto the back seat and sat in the car with the air-conditioning set to maximum. Once he had calmed down, he drove to the outskirts of the city and searched for a quiet spot. He parked his car and removed the bag. He decided to take it further along the canal, out of sight of the road. He struggled for almost ten minutes along the narrow pathway and then with a final effort flung into the water. He had hoped that it would reach the centre, but it had only rolled down the bank and floated for a moment on the edge before disappearing. Well, it had sunk anyway. Nothing, in his experience, that went into that canal ever came out of it again. He watched until the last bubbles rose to the surface. That much was done anyway.

And then came a roar.

'What kind of a bollocks are you? It's no wonder there isn't any fuckin' fish.'

Doyle gasped and looked to his left. In the fading light on the opposite side of the canal, a skinhead in a Parka jacket approached from a hundred yards away, an approach that would have been much quicker but for the oversize waders that flapped across his legs. He jerked his small fishing rod forward as he roared, the silver spinner wrapping itself around the tip.

Doyle turned his face away and headed back towards his car. The protest echoed around him as he passed under the arch of the canal bridge.

'Dump yer shit somewhere else, ya fuckin' bollocks.'

Doyle took a deep breath to steady his nerves. It was all right. The skinheaded fisherman wasn't going to go investigating what he'd thrown in. He was only mouthing off.

He was suddenly startled by the sound of his phone and he struggled to pull it from his pocket as he walked.

'Yes,' he panted.

He listened intently, his pace quickening as he neared the car.

'Oh! Christ, no!'

He hung up.

And then he ran.

He ran until his chest hurt.

***

Even though he knew that they had all seen the photograph, Donegan insisted on handing one to each man anyway. It made him feel better. Reassured him. Nothing was going to be left to chance.

'James Landers,' he announced to the room. 'Irishman, ex-British army, highly trained, extremely dangerous and, according to the last report from surveillance, is currently tucking into a tantalising feast of smoked salmon and mussels on a bed of home-baked brown soda in Room 16 of the Hayes Arms Hotel.'

He allowed for a weighty pause and looked around.

'I want to make one thing very clear, gentlemen. This one is to be taken alive. We have him in a confined area and that's where we're going to take him. We'll go through the setup of the perimeter in a minute.'

He eyed the ERU men. 'And I want to emphasise *alive.* This scumbag is responsible for five murders, maybe more. We're still waiting for the tally to come in. We know the *who.* What I want to know now is the *why.* This fella didn't just turn into a psycho overnight.' He opened the red file. 'I have his full profile here.'

The superintendent gave a gentle cough and stood up.

'Safety is of the essence here, men. The ERU will set up the perimeter, sealing off all exits. Civilians have been discreetly removed from rooms above, below and beside Room 16.'

Donegan rolled out a large sheet of paper on which a crude but accurate map of the hotel, showing all possible escape routes, had been drawn. On the top right-hand corner was a layout of Room 16. The group in the room stood up and moved forward.

'When do we go?' asked one.

'When we get the all-clear from surveillance,' replied Donegan. 'Sergeant, situate your men as you deem fit on the perimeter I've marked. This has become something of a face-slapping contest with our squad. So only my men go in for the capture. No offence, Sarge.'

The sergeant, who had served with Donegan a number of years before and knew him, leaned across the map.

'None taken, Frank,' he replied. 'But mark this well. If our Mr Landers wakes up, shoots the four of you and runs out the back door, then you're going to need mystic fuckin' Mary to ask him any questions. *You* may be prepared to risk your life to get a few answers, but my guys aren't really into that whole whodunit business.'

The superintendent lifted his eyebrows and gave an unintentional laugh.

'Well, I think you've made your point, Sergeant. Thank you for your dedication.' He picked up the plan of the hotel and held it out. 'Set up your perimeter.'

He waited until the sergeant was back with his squad before he beckoned to Reidy, Fox and McGrath.

'So, Frank,' said the super, 'let's hear it.'

'Right,' said Donegan. 'Alan and I will go through the door. Detectives Fox and McGrath will cover the fire-escape corridor and lobby respectively. We want to take him by surprise. Cuff him and get him out without any fuss.'

The superintendent looked at the four of them.

'Sounds like a steady enough setup. Get him out quietly and what we do with him after... well, that may be taken out of our hands.'

'And exactly what in the name of shite does that mean, Superintendent, if you'll pardon my bad Irish?' McGrath furrowed his eyes in confusion, his face unusually pale apart from the black bags under his eyes. 'Look, I've resigned myself to the fact that we're trying to clean up a mess here that can never be cleaned up. And the more I hear, the more I realise that we're only being told what we *have to hear*. So, what I want to know at this stage – and it may sound a little selfish in light of what's going on – but is there any way that we can hold on to our jobs when it's all over?'

'What makes you think that your job is in any jeopardy, Detective?'

'Because he's having one of his nervous breakdowns,' Fox intervened and slapped a weary-looking McGrath on the shoulder. 'Happens once every two rosters. I usually just give him a shot of steroids and a kick in the hole and he's fine after a couple of hours.'

The superintendent looked with concern at Donegan, who threw his eyes up.

'Don't even think about it, sir,' he said. 'You only see them now and then. I have to put up with this every day.'

The superintendent appeared unconvinced. He moved away from the table followed by a smiling Donegan.

'Just make sure that you don't fuck this up, Frank,' he whispered. 'The outcome of this will decide whether we end up with feathers in our caps or those shiny, store-security badges.'

Donegan watched the superintendent leave the room and returned to the table.

'What exactly is your problem, McGrath?' he asked, shaking his head in confusion.

'Nothing, Kig. I don't know, I just feel kinda hot and – I just don't know how I feel. I feel like I'm going to... to puke.'

The three of them took a quick step back as the contents of McGrath's stomach erupted in a geyser that would have done any special-effects man proud.

He wiped his mouth, gave a stupid smile and blindly reached for a chair behind him. Some of the ERU men stood up and looked with expressions of concern.

'Jesus Christ,' Donegan pulled the chair and settled McGrath into it. 'Don't just stand there, Fox. Get a doctor. What is it, Bob? What's wrong with you?'

He stood back as McGrath's shoulders lifted. All he emitted on this occasion was a forced groan and a belch.

'I'm OK, Kig. I've felt queasy for a couple of hours...'

He turned his head to Fox who was on the phone asking the station orderly to send for a doctor.

'Any doctor will do. He's after throwing up – and he's gone a sorta quare colour.'

He cupped his hand over the mouthpiece and turned back to them.

'It's probably those rolls you had. Or the orange, it got hot, remember?'

McGrath heaved again. 'Oh, God. Food poisoning!' he croaked. 'How come you're not puking? You had the same as me.'

Fox gave some more information on the phone and then turned.

'C'mon, Bob. You've seen my fridge, haven't you?'

'Jesus, I ate out of his fridge as well.' McGrath tried to smile. 'We'll never find an antidote now.'

Nerves, thought Donegan. He'd seen it before.

'If you've quite finished, Detective,' he said aloud, 'you might go and find a bucket and a bottle of Jeyes fluid, before we all catch whatever it is that you've got.'

He turned his back on Fox and McGrath moved to

the middle of the ERU squad and eyed the sergeant.

'I want the best man you have to replace McGrath. I don't want your best marksman or the fella who can jump tall buildings in a single leap. I want the man with a touch of a brain in his head.'

The sergeant reached back without even looking and pulled at a Kevlar jacket like a man selecting a pup from a litter.

'Mike Healy – best man I ever saw to think something through.'

Donegan looked at him for a moment and then pointed him in the direction of the vomit-covered table.

'Welcome to our world, Mike. You'll be taking the place of Detective McGrath, so lose the attack gear and change back into civvies.'

McGrath stood up and steadied himself.

'No way,' he protested, and wiped a shaking hand across his mouth. 'You don't think I'm going to let you endanger this young fella by letting him go in there with Fox. This is my capture too, remember.'

Donegan shook his head slowly. 'You can't even stand up straight,' he said.

'Give me a couple of minutes. I'll be fine.'

'Well, if you can clean up that puke, I'll consider you fit,' Donegan said.

McGrath nodded and left the room.

'You can cancel the doctor, so, Fox,' said Donegan. 'It's nothing much, he just needs to steady up.'

'Right,' said Fox and went to the phone.

All eyes turned to the walkie-talkie, which was crackling to life on the table. The ERU men stood up slowly together, waiting for the word, McGrath and his nervous stomach forgotten, in spite of the sickly stench in the air.

'Charlie one five. Target has settled. Awaiting instructions.'

The sergeant looked at Donegan, who stood back.

'Let me know when you're in position, Sergeant,' he said. 'Don't take any longer than you have to.'

The sergeant tapped the shoulder of his men as they left the room, like a football manager in a dressing room.

McGrath came back and started the clean-up. The raw stink of disinfectant covered over, but could not completely obliterate, the smell of puke.

Reidy offered McGrath a plastic cup.

'Here, drink this. It's nice and cold from the machine in the hall.

McGrath took it with a shaking hand and steadied it with the other.

'Are you sure you're up to this?' asked Donegan.

McGrath gulped the water and put the cup on the table. Then he continued with his mopping-up operation.

'I'm fine. I think I got the poison out of my system.'

Donegan, Fox and Reidy looked at the sludge he was sweeping into his bucket.

'You certainly did that,' said Fox.

The superintendent returned to the room, straightening his jacket and creasing a stray hair back with his palm. His nostrils twitched, but he passed no remark.

'I've just reiterated what you said earlier to the ERU, Frank. I made it very clear to them.' He clapped his hands. 'So,' he said with a smile, 'this is where we all look good. Sergeant Reidy and yourself make the arrest with Detective Fox and a very pale-looking McGrath as backup.'

'That's about it, Super.'

'Good, good. Then all we have to do now is wait for the word to go.'

A ghostly silence fell over the room for a minute or so, each man running the plan through in his own mind. Fox removed his .38 automatic and broke the silence by cocking it, inspecting the chamber and then allowing it to slam shut.

The superintendent looked at Donegan and back at Fox.

'Do you think you'll have enough bullets for the job, Detective?' he joked.

Fox stood up and jammed the gun back in his belt holster. He selected one of the walkie-talkies on the table with an earpiece hanging from it, handed it to McGrath and then took another. He winked at Donegan.

'A man can never have enough bullets, Super,' he said.

Whatever response the superintendent had in mind, it would have to wait for now.

'Charlie one five. Full back line in position.'

CHAPTER TWENTY-TWO

Landers removed his shoes and lay back on the bed. He unfastened the buttons of his polo shirt and massaged the sides of his neck, relaxing and closing his eyes. He felt comfortable and satisfied after his meal, safer that he was off the street, that he had ditched all ties and that he was anonymous once more. Just another middle-income travelling salesman staying in a hotel for the night.

He contemplated showering for a moment and then changed his mind. Getting undressed seemed like too much of a chore. He was so tired.

When he awoke, his hands rested by his sides. He listened for the noise. What was it?

He blinked and sat up slowly on the bed. He had only drifted for seconds. There was that sound again.

He cursed silently as he realised what it was and pulled the suitcase from beneath the bed. The green light of the mobile phone dial flashed on the clothes.

'Yes.'

The blood drained from his face as he listened to the barely audible whisperings of sheer panic. The voice squeaked with urgency. It was vaguely familiar.

'Get out, get out of the hotel now! They know who you are and they're coming to get you. They know everything about you.'

'Doyle? Is that you?'

'Yes. Yes. Get out of there now. Your escape is planned. Listen exactly to what I've been told to tell you.'

Landers pulled on his shoes and moved around the room as he listened to the escape plan.

'How much time do I have?'

'Minutes... seconds maybe. Do what I've told you. Our contact will meet you there and smuggle you out. Once he does that, you're on your own.'

Landers knew that the clock was ticking. There was no time for questions. To hell with the money. That could be settled later.

'We'll talk in due course, Mr Doyle,' he said. He put the mobile phone in his jacket pocket and then searched frantically in the suitcase for his .22 and silencer. When he found it he stood up and slipped it into his right sleeve. He took a deep breath as he opened the door. He was ready to return fire if necessary. The narrow corridor was empty.

Turn left, Doyle had instructed. On to the end and then right.

Landers braced himself. The boards creaked beneath the thin carpet. He increased his pace. On to the end and then right. The red fire-escape door faced him. He pushed it open slowly and looked down as far as he could through the grey steel stairway. Voices whispered in the corridor behind him. He closed the fire-escape door gently behind him and began his descent. His soft shoes made no sound, although the light above him cast a strobe of shadows through the meshed steps onto the floor below. He moved faster now, knowing that the hunt was beginning above him. He stopped on the concrete and braced himself against the wall, his face turned towards the corner. The sweat dripped from his eyebrows and he blinked through the stinging.

Obeying the instructions of Doyle, he whispered softly. 'It's the messenger of the gods.'

He held his breath to listen. He could hear nothing but the pounding of blood in his ears. He released the .22 in his sleeve and closed his palm around it. And then he stepped out.

Fox stood no more than ten paces away with the .38 automatic at arm's length, his left eye quivering slightly as he took careful aim. Landers looked at him and nodded.

'I'm the messenger of the gods,' he repeated.

Fox steadied himself and looked up and over the sights of the gun. He took a number of controlled breaths like a man who had been taken by surprise and was now composing himself.

'I couldn't give two fucks what your nickname is, Landers,' he replied. 'I'm an armed garda and you're under arrest. So, lift those hands so I can see they're empty, like a good man.'

'But – Doyle sent you to...'

'Don't try any of that smart shit with me,' Fox raised his voice. 'Give me the slightest reason and I'll blow ten fuckin' holes in you. *Now raise those hands and face the wall.*'

Landers narrowed his eyes in confusion as he tightened his palm around the .22. So many things were running through his mind. The first was that he had been set up to take the rap for them all. But no. He could lead them back to Doyle any time. Doyle was not responsible for this.

And then it dawned on him. His contact was now taking matters into his own hands. You could never trust a crooked cop.

'Do not test me.' Fox eyed him through the sights again as if reading his thoughts. 'Get your hands up and face the wall. Now.'

Fox had barely glimpsed the barrel of the small pistol before Landers turned his wrist a fraction and fired the first shot. It grazed across his cheekbone with the pain of a razor cut.

Fox did not hesitate. He fired three rounds in rapid succession hitting his target square in the centre of the chest. Landers bared his teeth in pain and defiance as the force drove him backwards. He gripped at the steel railing of the stairs and raised his hand to shoot again. The fire-escape door behind Fox burst inwards and the ERU sergeant shouldered him out of the way and fired a single shot from the automatic shotgun. It lifted Landers out of one of his soft shoes and threw him back like a rag doll against the wall. The discharge from the gun was deafening in the small concrete area. Fox waited for a moment before lowering his automatic and waving the smoke from in front of them.

'Je-sus Ch-rist,' he shouted at the sergeant.

They both looked down at Landers. The sergeant turned quickly and raised his hand to stop the charge of the others in his squad through the door.

'Back ye go, lads. This is our business now.'

Fox leaned down beside Landers and went through what he knew was the futile exercise of checking for a pulse. No man can breathe without lungs. He searched through his pockets and stood up when he heard the voice.

'Are you all right, Fox. Are you all right?' McGrath was running awkwardly down the narrow stairwell. 'Are you all right? Answer me!'

'Yeah. Yeah,' Fox muttered. 'I'm fine.'

'What the hell happened?' Donegan shouted from the balcony at the top, Reidy beside him, both with revolvers drawn.

'Yeah, everything's just a big bowl of stewed apple down here, Kig.' Fox's tone was sarcastic. 'And exactly what the fuck were the two of you *doing* up there?' he shouted. 'How did he get past the two of you to me?'

Donegan moved quickly down the steps.

'Calm down, Andy. Calm down. We went to his room and he was gone. We had to check all the others in the corridor. What happened to your face?'

Fox pressed his finger against his cheek and inspected the blood. 'It's nothing.'

Reidy looked down at Landers.

'Well, it looks like he won't be getting up,' he said dryly. 'What did you shoot him with? A bazooka?'

Fox holstered his gun and the others followed suit. He turned around and moved out of earshot of the ERU sergeant, who held the shotgun down at arm's length. He beckoned a nod to McGrath and Donegan moved beside them.

'There's something very, *very* wrong with what's happened here,' he whispered. 'Someone tipped him off. A fuckin' blind man could see that.'

Donegan knew he was right, but now was not the time.

'Maybe he just got lucky and heard us coming,' McGrath offered.

Fox shook his head in dismay.

Reidy positioned himself in front of Landers and dropped his eyes. He stared for a moment at the horrific wound inflicted by the shotgun blast, then turned and walked past the others towards the fire-escape stairway.

'He doesn't look all that lucky to me, Detective,' he said without looking back.

***

'A man was shot dead tonight and a garda injured in a shootout with members of the Garda specialist Emergency Response Unit and members of the Metropolitian Crime Squad. The shooting occurred when gardaí stormed the Hayes Arms Hotel to arrest the man whom they suspected of the importation of large quantities of cannabis for distribution on the Irish market as well as involvement in a recent spate of murders in Dublin. Our southern correspondent spoke immediately after the incident to the superintendent in charge of the investigation.'

All eyes in the room looked up at the small television screen.

'Well, yes. That is correct, Michael. We had this man under investigation for a number of months, and following that investigation, we were satisfied that he was one of the main importers to this country. In addition to this, we believed him to be involved in a number of recent murders in the city. A decision was taken this evening that he be arrested, and a plan was put in place for that purpose. During the arrest, the man produced a firearm, shot one of our officers, not too seriously, I'm glad to say. However, the tactical unit returned fire. And, tragically, there has been a loss of life.'

'Has the man been identified yet, Superintendent?'

'Well, we know that the deceased man is British. We have been in touch with the authorities in England. That's all I'm prepared to say at the moment.'

The room fell silent again as the bulletin ended. One detective stood up and switched the television off. The ERU sergeant huffed in disgust as he turned his pen between his fingers.

'"*Stormed* the hotel"! What sort of shit talk is that? We didn't storm anything.'

He looked around to his men who were writing.

'I don't want to see that word in any of those statements, especially your one, Healy,' he warned. 'This was just a simple case of a fella shooting at a guard and the guards firing back – more times. Most of you just heard the shots anyway. Don't make it too complicated. Leave the bullshitting to the officer in charge.'

Donegan could not help but smile as he moved like a schoolteacher between the desks and collected the short statements made by the ERU squad. Most of them displayed the three-monkey syndrome. They saw little, heard little and would certainly say nothing of importance.

He looked across the room at McGrath, who was engrossed in his statement. Beside him, Fox chewed the end of a plastic pen, his eyes raised in thought. Donegan knew that he was not concentrating on the job in hand.

'Get it done, Detective,' he said as he approached.

'Why do we have to do it now? An hour after it happened.'

'You know why. It's policy. Besides, it's better to get all of it down while it's fresh in your mind.'

Fox pushed the three sheets of paper along the desk.

'That's everything that happened,' he said. 'I've left out a few small details, I think it's only fair to tell you.'

Donegan frowned as he pulled up a chair beside the desk. He could feel the ears of the idle ERU men straining behind him.

'Get out if you're finished,' he shouted.

He waited until the clattering of chairs had stopped and the door slid shut.

'If you've got something to tell me, Detective,' he whispered, 'spit it out.'

Fox scraped his chair closer. McGrath stopped writing to listen.

'You're the only one who *really* thought that there was a mole, Inspector. Well now, we believe it too.'

Donegan raised his eyebrows. 'I thought that you and McGrath believed me from the start.'

'Nah, Kig. We said that to make you feel better. Just in case you thought that you were turning into one of those strange wackos who goes around telling everyone that the world is going to end.'

Donegan smiled. 'So, what made you change your mind?'

Fox dabbed at his cheekbone and looked at his fingertips.

'Just before the shit hit the fan, he mentioned a name – Doyle – something about him sending me. He knew that I was a guard, but he didn't seem shocked – looked like he had been expecting to see me there, expecting *someone* to be waiting for him, and that someone was supposed to be a guard.'

Donegan moved closer and rested his elbows on the desk.

'Who else knows about this?' he asked urgently.

'Just me and McGrath here. No one else.'

'Good. Keep it that way. We're bound to find something that can lead us back to the mole if we keep what we have under wraps.'

Fox reached into his jacket pocket and took out a mobile phone.

'Maybe this can be of some assistance,' he grinned. 'I took it out of Landers's pocket. We can trace all his calls back. I'll bet our man Doyle is in here somewhere.'

'Great work,' whispered McGrath forcefully. 'Now we can add tampering with case evidence to our long list of charges. Is there any other fuckin' rule that we can break now that we've missed?' He laughed unintentionally. 'Ah well, what difference does it make now?'

All three men grinned.

'The best part of the game is breaking the rules,' whispered Fox.

The ERU sergeant approached and slammed the sheet of paper down with his palm on the desk.

'This is all I have to say on the matter, Frank,' he said. 'If any man in my unit has written something – well, something foolish – let me know.' He looked down at the mobile in Fox's hand and started to guffaw loudly as he went to the door. 'I think he's right, Inspector,' he joked. 'I think it's time ye phoned a friend.'

***

Although the night was particularly warm, Mitchell Doyle had lit a roaring fire in his study. First into the blaze of firelighters and small cuts of timber went the half-inch thick dossier. Photocopies of files and photographs. Maps of streets that he and his contact had scrupulously prepared. Notes of sightings and haunts where the victims could be found on any given day. As soon as the first pages began to curl in the fire, he held the letter he had prepared for the journalist Tom Farrell over the flames and held it there until they drew along the paper and singed the hair on his knuckles.

Pat Doherty's death was old news now anyway.

Last into the evidence pyre went the cheap box of surgical gloves, the empty envelopes, the writing paper and the plastic biro.

He took the long poker and sat back on the low coffee table staring ahead, looking but not really seeing, hypnotised by the flames. He rested the black tip of the poker on the carpet and turned the brass handle gently between his fingers as he gazed ahead, like an old man on a park bench contemplating what life had left to offer.

He awoke suddenly from his trance and jabbed angrily at the cluster of burning pages with the poker. Sparks blew and drifted upwards as the sheets parted and burst into flame. He replaced the poker on its brass holder and sat back again, lowering his face into his hands.

Although the entire plan had taken a sudden nose-dive into failure with the death of James Landers, what was most important now was that the trail of the Garda investigation would end there.

The telephone call half an hour earlier had settled him somewhat. There were no leads to go on. There were still mutterings about an insider who had given information on the victims, but this would die down in time. The top brass would be satisfied that the killer had been found and the matter would be left at that. The media appetite would be sated with a couple of suggestions that linked the murders of the Wolfman and Ivor Danby.

'I knew that you'd get nervous when you saw the news, but relax, it's all been taken care of. Right now, it's cleanup time. Don't leave anything lying around that could link you to our deceased friend – just in case. And that, as they say, Mitchell, is that. Talk to you next week.'

Doyle had so many questions that he had wanted to ask, but his contact had done all the talking. Like a politician on a talk show who did not want to hear the opinion of his opposite number, he had forced Doyle to listen. It was evident from his tone that he was displeased at Doyle for not calling off Landers as he had advised him to do, but there was also a sense of relief.

Doyle lifted the poker once more and scraped at the slivers of ashes in the grate that remained. A single, blue flame gulped at the remaining pieces of paper, and in a second they were gone. He replaced the poker and stood up, arching his back and blowing gently at a feather of grey ash that had settled on the joined bronze crests that hung above the tall mantel. The crests, a wedding present from his brother-in-law, had been in the room for over thirty-eight years. It had been a long time since he had really looked at it.

It celebrated the union of two wealthy families.

He moved his finger along the names at the base, wiping at the light coating of dust.

Doyle and Haskard.

He turned quickly to his side as the door of his study creaked open. His wife entered and looked at the grate.

'Mitchell Doyle, your daughter has been waiting for the past twenty minutes,' she scolded. She looked curiously at the smoking ashes. 'What are you doing in here?'

He smiled and moved towards her. 'Just a few old documents that I've been meaning to get rid of. You know what I'm like.' He put his arm around her and they turned for the door. 'I just hate getting rid of old things.'

She leaned back on his arms to check that the fire was quenched and then flicked the light switch. As they stood together in the hall, she raised her finger to her lips.

'Don't take too long, now,' she whispered. 'Make it one of those very short stories of yours. She looks exhausted.'

Doyle gave her a quick peck on the cheek. 'Ten minutes at the very most,' he said and winked.

'I've heard that before, Mitchell.' She smiled as she went down the hall.

Doyle stepped into the sitting room and closed the door gently behind him. He tiptoed across the carpet to the dark-oak bookshelf. Although his daughter's eyes were closed, he could sense that she was waiting. He selected a large leather-bound book and sat down on the armchair. Her favourite music played softly from the stereo.

'And what shall it be tonight, my little princess?' he whispered as he opened it on his lap.

Her eyelashes flickered for a moment and then she opened her eyes. She gazed blankly at him as she closed and opened them again, her mouth turned down as if in disappointment at the lateness of his arrival. He looked back and waited for her to speak, willed and prayed for her to speak as he had done every night for the past three years.

He smiled through the welling tears and sniffed.

'I know, Princess,' he said as he looked down at the book and gently turned the pages for a moment before settling his hands on the charcoal drawing. 'It's time for your favourite story again. It's a long one, so mother will be cross. I'll read until she comes in and scolds us.'

The expression on her face did not change. Her eyes continued to open and shut slowly.

'The Sword of Damocles,' he announced in a whisper, and began.

The words flowed as he read, so well did he know the story, so many times had he read it. He looked up at her as he spoke, and although the words from his mouth related the story, his mind had once again returned to the fateful day three years previously.

Laughing and joking with the staff of his engineering plants at their annual golf outing.

'Don't ever call me *Mr* Doyle in a clubhouse,' he had told the new, young assistant manager of his Tallaght plant. 'We're all equal in the eyes of Golf.'

'And you, Jimmy,' he called across the room from the bar counter to one of his factory-floor operators. 'I was watching you out there today, and if I ever see you with a golf club in your hands again, I'm going to call the guards.'

Laughter resounded around the clubhouse. What an enjoyable day!

He slapped the man next to him on the back as the barman in the white shirt placed the phone on the counter. 'It's for you Mr Doyle. I mean, Mitchell.'

'You're learning.' He smiled and picked up the receiver.

The laughter and joking continued around him, his companions unaware that he was listening to news that would change his life forever. He placed the receiver back slowly and staggered off the stool.

The laughter stopped as they watched him lean to one side and grip at the counter ledge to steady himself.

'What is it, Mitchell? What's the matter?' The words seemed faint in the distance.

'It's my daughter, Susan, my daughter...' Someone else seemed to answer for him.

Stephen, one of his company directors, had driven him to the hospital. He had sat numb in the passenger seat on the journey, immune to the words of comfort that it might not be as bad as it had sounded.

The doctor met them in the corridor, and Doyle saw, to his dismay, that his expression was one of deep concern. He took Doyle by the arm and led him into an empty waiting room. He spoke quietly and gravely.

'She's in theatre, Mr Doyle. She received a severe blow to the side of her head...' He pointed with his silver pen. 'Here, just behind the temple. They're operating on her at the moment to relieve the swelling.'

Doyle's mind spun in confusion.

'How? What happened? Will Susan be all right? When can I see her?'

He took the doctor by the arms suddenly and squeezed. 'Tell me that she's going to be all right,' he pleaded. His eyes narrowed, his voice grew deeper. 'Tell me.'

Stephen, who had been waiting outside the open door in the corridor, came quickly into the room.

'Easy, Mitchell. Easy,' he said, as he released Doyle's grip on the doctor's arms.

'Tell me,' Doyle shouted as he was moved back.

'We're doing everything we can,' the doctor promised. 'We'll know the extent of the damage, if any, after the operation.'

Doyle breathed heavily as Stephen eased him onto a chair. His limbs tingled and he felt faint. 'Get my wife,' he gulped hard. 'Get Emily.'

CHAPTER TWENTY-FOUR

Susan Doyle could have not picked a worse time to make a withdrawal from her deposit account at the local bank. But she had a spare couple of hours and it seemed like the ideal opportunity to get her money and pay for her flight ticket. All week she had talked of nothing else except the planned three-month holiday, drawing smiles from her parents who never grew tired of watching her growing excitement. Three months with her pals on an archaeological tour of Rome and Greece. 'I'll bring you back something beautiful for your collection, Dad,' she had promised.

The queue in the bank tailed back to the door and moved at a snail's pace.

But she didn't care. She closed her eyes and felt the hot, Italian sun shining down on her. The smell of freshly cooked pizza. The taste of red wine from the local vineyard and the wonderful company of her friends. Like her, all thirty-somethings, unmarried and loving every minute of it.

She opened her eyes and took another three short steps along the queue. The woman in front of her complained in a mutter about the poor quality of service.

'*Down on the fucking floor or you're all dead.*'

Some in the queue reacted quicker than others.

She turned to see the two men in army surplus gear and balaclavas enter the bank, one shutting the door behind them. The other moved the shotgun in a wide arc.

Her hands shook as she lifted them in surrender. And she froze to the spot.

He approached her menacingly and raised the weapon up and behind him.

'I said on the floor,' he roared, and brought the butt of the shotgun down across her head.

The operation had taken just under eleven hours. Doyle stood up as the doctor entered the room. He motioned Doyle back to his chair and sat down beside him.

'Mr and Mrs Doyle,' he began. Although he had the words, he struggled to get them out. 'The operation relieved the swelling on Susan's brain, but she has not regained consciousness. She's... she has lapsed into a coma.'

Doyle closed his eyes. His wife sobbed quietly.

'What exactly does that mean, Doctor?' he asked. 'I mean... is she going to live? Will she recover? Tell us the truth now, man. Don't colour it,' he warned.

The doctor clasped his hands together and leaned towards them.

'Well, Mr Doyle. It's too early to say yet. It all depends on the depth of the coma. On first examination it would appear that it is not severe. She is breathing unaided, which is always a good sign.'

'When will you know for sure?'

'Well, the next couple of days will give a very good indication.'

His wife sniffed her tears back and spoke. 'Can we see her, Doctor?'

The doctor nodded and placed his hand on hers. 'Of course. But just for a couple of minutes, I'm afraid.'

The coma lasted for twelve days. Doyle and his wife had kept a vigil in the hospital throughout. On the twelfth day, the sensational news came from the young, tired-looking doctor on watch that Susan had opened one of her eyes.

The jubilation was soon to be replaced with heartache.

Indeed Susan had awoken from the coma, but she had suffered severe brain damage. Muscular weakness and paralysis had set in. She lapsed in and out of consciousness, which suggested that she was suffering from progressive brain damage.

***

The door of the sitting room opened behind him, and Doyle pretended to be asleep.

'You don't fool me, Mitchell,' said his wife as she

stood in front of him. She took the book from his lap and turned it. '*The Sword of Damocles*,' she huffed. 'Will you ever grow tired of this nonsense?'

'Never, my love.' He opened his eyes and took the book from her. 'It's about all things great.'

She pulled the blanket over Susan and released the brake on the wheelchair. 'Well, it's way past her bedtime,' she fussed. 'It can wait until tomorrow.'

He leaned over the arm of the chair and kissed his daughter. 'Good night, Princess.'

The door closed behind him.

He rested back and thought about the day that the gardaí came to his house to tell him that they had captured the men responsible. The men who had stolen his daughter's life. The men who had grinned as defendants in the court when the judge handed them both a seven-year sentence.

The two men whose solicitors were now appealing the case three years later on the grounds that one of the gardaí had perjured himself to secure the conviction. They felt confident that they could prove it and get their clients the justice that they deserved.

Doyle felt the same way. He had prepared carefully to ensure that they would receive justice. And had covered his tracks with the help of his contact. Both men were to be executed on their release by the avenging messenger of the gods. And suspicion would never return to his door. Just another two criminals made to pay for their crime by the elusive Mercury Man.

But now his messenger was dead. Vengeance would have to be put on hold.

Still, there were more men like Landers to be found.

Someone would fill his shoes. But they would have to be filled quickly. He would phone Haskard in the morning and make the necessary arrangements.

***

Almost a week had passed since the shootout in Hayes's Hotel and, although it remained the topic of conversation in the squad, things were beginning to return to near normality. Detectives had resumed the cases that they had been working on before the arrival of James Landers on the streets of Dublin. His reign of terror was over and his body had been hastily returned by private jet to Britain under a discreet plainclothes military escort.

One of the tabloid papers showed a blurred photograph of the coffin being lifted onto the plane by two men. Underneath, a few lines on the life and death of Paul Winters, the drug-dealer and killer for hire who took the nickname the Mercury Man and left a calling card on his victims. Information to the media from the authorities in England was that he was a deranged psychopath who murdered for the fun of it. They believed him to be responsible for at least three drug-related killings in Britain during the past year alone. Any effort to get further information or to find relatives or friends of Paul Winters would prove futile.

He was dead now and the problem had passed.

Some journalists who were more determined than others pressed on, but were met with a wall of silence from the squad.

Five murders had been solved and the matter was to be left at that.

The superintendent sat back on his leather chair and rubbed his forehead in disbelief. 'I don't believe what you're asking me to do, Inspector,' he said. 'You want me to keep the investigation at full speed because you suspect that a guard was involved. Have you any idea how much bullshitting it's taken to put this whole thing to bed in the last week? I haven't told as many lies since I was in national school.'

He stood up and walked around the desk.

'Tell me what you have to go on, Frank. And I want to hear it all.'

Donegan coughed gently as he opened the thin folder.

'Well, first of all, there's the search done on the computer, that happened on...'

'Aw! Jesus Christ, Frank,' the superintendent protested. 'We've been down that road before and it's a dead end. I did what you asked me to and tried to find out who checked the computer files that day. I even got that egghead from technology over to search for the code used. And he couldn't do it. So it's obvious that someone hacked into the system and got the information that they wanted. Why are you insisting that the information leaked from inside the job?'

Donegan was unconvinced.

'Super, I want you to give me one more week on it. And two men. Fox and McGrath. That's all I ask.'

'Frank, we've wasted enough time on this already, not to mention the Doherty file which will be firing out gigantic amounts of public shite in a few days time.

By the way, I pulled the surveillance off that journalist Tom Farrell. The finance on this whole thing has gone through the roof.'

Donegan stood up. He appeared to be in a hurry to settle the issue.

'Yeah, yeah, whatever. Farrell was a non-runner anyway. But I really think that we should give this one more shot. All we want is the time, and you can keep the overtime.'

'We!' the superintendent seemed surprised. 'So you're not the only one who believes that we have a problem. Fox and McGrath believe it too, do they? Did they form their own opinions or was it just because you said so?'

Donegan swallowed his anger. This was not the time for a conflict.

'I guess they're like me. Curious to see where this whole scenario began. Somewhere out there is a man who paid James Landers to murder five people, and as far as I'm concerned, got a little help from our job on the way.'

The superintendent snapped his fingers.

'Yes – the money in the case,' he said. 'How did the print men get on with it? Any luck?'

Donegan shook his head.

'The only prints on the money belonged to Landers. All fifteen thousand pounds of it. Whoever made the pay-off to him is a very clever person. Paid him in sterling, too.'

'Mmmm, yes,' mused the superintendent. 'He must be. And nothing else was found that could give us any further leads.'

He cheered suddenly and clapped his hands.

'So, Frank. What other possible leads could you have to convince me to give you another week on this? Everybody else seems content that our killer has been caught. And to be perfectly honest with you, Frank, everybody else would prefer it to be left at that – on both sides of the water, if you get my meaning.'

Donegan gave a short laugh.

'So the contractor gets off scot-free. Is that the general consensus?'

The superintendent waved his hand to dismiss the very idea.

'Certainly not. As far as the media are concerned, the investigation is ongoing to find the person who hired Landers. Probably a drugs baron – you know, the usual crap we feed them.'

'And the reality of the situation is?' The superintendent sat down and raised his legs slowly onto the desk.

'Well, Frank. The reality is that it's a dead duck. And that's on instructions from the real God himself in the department. The one who wears a suit and spins around in a Merc. This goes way above ordinary men like us. A promise has been made by someone and it must be kept.'

Donegan could see where the speech was leading.

'Are you going to give me the week to wrap this up?'

The superintendent looked at him for a moment and then smiled as he threw his arms out in surrender.

'Well, Frank, if that's the only lead that you have - then why not? Of course, if you step on anyone's toes,

I'll deny that this conversation ever took place. A bit like that old TV programme – em – *Mission Impossible* where they were told...'

'Yeah, yeah, I know the one.' Donegan snapped the joke closed.

The superintendent removed a pen from his pocket and leaned over a document on his desk. Donegan moved towards the door and opened it.

'Inspector, let me know if you find anything of importance,' said the superintendent without lifting his head.

'You'll be the first to know as usual, Super,' replied Donegan and pulled the door closed.

He took a deep breath and headed for his office, where Fox and McGrath were eagerly waiting. They stood up together as he entered.

'Well?' said Fox. 'Have we got the all-clear or what?'

Donegan moved quickly around his desk and sat down.

'Yeah,' he answered. 'Now show me what you have.'

Fox held out the four sheets.

'These are the calls that Landers made and received from the mobile phone in the past two weeks. The ones I've highlighted came from a phone belonging to one Mitchell Doyle of 3 Fairfield Square, Dublin 4. He was the last one to phone Landers. Look at the time of the call.'

Donegan flipped the pages over to the last and looked down at the number and time.

'Christ, a few minutes before we moved on him in the hotel! This Doyle was a regular caller,' he said as he turned the pages back. 'What about the other numbers here?'

McGrath had followed that up.

'All three are phone boxes,' he replied. 'And all within a two-minute walk from Doyle's house.'

Fox leaned forward and placed another sheet on the desk. 'We did a check on Doyle's number for calls made and received. That mobile number comes up regularly, including a call to Doyle seconds before he phoned Landers at the hotel.'

'Who owns the mobile phone?' asked Donegan.

Fox shook his head. 'We'll never know. It's one of those pay-as-you-go jobs with no registration. So there's no way to find the owner.'

'Fair enough.' Donegan was disappointed. 'What else do you have?'

'We did a full background check on Doyle,' he replied. 'Respectable, wealthy. Owns a line of factories making... em...' He faltered.

'Iron things, you told me earlier.' McGrath helped him on.

Fox glared at him, then smiled.

'Yeah, iron things. Anyway, there was nothing unusual until we found that his daughter had been brain-damaged by some gouger during a bank robbery nearly four years ago. Struck her on the head and crippled her. Him and his accomplice got seven years for it.'

He paused for breath. Donegan raised his eyebrows in curiosity and beckoned to him with his hands.

'Let's hear the rest, Detective,' he said excitedly. 'Don't stop now.'

'Well, one of our lads may have coloured the truth a bit during the trial – got a bit over-enthusiastic in the witness box.'

Donegan pinched at his closed eyes. He knew what had happened next, but asked anyway.

'And?'

'And it's gone to an appeal. To be heard in a few days' time. It looks like the two gougers will walk out the door. They did it for sure. They were caught with the weapons and what was left of the money. The lads just bollocksed it up, that's all.'

Donegan sighed. 'Ah, well, you can't blame policemen for trying too hard. As the Americans would say, "Shit happens." Will the gougers get off on the appeal for sure?'

McGrath laughed. 'They will unless a few other guards perjure themselves – which is always a possibility in awkward situations.'

Donegan leaned forward on the desk and clasped his fingers under his chin.

'So, Landers was to kill these two gougers when they were released and it was all to fit neatly into the Mercury Man file. Is that what the plan was?'

'Appears that way now,' said Fox. 'Clever enough when you think about it. If Landers had succeeded, got paid and got away, how could any case ever be proved against Doyle? He'd be just another relative who was shocked but thrilled that justice had been done. And in the unlikely event of someone having the slightest suspicion about his involvement, there isn't a damn thing that could be done about it.'

Donegan looked down at the pages for a moment. The room fell silent.

'So how do we trap him, lads?' he asked finally.

Fox and McGrath looked at one another.

'We've been thinking of a way to do just that,' said McGrath. 'Though you might consider it a little drastic.'

Donegan stood up and moved to the front of the desk.

'Nothing – and I mean nothing – could be considered drastic at this stage.' He tried to smile. 'As long as it doesn't end with flashing cameras and the three of us in handcuffs, I'm willing to risk it.'

Fox stood up and punched him on the shoulder with enthusiasm. 'That's the spirit. Now, we need an illegal phone tap and one item from the evidence room.'

'Jesus Christ,' Donegan muttered as he looked at both men. 'Why does it have to be an *illegal* phone tap?'

'Do you think you could get us a legal one?' quipped Fox.

'Point taken.'

McGrath smiled. 'We can settle this matter in the next twenty-four hours. And maybe get your mole as well.'

Donegan brightened. 'Well, now, that would be a bonus,' he said. 'And by the way, as far as the superintendent is concerned, it's our mole.'

'What did he say about keeping the mobile phone and Landers mentioning a fella by the name of Doyle?' asked Fox. 'Surely that got him thinking?'

'I didn't tell him,' replied Donegan. 'I didn't see the point in it. As far as the upper echelons are concerned, the entire matter has been "put to bed" to use the super's words.'

Fox looked at McGrath and then back at his inspector. 'You know – if I didn't know you better, I'd say that you probably think our superintendent is the mole?'

A smile broke across Donegan's face. 'Well, Detective Fox. If I was a vicious bastard, which I'm not, I'd probably say that you were right.'

***

Doyle slammed the morning paper on the table causing the silver cutlery to rattle and jump. 'Garda Inquiry Into Case'. The article on the court appeal of his daughter's assailants had made a column on the front page of his chosen newspaper. Not because of the crime that they had committed three years before, but because of the internal Garda investigation into one of the officers who had brought them before the courts for the robbery and assault.

It was an accepted ruse by the defence to leak such information to the press a couple of days before an appeal was to be heard. It helped to 'soften the bench' as it is known as in legal circles.

Doyle settled the cutlery and china back in its place just as his wife came into the room.

'What happened, Mitchell?' Her voice was filled with concern.

He eased her worry quickly. 'Nothing, love. I knocked some of the cutlery off with my elbow, that's all. I'm an awkward so and so in the mornings. You know that.'

She examined his reddened face and looked down at the folded paper on the table.

'It's about them, isn't it?' she said. 'Please don't take me for a fool, Mitchell. I've read the papers every day as well. I've seen what was happening.'

She moved from the door and picked the newspaper up. She stuttered as the words came out.

'That case is starting today, isn't it? Those – those men who – did that to Susan are going to get out. They're going to be set free because that guard perjured himself to put them in jail.'

Doyle was taken aback. In all the time since the capture and conviction of the men responsible, she had never once mentioned their trial or conviction. Never mentioned their names. She had cried at the news of their imprisonment. That was her only reaction.

And then, all she cared about was looking after their daughter. All offers from Doyle to hire a nurse to do the job were turned down. From early morning until he had read the story at night, she had fed and changed their daughter and attended her every need, just as she had done when Susan was a helpless infant.

He took the paper from her.

'Yes,' he said quietly. 'That's why I'm upset.'

She put the paper back on the table and looked at him. She ran her hand down the side of his face.

'Don't worry, Mitchell.' She smiled. 'God will deal with them.'

He reached out to her, but she had already turned. He was alone again in the room. He sat down and looked at the black-and-white photograph of the men who had destroyed their lives.

'God will deal with them.' He swallowed hard as he repeated the words. If she only knew what he had done! It would surely kill her if she knew that he had instigated the needless murder of five people to avenge their daughter. If only he had the gift of second sight, like Tiresias.

He unfolded the paper and read it until his wife arrived with breakfast.

They sat and ate in silence. He could picture the grand finale. Everything had been arranged and was out of his hands. The telephone call to Haskard from the coin box down the street three days previously had seen to that.

'Robert, it's Mitchell. I want you to find me a replacement as quickly as possible.'

He looked out at the passing cars as he listened to the wave of objections.

'Can you do it or not?' he had asked angrily. 'Yes, I know it's a risk to take. But I'm prepared to take it. I want a replacement. Make the necessary arrangements and contact me with the details. Yes, fifty thousand pounds in sterling. To be done on my terms. The details and payment will be given in the usual way.'

He listened as Haskard first objected to the plot, then mentioned various names and promised to do what he could. Finally he stated that, to avoid suspicion on Doyle, he himself would make all the necessary arrangements as well as the final touch.

'Thank you, Robert,' Doyle had said when he was finally satisfied that the matter had been settled. He rubbed the receiver with his sleeve for good measure.

The doorbell rang just as he finished his breakfast.

'I'll get it.' He stood up and went to the front door.

The postman whistled on the step below him and looked up.

'Mitchell Doyle,' he said casually, and held out his folder. 'Sign here, please.'

Doyle took his post and glanced down at the registered letter. He examined the printed typing on the front as he squiggled his signature across the folder held by the postman.

'Thank you,' he said and went inside.

'Anything for me?' his wife enquired from the door of the dining room.

He examined the envelopes and held out one. 'Looks like one from Jennifer.'

Emily's sister lived in England.

He returned to his study and frowned curiously at the white registered envelope.

He picked up his duck-handled letter opener and sliced across the crease. The contents were familiar to him. It drew the breath from his entire being. He dropped the card on the desk.

'Messenger of the gods.'

Doyle squeezed his fists to stop his hands from shaking.

'Who knew? How could this happen?'

He picked up the receiver and dialled, rocking back and forth as he waited for a reply.

'Yes.'

'I've just received something very unpleasant in the post.' He tried without success to hide the fear in his voice.

'What?'

'I'd rather not say. I want to see you. As soon as possible.'

'I can be there some time this evening. What seems to be the problem?'

'Landers may not have been as secretive as we had hoped. Someone else knows.'

The voice tried to calm him.

'Relax, Mitchell. It's like I said. The file has been closed. I've seen to it. Even if it is someone that Landers told – there's nothing that they can do about it now. There was nothing found on him that could lead back to either of us.'

Doyle grew angry at the nonchalant attitude.

'You're not the one sitting here looking at this blasted card,' he insisted.

'Calm down, Mitchell. Calm down. I'll call to you this evening and we can talk then. Don't do anything foolish. I have to go now.'

The line went dead before Doyle could speak again. He sat for a moment with the receiver to his ear before lowering it slowly. He picked up the card and went to the fireplace. His hands still shook as he took the box of matches and lit one. He gazed at the black lettering on the card until it was half burned and then placed it carefully in the grate. And he watched with fear in his eyes until it had changed to a roll of ash.

CHAPTER TWENTY-FIVE

Everything was in readiness.

Fox and McGrath sat in the dirty, red van at the top of the street. Although their view of the entire house was somewhat restricted, they could still see the all-important front door and driveway. The news from Donegan that the telephone call made by Doyle that morning had been to the untraceable mobile phone, and that a meeting had been arranged for that very evening, sent a shiver of excitement through them both.

'I'll be with you both shortly,' Donegan had promised them. 'Keep me a space.'

Fox rose from the steel floor of the van, bent in

half and pressed at his aching knees. He moved noisily around as he slapped at his rear.

'Jesus. My arse is gone completely dead. All the blood is gone out of it.'

'Sit down, for fuck's sake,' whispered McGrath pulling at him. 'That noise can be heard a hundred yards away.'

Fox pulled a dusty cushion beneath him and lowered himself slowly onto it.

'I'm going to need an arse transplant after this,' he continued to complain. 'I hope that we won't have to run after anyone 'cos my legs are dead as well.'

McGrath sat in the lotus position looking out the shaded back window. He looked calm and relaxed.

'This is going to be worth the wait,' he promised in low voice. 'I'm looking forward to seeing the fella who was responsible for all this shit.'

'Doyle, you mean?' enquired Fox.

'Nah. The ghost with the mobile phone. He has to be the brains behind it.'

'Why do you say that?'

McGrath turned his head from the window.

'Well, he was the first one that Doyle called after he got our little registered letter, wasn't he? He sees the card and panics, just as we thought. If he was the brains, then he'd have thrown the card away and done nothing. He's scared, so he calls for help.'

'Right, right, I get it,' said Fox, sorry now that he had asked at all. 'What have you in the flask?'

'Soup,' replied McGrath and turned back to the window.

Fox looked at him in disbelief.

'Bob! It's the middle of the fuckin' summer. We're sitting in a furnace with our T-shirts drenched in sweat and you bring a pot of soup to warm us up. What sort of a strange bollocks are you at all?'

McGrath was unshaken. He continued to keep watch.

'The soup is not for now,' he said. 'Have you ever noticed how cold it gets when the sun disappears in the evening? You'll be glad of it then. Wait! Hold it – movement.'

Fox grimaced as he moved beside him at the back window and squinted.

'What is it?'

They both watched as the wheelchair was pushed out onto the path. Emily Doyle smiled as she settled the light, tartan blanket around her daughter's shoulders, her voice barely audible as she spoke and then laughed.

They watched as mother and daughter approached, the mother chatting, the daughter with her eyes lifted to the heavens, her head held in place, her face expressionless.

Fox and McGrath leaned back from the window as they neared. Fox winced as the pain stabbed at his calf muscle. He bared his teeth. McGrath lifted his fist and positioned it just beneath Fox's chin.

As if in divine punishment for their peeping-tom activity, one of the neighbours appeared in a gateway and stopped Mrs Doyle and her daughter within ten yards of the van.

McGrath's eyes widened in fear as he watched Fox ease himself off the floor and stretch out his leg with a gasp of relief.

He waited until Fox had settled and they looked out again.

Emily Doyle and her neighbour chatted while Susan looked straight ahead.

Neither McGrath nor Fox were listening to the conversation. Both of them were looking at the young woman in the wheelchair.

After ten minutes or so, the conversation ended and they went on their way.

McGrath and Fox sat in silence for a moment, both of them knowing what the other was thinking but half ashamed to say it.

'She's a beautiful-looking girl,' said McGrath finally.

Fox nodded, pleased that all he had to do was agree. 'Yes. Yes she is. It's a terrible shame that something like that should happen.'

'I can understand why her father would want to kill those fuckers,' McGrath toughened the conversation as he straightened up. 'If I had a daughter and they did that to her – policeman or not, I'd go for the ultimate retribution as well.'

Fox gave a soft laugh and covered his mouth.

'No, you wouldn't,' he argued. 'You've got too much respect for law and order. Leave it to the judge and all that shite. Vengeance is mine sayeth the Lord. I heard you at it before, arguing against vigilante gangs.'

'Mitchell Doyle isn't a vigilante,' said McGrath.

'What the fuck do you call killing five criminals?' Fox raised his voice. 'In some South American countries, that would be considered an act of war.'

'He had them killed so he wouldn't be caught,' McGrath whispered.

'So he's just a murderer then,' Fox stared at him. The temperature of the argument was rising.

'We can settle this with a simple question. But answer truthfully, all right.'

Fox stretched out his legs and yawned. 'Let's be having it then.'

'You're Mitchell Doyle. She's your daughter. The men who turned her from a beautiful woman into what she is now are going to get away with it. And you have all the money that you need. What do you do?'

Fox clasped his fingers behind his head and pursed his lips in thought as he looked up at the roof of the van. He closed his eyes for a moment.

'If I didn't have to face the consequences, I'd kill them,' he answered.

McGrath resumed his lookout. 'The defence rests,' he said dryly.

'Whoah, wait a minute,' Fox pressed him. 'That would still make me a vigilante though, wouldn't it?'

McGrath shook his head without looking back. 'A vigilante is just some arsehole who goes around pretending that he cares about justice and the law. Hitting young fellas with baseball bats and frightening people in their homes. Ninety-nine per cent of the time he's just a lowlife scumbag himself with no job and a severe personality disorder.'

'Oh, holy shit!' said Fox quietly. 'We're off on one of those journeys into the criminal mind now, are we?'

'Mitchell Doyle isn't a vigilante,' McGrath continued. 'He's just a father who wanted an eye for an eye. You can't blame him for that.'

'This whole thing is really getting to you, isn't it?' Fox asked.

McGrath spun his head back. 'No it isn't,' he snapped. 'I just think that...'

They both froze as the sound of the side door being tapped with a metal object.

'Open up,' said Donegan.

Fox pulled at the handle.

'What in the name of... I thought you two did the surveillance course. It sounds like the fuckin' *Jerry Springer Show* is going on in here.' He was visibly angered. 'All you have to do is watch the house and not let anyone know that ye're hiding in the back of this van. Is that too much of a job, lads? Christ, what did ye do when ye were watching Doherty? Put on the siren and start drinking a bottle of whiskey?' He puffed in the heat as he removed his jacket and threw it in the corner.

'Is Doyle a vigilante?' asked Fox to add to his dismay.

Donegan thought about the question for a moment.

'Is there coffee in this?' he asked, as he picked up the flask.

'Yeah. It's lovely and flavoured. Have a cup,' said Fox. 'Answer the question, Kig. Is Doyle a vigilante?'

Donegan sat down on the opposite side of the van and spun the plastic mug from the top. He tilted the flask and grimaced as the creamy mess flowed into the mug.

'Which one of you lunatics brought mushroom soup on a day like today?'

McGrath's shoulders lifted and fell in silent laughter as he looked out the window.

'No, he's not a vigilante,' Donegan snapped. 'He's a

murderer and a father who wants to kill the men who all but killed his daughter. And he's a criminal. Is that the answer that you wanted? Who gives a shit anyway? He's broken the law and we're going to see that he pays.'

He poured the soup back into the flask and put it back between the front seats.

'Why the hell didn't you soundproof the floor of the van with carpet, McGrath?' he said as he moved back to the window, the tip of his shoe drumming on the hollow steel.

'It won't make any noise if you don't move around,' replied McGrath calmly.

Donegan eyed him through the sweat. 'I can see this is going to be a long evening.'

After three hours in the van, relations were strained to breaking point. McGrath had remained almost motionless at the window throughout, while Donegan and Fox had spent the time moving around spider-like in an effort to keep the circulation going. The final straw came when Donegan produced his cigarettes.

'Light that and you're a dead Garda Inspector,' warned a sweat-soaked Fox.

'If I don't have a cigarette then we're all going to die,' Donegan snarled at him.

McGrath and Fox said nothing.

'All right, all right. I can wait. I don't know what brought me into this friggin' van with you two anyway,' he grumbled. 'I'm the man in charge. I should be in a hotel down the road waiting for the word to come up here. Jesus. The things I do for this job.'

Fox watched as McGrath wiped the beads of sweat

from his eyebrows and flicked it onto the floor. Donegan had loosened the knot of his tie down and it rested on his stomach. The sweat on his chest and armpits spread across his light-green shirt. All three gasped in the warm air.

'Anyone for soup?' asked Fox and gave a laugh that drew a smile from the others.

'I can't stay here much longer,' Donegan gasped. 'It's all right for ye fellas. Ye're nearly twenty years younger. If I stay here any longer, I'll be dead in a few minutes.'

Fox could see the pained expression on the face of his inspector. He knew that he could not last much longer in the heat of the van.

'Wait until the coast is clear,' he said. 'I'll give you the word to go.'

'Thanks, Andy,' Donegan tried to smile through his discomfort. 'I'll never make the same mistake again.'

Fox rose up on his knees and looked out through the front windscreen. He was about to give the all-clear when he sank back and scrambled noisily past Donegan.

'Quiet, will you,' snarled McGrath.

'Quiet, my arse,' Fox growled at him. 'Look whose mean machine is just coming up the street.'

Donegan moved beside them and they waited for the car to appear. It drove slowly and pulled into the kerb in front of Doyle's house.

The driver got out.

'Fuck - me - pink,' whispered Donegan.

'Now there's a turn up for the books,' said McGrath.

Detective Sergeant Alan Reidy closed the driver's

door and walked up the steps. He pressed the doorbell and looked around for a moment before being ushered inside.

The three men in the van looked at one another in silence.

Fox raised his eyebrows. 'Now, this is what our English counterparts would call an extremely sticky fuckin' wicket,' he whispered and rested back against the side of the van.

Donegan breathed deeply through his nose as he contemplated the next move. The heat and discomfort of their surveillance operation had paled by comparison with the position in which they now found themselves.

'I've already made my mind up, lads,' he announced suddenly. 'But this is something that we all have to agree on. The choice is simple. We can drive out of here, pretend it never happened and "put it to bed". No risk taken. No loss. And only the three of us will ever know. We can lie in wait for years until we find some other crumb of evidence.'

He reached for his crumpled jacket in the corner of the van and removed a folded sheet of paper.

'Or we can go execute this warrant, search the house and arrest Doyle and anyone else in there on suspicion of being accessories to five murders. Our detective sergeant is the mole. Are either of the two of you as curious as I am to know why?'

McGrath took a deep breath and exhaled. 'Let's all just take a minute to assess exactly what we have here,' he advised. 'We have phone records that connect Landers to Doyle. We now have the connection between

Doyle and Reidy. And we know that it was him who got the information from the computer system, but we can't prove it. And the fact that Landers mentioned the name 'Doyle' to Fox in the hotel. It's all a kinda hairy-hole, circumstantial file at the moment, isn't it?'

Fox looked at him and gave a nervous laugh.

'You big girl's knickers, Bob. Why chicken the issue now?' he said.

He waited for the seconds to pass and for McGrath to give a resigned nod.

He pulled the sliding door of the van back and the three of them stood out on the road. They walked along the path in silence. Donegan led them up the steps and rang the bell. After a few minutes Doyle answered the door. He stood back and held his hand out as if he had been expecting them.

'Come in, eh... Inspector, is it? Come in. You're all very welcome.'

Donegan stepped inside and moved past him quickly, at the same time handing the warrant back to Fox.

'Read it to him,' he ordered and went through the open door of the study. Detective Sergeant Alan Reidy sat on the crimson-leather armchair with his legs crossed. He did not flinch or pale or show any of the reactions of astonishment that Donegan had hoped for and expected. Fox and McGrath entered the room, followed by Doyle, who was looking at the warrant with interest.

'This is most exciting,' he said as he took his reading glasses from his study desk and put them on. 'I've seen all this on television before, but this is the first time that I ever saw a real one. Murder you say.' Although his voice was calm, his hands shook gently. But this could have passed for age.

Reidy looked up at Fox and McGrath and smiled. 'Sit down, lads.' He pointed to the long sofa. 'You too, Inspector. The three of you look like you spent the evening in the back of that surveillance van that McGrath signed out this morning. Now what's all this fuss about? And why the warrant?'

The three of them sat down and Donegan rested his elbows on his knees. He narrowed his eyes at Reidy. 'So you were the one who gave the information on the victims to Mr Doyle here to pass on to Landers, the hired killer.'

'What information, Inspector? What are you talking about?' Reidy furrowed his eyebrows intentionally.

Donegan knew he could never prove in a court of law that Reidy had downloaded files from the computer system. And it was obvious that Reidy knew it as well. The ace card was his very presence in the house of the man suspected of planning the murders. And he would play it shortly, but not yet.

'May I see your mobile phone, Alan?' Donegan asked.

Reidy smiled as he reached into the inside pocket of his jacket and took it out.

'This is all very irregular,' he said. 'None of this is being done in compliance with the law. And we know how important that is to us all. What's that old saying, Inspector? When the rules cease to operate efficiently – forget the rules. Yes, that's it, isn't it?'

Donegan glared at him and handed the phone to

McGrath. 'I can arrest you and bring you to the station if you like,' he snapped. 'Is that what you want?'

Doyle folded the warrant and placed it on the coffee table as he sat down in the armchair opposite.

'Why exactly are you here, Inspector?' he asked casually.

Donegan looked directly at him and stood up.

'I believe that you are the man who hired James Landers to commit five murders in a bid to cover up the planned killing of the men who were responsible for what happened to your daughter. We have telephone records of calls made from here to Landers, right up until the minute before he died. This...' he sneered at Reidy. 'This policeman here gave you all the information on the victims' files, which he took from our computer system – and he was clever enough to cover his tracks.'

He turned back to Reidy. 'But not all his tracks. Not today anyway.'

Doyle sat back and rolled his thumbs.

'These obscene telephone calls that I've been receiving, Inspector. Has anything been done about them? I've made several complaints to my local gardaí during the past three months. I gave them the number of the caller as well, but they said that it couldn't be traced. I'm sure that they have all this on record if you check. Finally, I decided to take matters into my own hands and got one of those caller identification gizmos. I got the number of this "crank caller" and decided to call him back every time that he called me. Fighting fire with fire, so to speak. To be honest, I was beginning to enjoy it a little too much. I hope that my behaviour won't be considered a crime or anything.'

Donegan could feel his heart sinking in his chest. He wished now that he had taken the option of driving away in the dirty, red van and having a few pints with Fox and McGrath. He was down to the last roll of the dice.

'Why is Sergeant Reidy here?' he asked.

'What do you mean, Inspector?'

'His presence here alone is proof of his involvement,' replied Donegan looking at Reidy. 'There isn't a jury in this country that would fail to make the connection.'

'Different number,' McGrath interrupted as he handed the phone back to Donegan who in turn threw it on Reidy's lap.

'Is visiting someone against the law now, Inspector?' asked Doyle curtly.

Donegan smiled at him. 'Well, in light of all the evidence, circumstantial as it may be, I think that his presence in this house may just be the missing piece of the jigsaw.'

'Inspector?' enquired Reidy gently.

Donegan turned to him.

'Is it against the law for a son to visit his father?'

Fox and McGrath looked at one another. Donegan's jaw fell.

'Cut the bullshit, Reidy,' Fox blurted out. 'I know your father. I met him at your mother's funeral six years ago. Have you forgotten that the two of us had a few pints with him afterwards? Forgotten that, have you? Well I haven't.' He nodded in Doyle's direction. 'And this joker ain't him.'

Fox, in his eagerness to prove the case, had, unlike the others, been blinded to the reality of what they were being told.

Reidy stood up and went to the glass drinks cabinet. 'I am the result of what Mitchell once described to me as "a youthful indiscretion". My mother never told her husband, of course. I didn't know myself until she died. I discovered the truth in a letter that she left for me.'

He gave a smug laugh as he poured the brandy into the crystal glasses. 'I was a love child of the sixties.'

'A bastard, you mean,' Fox could not resist the chance.

Reidy was unshaken by the insult. To prove it, he handed the first glass to Fox.

'How can a man with two fathers be a bastard, Detective?' he said.

He gave the second glass to his father and turned back for the others.

'Enough of my family history,' he said. 'You men have a very serious decision to make after what you've heard. You can arrest my father and me...' he turned with the glasses and handed one each to Donegan and McGrath. 'You can take us to the nearest station and hold us for twelve hours of boring questions on phones and computers and bank accounts and other ridiculous connections, to which every answer will be, "I haven't the faintest idea what you're talking about, Inspector." And after twelve hours we will be released without charge, and then copious amounts of shit will hit the fan.'

He stared hard at Donegan.

'You and I know that to be the truth, Inspector.'

Donegan averted his eyes and sipped his brandy. He knew that Reidy was correct in what he was saying. Although it was too early to concede defeat, arresting either of them at this stage after what had been said would be a suicidal career move for all three of them. McGrath and Fox would have to be considered.

He put the glass down on the table and turned to survey the array of gold statuettes along the mantel.

'The one in the middle is Jupiter,' said Doyle, following his gaze. 'The supreme god of the Roman pantheon. Protector of laws, justice and morals.'

Donegan examined each one in turn. 'And Mercury?'

'He's there at the very end, Inspector. A thief, a scoundrel...'

'A messenger?' Donegan interrupted.

Doyle nodded and smiled. 'Whenever he was called upon, yes. The others are probably of little interest to you. Athena, Tiresias.'

Donegan turned to Reidy. 'So, the girl in the wheelchair is your half-sister, Alan.'

'Her name is Susan,' Reidy corrected him. 'And, yes, she is my half-sister.'

'You must have been pretty cut up when she got hurt?' Fox suggested.

'As any brother would have been,' Reidy was composed. 'Please lads, you forget who you're talking to here. Don't try that psycho, anger-drawing crap where I end up getting all mental and making some insane admission to every crime ever committed. I've driven that truck around the yard before as well, remember.'

Donegan's mobile phone rang and he pulled it from his jacket pocket.

'Yes, this is Frank Donegan. Yes, I'm the one who wanted to know if there were any developments.'

He turned his head slowly and stared at Doyle as he listened.

'I see. And when did this happen? Just now? Well, that is a surprise...'

'Yes, I'm sure he is. Thanks for letting me know.'

He replaced the phone in his pocket and sat back.

Doyle raised his eyebrows. 'Developments, Inspector?'

Donegan gave a thin smile.

'Yes. I suppose you could say that it was a development, Mr Doyle,' he replied.

Reidy turned the crystal glass in his hand. It was time to call the bluff.

'So – are you going to execute that warrant or not, Inspector? If you are, then I ask that you give us a little time to phone our solicitor.'

Donegan rose to his feet. He took the warrant, folded it and placed it in his pocket.

'You're a clever man, Alan Reidy,' he said. There's no real point in searching this house or arresting either of you, is there? I'm sure that you, being the perfectionist that you are, have left nothing to chance. You know, if I was a quitter, I'd say that you and your new-found father had just got away with murder.'

His voice lowered menacingly. 'But I think you know me better than that, pal. I don't give up the chase that easily.'

Reidy lifted his glass in salute. 'I would expect

nothing less from a policeman of your calibre, Inspector. Unfortunately, we won't have the opportunity to work together again. I'm resigning from the job as of today. Mitchell here has asked me to oversee the security in his newly acquired plant in South Africa. The pay is much better as well.'

He looked at Fox and McGrath. 'Maybe you two would like to come out for a holiday some time,' he added and a smile cracked on his lips. 'Fabulous weather.'

'Go fuck yourself, Reidy,' said Fox in disgust.

Doyle clucked his tongue. 'There's certainly no need for language like that, Detective.'

'All right. That's it,' ordered Donegan. 'Let's go, lads.'

Doyle stood up and extended his hand.

'I think you're making the right decision, Inspector. It saves everyone a lot of unnecessary embarrassment. Not to mention the enormous civil bills.'

Donegan ignored the outstretched hand and gestured towards the door.

'Go ahead, lads. I'll be with you in a minute.'

He waited until Fox and McGrath had left the room and the latch of the front door sounded.

'What will you tell your daughter now, Doyle?' he asked.

Reidy approached and stood in front of him. 'What do you mean?'

Donegan smiled at him.

'How you and your sick-minded Daddy killed five people for nothing. Even if Landers had gotten away from us, the whole thing was just a total waste of time, money and lives.'

Reidy and Doyle remained silent.

'That call I got a few minutes ago,' Donegan continued. 'It was from the courts. The appeal collapsed after just three hours. I guess the judge believed the guard after all. Not only that, but he added another four years to the sentence. Those men are going back to prison to serve the full term, even as we speak. You killed those people for nothing, Mitchell. Just remember that, every time you look at your daughter.'

He had moved away as Reidy began to object and Doyle slumped in the armchair. He stopped at the sitting-room door.

'South Africa won't be half far enough away for you to feel safe,' he said with a sour smile. 'I'll make this case my little hobby until I retire. And then I'll pass it on to some enthusiastic young policeman to keep the home fires burning for whenever you return.'

He left the room, pulled the front door closed and joined Fox and McGrath on the path below.

He slapped Fox on the shoulder and the three of them moved away.

'I can't believe it,' McGrath said. 'We know they're responsible – and there isn't a shaggin' thing that we can do about it.'

Fox laughed. 'Maybe you should become a vigilante and sort this whole thing out once and for all, McGrath.'

'When the rules cease to operate efficiently – forget the rules,' mused Donegan. 'I said that to him in my office the first day he joined the squad.'

Fox tried unsuccessfully to stifle a grin.

'Looks like he took the advice fairly seriously, Kig.'

He laughed. 'What words of wisdom did you give to us when we joined? I can't remember.'

McGrath stopped at the van, folded his arms and rested back against it.

'He told us to do our jobs without fear, favour, malice or ill will,' he said.

Donegan looked at the ground and shook his head slowly. He looked up at the two of them.

'And *did* ye listen?' he sighed. 'Huh! Did ye fuck!'